Praise for Award Winning *Whispering Vines* by Amy Schisler

"The heartbreaking, endearing, charming, and romantic scenes will surely inveigle you to keep reading."
Serious Reading Book Review

"Schisler's writing is a verbal masterpiece of art."
Alex Jacobs, Author, The Dreamer

"Amy Schisler's Whispering Vines is well styled, fast paced, and engaging, the perfect recipe for an excellent book." *Judith Reveal, Author, Editor, Reviewer*

Praise for Award Winning *Picture Me* by Amy Schisler

"This book kept me turning the pages until the end, great suspense!"
Harps Romance Book Review

"Interesting little mystery!! An awesome story with great characters, so I am giving it a full four fangs!"
Paranormal Romance and Authors that Rock

Praise for *A Place to Call Home* by Amy Schisler

"The action begins on the first page and does not stop until the ending. This debut novel is a novel of hope as well as one of adventure."
Elena Maria Vidal, [illegible] *Tree*

Also Available by Amy Schisler

Suspense Novels
A Place to Call Home
Picture Me

Contemporary Fiction
Whispering Vines
Island of Miracles

Children's Book
Crabbing With Granddad

Island of Miracles

Island of Miracles

By Amy Schisler

Chesapeake Sunrise Publishing
Bozman, Maryland

ISBN: 978-0-692-77575-2

Published by:
Chesapeake Sunrise Publishing
Amy Schisler
Bozman, MD
2017

Acknowledgements

First and foremost, I'd like to thank all the men and women who serve our country whether they be first responders who show up when needed, overseas military personnel looking out for our interests, or those protecting our borders here at home. Our country and its people are kept safe every day in a myriad of ways thanks to the bravery and dedication of those who leave their families, their communities, and the safety of their homes to ensure that we, Americans, may continue to live well and protected in the land of the free.

Thank you, Ken, Rebecca, Katie Ann, and Morgan, my wonderful family who support my writing, my research, and my crazy, often manic, need to be in control that helps me maintain my creative juices, be organized, and meet my deadlines. Thank you, Judy and Richard MacWiliams, my mom and dad, for you unwavering support. I couldn't do anything that I do without your love and support.

Thank you, Ty, my nephew and advisor on all things having to do with the Coast Guard. Your input and ideas were invaluable in shaping Aaron's storyline and character. Thank you to my many muses who sat on my shoulder while I was writing this book, Father Darryl Millette, Anne Novey and Anne Kennedy, Ronnie Zollo, Mitzi Meade, Michelle Lloyd, Marian Grammer, Tammi Warren, Shannon Dolgos, Mary Sifka, and George Sprance.

Thank you, Judy Reveal, my editor and proofreaders, Mindy Howell, Mary Leve, Katie Lowman, Debbie Nisson, and Crystal Reynolds. I appreciate all your help more than you know.

To my nephew, Ty Schisler, and to all the men and woman who protect us both at home and abroad. Semper Paratus!

An interesting observation to be made within the Matsé of the Amazon is their acceptance of polygamy. Men openly take many wives, often of their own bloodlines, as not only a normal practice but one that elevates the perception of their virility within the tribe.

From the *Studies of Indigenous Peoples*
by Walter Middleton

CHAPTER ONE

It was so hot when Katherine Leahy woke up that July morning that she thought for a moment the air conditioning must have stopped working. But as she lay in bed with beads of sweat running across her back and onto the sheets behind her, she heard the faint hum of the fan as the air ran through the coils within the walls of her Georgetown Brownstone. Late July was always hot in DC, but this year, the air seemed even more stifling than usual. Katherine watched the flies trapped between the storm window and screen. They were just barely flying, as if even they could not tolerate the abominable heat that hung over the city like a wool shroud suffocating all the inhabitants, human and insect alike.

Despite the heat, Katherine smiled as she thought back over the previous three days. After Mark left for the airport well before sunrise, Katherine laid in bed and cried. She cried tears of joy for the time they were together and tears of sadness for the days they would be apart. Eventually, she drifted back to sleep as she thought about the precious hours they had spent in each other's arms.

She finally rolled out of bed, showered, dressed, and headed to the kitchen where she made herself a cup of strong coffee. Taking the steaming mug with her, she went back to the bedroom to fix her hair. She stopped in the hallway when she heard an unfamiliar ring.

"Oh no," she whispered to herself. "Mark must've left his cell phone."

Getting down beside the bed and pushing the covers up out of the way, she reached under the bed and picked up the phone that stopped ringing just as she located it. Katherine guessed that it had fallen out of her husband's pocket and slid under the bed the night before when they were ripping off each other's clothes. She smiled to herself as she held the phone in her palm and remembered the passionate moments before they fell onto the bed. Another ring ripped her out of her the memory.

"Hello," Katherine answered.

"Hello?" the voice on the phone said in a questioning tone. "Who, who is this?"

"This is Katherine. May I help you?"

"I'm so sorry," said the woman. "I must have dialed the wrong number."

"Maybe not," said Katherine. "This is my husband's phone. Who were you calling?"

"Oh," the voice said with surprise. "I was calling my husband, Mark."

The phone slipped from Katherine's hand and slid back under the bed. She sat for a moment unable to move. This is a mistake, she reasoned. The caller had made a mistake. It was pure coincidence that their husbands had the same name. This was definitely a mistake.

Katherine's hand shook as she reached for the phone again. When she looked at it, she realized it wasn't Mark's phone after all. She breathed a sigh of relief. He must have picked up another person's phone when he was out yesterday.

He had gone out yesterday, hadn't he?

Of course, he had, she recalled. He had gone to the gym. He had his phone when she called him in the afternoon to tell him she loved him, so he must have picked up this one by mistake sometime after that.

But how could he not have noticed? This isn't the same brand as his. He must not have been paying attention. He was off, after all, no need to look at his phone…

Her inner voice tried to rationalize with the other voice in her head, the one that held doubts that Katherine didn't want to acknowledge.

The phone rang again. Katherine stared at it, unable to make up her mind as to what to do. She looked at the caller ID. It said 'home.'

On the third ring, Katherine answered the call.

"Did you say Mark?" Katherine asked. "Is your husband's name Mark?"

The caller sounded flustered at such a greeting, and she hesitated before answering. "Yes, that's what I said. Who is this, and why do you have my husband's phone?"

"I think there must have been a mix-up, that my husband took your husband's phone by mistake. Does your husband use the gym on Wisconsin?"

"Wisconsin?" she asked. "I'm sorry. I don't know what you mean. Oh, wait," she said as if things were just beginning to click in her mind. "Of course, he's in DC this week. I don't know the name of the gym he uses or what street it's on, but I'm sure that's where the mix-up occurred. He goes to the gym every day."

Katherine smiled. "Mine does, too. He never misses his workout. They must have somehow switched their phones while changing or something. What would you like me to do with his phone?"

The caller thought about it. "Well, let me check his schedule." There was silence on the other end for a few minutes, and Katherine held her breath in anticipation.

"He's due back home this afternoon, then he flies out again on Monday and will be gone until the next day." She continued thinking through her husband's schedule as Katherine's feeling of panic began to return. "He'll be back in DC in seven days," the woman was saying. "I hate for him to not have it before then, but it doesn't make sense for you to send it if there's a chance it might take that long to get here, unless of course you don't mind sending it overnight."

The woman on the other end of the call was waiting for an answer, but Katherine couldn't say a word. How many coincidences could there be surrounding one phone call? She hated to ask the next two questions, but she knew she must.

"I'm sorry, but I need to ask you something," Katherine said. Taking a deep breath, she proceeded. "What is your last name?"

Again, the woman hesitated. It wasn't the answer she was expecting. "Leahy," she said with apprehension. "Would you like our address?" she asked slowly. She obviously thought Katherine had agreed to send the phone overnight and must be wondering if Katherine had a screw loose.

"Mrs. Leahy," Katherine began. "You said your husband flies out again tomorrow."

"Yes," she said with a note of annoyance in her voice.

"What does he do?" Katherine asked. "Your husband, what is his job?"

"He's a pilot. What is this about? Are you going to send him his phone or not?" Katherine could tell that the woman was either very irritated with her or, like Katherine, was on the verge of panic.

"Mine, too," Katherine said quietly. "My husband, Mark Leahy, is a pilot. He'll be back home in DC in seven days."

After several seconds of silence, Katherine held the phone out away from her ear to make sure the call hadn't been dropped. She noted that it was after 8:30. She'd never make it to work on time. She was about to say something, though she wasn't sure what, when she heard ringing from the other side of the phone.

"Hold on a minute," the woman said quietly, and Katherine listened as she answered what must have been her cell phone.

"Hello. Mark? Oh, you did? In the hotel room? Uh-huh. Okay. Yes, I'll see you tonight. No, everything's fine. All right. Me, too." Katherine waited for her come back to the phone.

"He says he left it in the hotel room and that they are holding it for him at the desk," the woman told her quietly. "But you're not at a hotel, are you?"

Katherine closed her eyes and put her hand to her head. She took a deep breath and exhaled as she looked up at the room she shared with her husband. No, at the room she shared with someone else's husband.

"How long have you been married?" Katherine asked.

"Fourteen years," she answered. "We have three children."

Katherine thought she detected tears in the woman's voice, and who could blame her? Her pain must have been far greater than Katherine's if that was even possible. Now that she was thinking about it, Katherine didn't feel any pain. She felt hurt, anger, confusion.

What should I be feeling. Is there a standard way to feel in this situation?

"And you?" the woman asked hesitantly.

"Eleven months," Katherine answered. "We were married on the beach in Mexico," she told her. She didn't know why that seemed important at the moment.

"What do we do now?" the woman asked after a moment of silence. It was like one of those moments of silence that showed respect to someone who had died.

"I don't know," she said honestly. "I just don't know."

Katherine sighed into the phone. "I'm sorry," she whispered as she closed the phone and disconnected the call and herself from Mark's other life.

She heard her cell phone ringing but did not move to answer it. She waited until it signaled that she had a message, and then she hesitantly pushed the play button.

"Hi my sweet. We're about to take off, but it seems I may have misplaced something." He hesitated. "I may have picked up Sam's phone at the gym by accident. I can't find it anywhere, so if you find a cell phone lying around, would you mind turning it off if it's not dead and holding onto it for me? I'll get it when I get home. I love you. Bye."

***

It was a week before Katherine was able to throw out Mark's clothes. Pictures, books, and other reminders of him were thrown into the trash in bits and pieces as she passed them in the hall, found them in a drawer, or came upon them in any way that caused her to actually notice their presence. Katherine was surprised at how little he had and even commented on it in an email to her brother.

> *"Why wasn't I suspicious? He hardly had any clothes other than his uniforms and clothes for the gym. He had almost no personal belongings. He said that was the life of a pilot, that they are among the last of the world's nomads. And I believed him. How stupid am I?"*
>
> *"You're not stupid, Sis,"* had been Zach's reply when he finally emailed her back. Katherine had no idea just what Zach did in the Army. His job

was covert, and she often went weeks without hearing from him.

"You've always had everything handed to you like a princess. Even when we lived in those God-forsaken jungles, the people treated you like a pale-faced goddess. It's no surprise to me that you fell into the fairy tale trap."

His words stung, but she knew that he was right.

"But I was so blind," she answered back. *"Mark always said he hated Facebook, that it held no interest for him. He wouldn't even let me post pictures of him, not even of our wedding. He was so annoyingly private, and he insisted that I be the same. Well, guess what, he did have Facebook. He just didn't want me to know about it. He must have his security settings set up so that he can't be searched for, but I found his wife, and he's listed as her husband. There are pictures of them together and their kids. It's all there, proof that he had a whole other life. I was such an idiot to fall for his lies."*

She hadn't heard back from Zach after that, which was just as well. What could he say? She had been an idiot, and he couldn't argue the contrary. Mark hadn't allowed any wedding pictures to be taken other than one of the two of them on the beach at sunset, toasting with their complimentary champagne, a gift from their hotel. A stranger had taken it for them. It sat on the table by their bed until Katherine smashed it on the floor and swept the pieces into the trash.

Katherine realized that it was time to face the inevitable, especially since Zach knew what had happened. She couldn't ask him to keep it a secret forever. She summoned the courage needed to call her parents in Florida and shatter the idyllic retirement they were enjoying. She dreaded hearing them tell her 'I told you so.' She begged Zach not to tell their parents because she needed to find her own way to let them down. She might as well get it over with.

The conversation was short. With their daughter on speaker phone, both Walter and Mitzi could simultaneously convey their disappointment in their daughter. They tried to keep their lecture to a minimum, but Katherine hung up the phone feeling like a five-year-old. Why did she always revert to being a child where her parents were concerned?

A few days later, Walter called Katherine as she walked home from the Metro with what she supposed was good news.

"You're in the clear," he told her.

"What's that supposed to mean?" Katherine asked as she hung her keys on the hook by the front door and collapsed on the sofa.

"The marriage was a sham from the beginning."

"I know that, Dad. He was already married."

"Stop playing the victim card, and listen to what I have to say," Walter barked into the phone. "You asked me to help you fix this mess, and that's what I'm doing."

"You're right, Dad. I'm sorry. Please, go on." Katherine said, closing her eyes and tilting her head back as she listened.

"There is no record of your marriage with the Mexican Government. I hired someone to do some checking, and the name you gave me belongs to a man who's a known con-artist. He makes his living tricking couples into thinking they're being legitimately married, but it's a ruse. He's not licensed, and the papers he gives to the couple are fakes."

Katherine's eyes flew open, and she sat up on the couch. "Do you think that Mark knew that? Was he in on the deception?" She swallowed and looked around, wondering if anything she thought was the truth was even the least bit real.

"My guess would be that he knew exactly what was going on. He couldn't have gotten a legitimate license in Mexico or anywhere else, at least not one that would have been accepted by the US Government."

"Dad," Katherine hated to ask the question. "I didn't get my social security card. Mark did. He told me that I didn't need to go in person; I just needed to fill out some form he gave me. I never even bothered to check it out. I trusted him completely. Does this mean that all of my documents are fake?"

There was silence on the other end, and Katherine thought that the call had been lost, or maybe her father had simply hung up on her.

"Dammit, Katherine," he said after a minute, and Katherine heard something, a mug perhaps, being slammed down on a table. "Didn't we raise you to be smarter than this? What the hell were you thinking?"

Katherine didn't have an excuse. She could tell her father the truth, that she had never been married before, had never had to change her name, or get new documents. She had no idea what was involved. But she knew that there was no justification for not being more responsible. She had let Mark waltz into her life and take over without ever questioning who he was, where he came from, or anything else about his life that didn't fit into the perfect portrait of him that she had painted in her mind.

Katherine listened as her father explained what needed to be done to straighten everything out. Thank Heaven her mother had volunteered for so many causes and served on a number of boards while they lived in DC. Between her contacts and the people her father knew from his days as a student at Georgetown, this was all going to be taken care of quickly and quietly. Katherine just wished that the same could be said for her heart.

CHAPTER TWO

"Dammit, Katherine, open the door," Mark called as he continued pounding his fist against the red door that separated them. Sweat poured off him in the August heat. Katherine could feel the vibrations of his punches as she leaned against the wood, tears streaming down her face. She had changed the locks and blocked his number on her phone the same day she received the call from his wife three weeks prior, but now it took every ounce of strength in her not to unlock the deadbolt and let him in.

Tears flowed down her cheeks as she remembered the night they met. From the moment Katherine laid eyes on Mark, she was smitten. She and some of her co-workers had gone out for a drink after work. It was St. Patrick's Day, so they went to an Irish Pub in Alexandria. Katherine was enjoying the music and the crowd, not to mention the beer, but she had to work the next day and knew that dragging herself out of bed in the morning was already a nearly impossible chore. She decided that, if she was going to get in a run before work, she needed to call it a night. She said her goodbyes and started to get up when the man in the next booth caught her eye. She smiled, he waved, and they were married just six months later. It was like a fairy tale, until it turned into a horror story.

Drawing in a deep breath, she closed her eyes and reached into her pocket for her cell phone. This was the third time, since that fateful day, that he had shown up at the house. Each time, his temper grew worse, and for the first time since they met, Katherine was afraid of him. She had asked her neighbors to call the police if he ever showed up, but they were not at home, or preferred not to get involved, each time he arrived at her door demanding to be let in.

"Please," she whispered into the phone. "I need help. Send someone right away. A man is trying to break into my home."

Katherine calmly gave the dispatcher her address and waited while the woman assured her that the police were on the way. Willing herself not to look out the window, Katherine thought about how easily Mark could crush her with his bare hands if he so desired. At thirty-eight, he resembled a heavyweight boxing champ more than an airline pilot. He was tall and lean with chiseled muscles from many hours spent at the gym and the strict diet of one who pays close attention to his health. Katherine was in good shape, rarely missing her morning run, but she was no match for Mark.

The minutes crawled by as Katherine listened to the dispatcher's reassuring voice coupled with Mark's angry demands. Finally, she heard Mark curse before being addressed by the officers who had arrived on the scene.

"There's been a mistake, officers. I'm not sure who called you, but this is my house."

Katherine peeked through the narrow pane of glass that ran alongside the door and watched as Mark walked down the steps toward the policemen, his arms raised. She could no longer hear what he was saying as one of the officers approached the door. Opening the door just a crack, she whispered to the older man.

"Thank you for coming. That man is no longer my husband. This is my family home, and he is trespassing." Her voice trembled, and she swallowed hard as her eyes pleaded with the officer. She worried that the men would believe Mark's story, whatever it was he was telling them, and she wished that one of the officers had been a woman.

"Did he hurt you?" the officer asked. "Would you like me to call someone or have you taken to the hospital for treatment?"

Katherine shook her head. "No, thank you. Please, just make him go away."

The man looked from Katherine back toward Mark who was showing the other officer his identification. The kind looking gentleman turned back to Katherine.

"Would you like to file a restraining order, Ma'am? I can help you with that, explain to you the procedure."

Katherine looked past the officer to Mark. He turned and looked at her, giving her his saddest expression. "Please baby," he called. "Let's find a way to work this out."

Katherine thought about how hard she had tried to convince her parents and her brother, Zach, that Mark was the perfect man. Her father's doubts had bothered her but not enough for her to change her mind. She believed he would come around. Katherine was the only single woman left of all of her childhood and college friends and had been anxious to marry and start a family. Her parents talked about grandchildren non-stop, but they found no comfort when learning that she and Mark had eloped.

With tears streaming down her face, Katherine turned back to the officer. "Yes," her voice cracked, "please tell me how to file one." She opened the door and let the man enter.

***

Katherine didn't leave the police station until almost noon. As soon as she exited from the Smithsonian Metro stop, she was hit with a wave of oppressive heat.

How could any person be expected to work on a day like this?

She dreaded the discomfort she would be forced to endure in the cramped cubicle she referred to as her 'office.' She thought she would be farther along in her career by now. At thirty-two, she had been with the Smithsonian Magazine for way too long to still be doing this dead-end job. She wanted to do more than sit at her desk and solicit ads all day. She had majored in journalism to see the world, the beautiful parts, not the inside of a dark cubby hole in the Smithsonian Castle, no matter how stunning the view of the Washington Monument and National Mall.

From a young age, Katherine had been obsessed with the daily news. For years, her day began with the local news and the first thirty minutes of the CBS Morning Show. Unable to get enough to satisfy her addiction, she'd buy the Washington Post on the way to the Metro and peruse the headlines on the train, deciding which articles she would read on her commute and marking others to read over lunch or on the ride home.

That all stopped after she started dating Mark. Her journalism professors and co-eds from college would never understand this morbid avoidance of the news, but Katherine could no longer bring herself to hear the many travel warnings, bomb threats, and catastrophes that had become commonplace in the world. Since being with Mark, she didn't want to know if terrorists hijacked a plane or if some pilot lost control over the Mid-West.

She now thought back and wondered what other parts of her identity she had abandoned or restructured because of Mark.

"Bad morning," her friend, Megan, asked as Katherine dropped her purse into the drawer of her desk. Megan leaned over the short wall of the cubicle, sipping some sort of healthy concoction that was no doubt meant to soothe a hangover.

"I've had better," Katherine grumbled, slumping into her chair.

"Mr. Becker is on a rampage this morning," Megan warned, her dark brown eyes scanning the room for signs of their boss. "You've been late almost every day for the past three weeks." She looked sympathetically at Katherine.

"Mark showed up again this morning," Katherine said. Megan rushed around the divider and laid a soft, brown hand on Katherine's shoulder.

"I'm so sorry, Kate. Are you okay?"

Katherine nodded. "Yeah, but I had to file a restraining order against him and then had to wait for a judge to find time to rule on it. It wasn't a great way to start the day."

"You know what you need?" Megan asked. "You need a night out with the girls."

"Oh, Megan, I don't know," Katherine said, shaking her head and closing her eyes.

"I do. It's just the thing that will cheer you up." Megan headed back to her own desk. "Harry's Bar, tonight, right after work. Don't try to get out of it."

Katherine sighed as she weighed her options. It was certainly better than spending another night at home alone in fear that Mark would beat down the door.

***

"Come on, Kate," Megan said as Katherine sat at the table and stared at her nachos. Nobody else ever called her Kate. Megan, a believer in the science of names, said that Kate was a better name for her future success. "So he's a rat, and you got taken. It's been three weeks since you found out. You gotta bounce back, girl. Get over it."

They had been at the bar for over an hour, and by the looks on the faces of the other girls in the group, everyone was tired of Katherine's lack of enthusiasm.

"Get over it?" Katherine asked incredulously. "Get over it?" she repeated, her voice rising above the music of the band. It was the first night she had gone out since taking out the restraining order, and her nerves were already on edge. "Do you even know what you're saying? I thought I was married. Married! I thought this was supposed to be happily ever after, and all the time he was married to someone else. And they have kids for Christ's sake. And you say get over it!" Her voice grew louder with each sentence, and people at the nearby tables turned to look at her.

"Kate, calm down," Megan said, looking embarrassed. "You gotta get yourself together. You're causing a scene."

"My life has fallen apart, and you're worried about me causing a scene? I'm thirty-two years old, working a job I hate, living a life I don't even recognize, and now I'm not even married." Katherine's voice carried across the club as the band paused between songs. Eyes from around the room looked to see what they were missing in the darkened corner. "Who the hell cares if I'm causing a scene?"

"Jeez, Kate. Knock it off," Megan said, trying to keep her voice low. "He was a jerk, but he's gone. Your life is not over."

Katherine realized she wasn't going to get through to Megan. Megan was twenty-four, not long out of college, and still living in Maryland with her parents trying to save up for an apartment. She considered her job at the magazine a springboard to bigger and better things. *She's so like I was at one time*, thought Katherine.

"I need to go," Katherine said. It was no use trying to get Megan to understand. She was still entrenched in the hookup scene - sleep with a different guy every week until you find one good enough to stick with for a while. The concept of marriage was foreign to her.

Katherine pushed her way through the club and out onto the street. Where could she go, she wondered. She hated going home now. It held too many memories.

She walked the streets for close to a half hour until she realized that it was too late at night to be out there alone. The Nation's Capital had come a long way in recent years, but not far enough for anybody to be on the street alone at night. Until that moment, her safety hadn't been the slightest concern for Katherine. It was then that she thought about the way Mark had been acting lately, the numerous phone calls, the frightening scenes when he showed up at the house. A chill ran down her spine as Katherine looked around, making sure that she was alone while at the same time looking for a friendly face somewhere on the deserted street.

She walked swiftly to the nearest Metro and headed down into the lighted world of the DC subway system.

It's no safer down here than it was up there, but at least it will get me home faster.

Once at home, Katherine looked around the Brownstone that had been in her family for generations. The living room was a mess, as was the rest of the house. Her office looked no better. She hadn't vacuumed the house or done dishes or laundry in weeks. She wasn't sleeping and was barely eating. Had her mother still lived here, she would've scolded Katherine until she came to her senses. And her father, well, she couldn't even bring herself to think of how disappointed he would be in her. Again. Her trusting Mark and jumping into a sham of a marriage was bad enough, but the fact that she couldn't get her life together after three weeks was even worse.

She walked past the piles of mail strewn on the coffee table and the blanket thrown onto the couch. Did she feel like reading? Not really. She doubted her mind could absorb anything more detailed than a children's picture book, but she knew she wouldn't be sleeping, so why not try to read?

Katherine went into their family library and walked to the bookshelf. She fingered the books as she perused the titles. The few fiction books within her father's collection were priceless first editions, including a leather-bound copy of *Moby Dick*, which her father claimed was the inspiration for his studies. Though Queequeg, his tribe, and even his island were pure fiction, her father always claimed that the character sparked his interest in indigenous peoples.

The rest of the books on the shelf, were her mother's books. Mixed in with those were the ones that Katherine had added since moving back into the house three years ago. Titles jumped out at her as she ran her finger across the spines. Classics like *Gone with the Wind* and *The Great Gatsby* sat next to modern day bestsellers by Mary Higgins Clark and James Patterson. As Katherine gazed at the books, her finger stopped at one she remembered reading a few years ago before meeting Mark. It was Jacqueline Mitchard's *The Pilot's Wife.*

Katherine caught her breath. She closed her eyes and thought about the plot of the book. A pilot was killed in a crash, and while digging into the events leading up to the crash, his wife discovered that he had led a double life. He was married to her and another woman at the same time. He had a family, children, or was it a child? She couldn't remember. But there it was, her story in a work of fiction.

But this wasn't fiction. It was real life, *her* real life. And she wasn't the wife of fourteen years or the mother of the pilot's children. She was the other woman. The one whose story was not told in the book, the one nobody cared about or wondered how she was holding up, the one with nobody to lean on except for parents, who always saw her as a disappointment, and a brother, thousands of miles away on tour in Afghanistan.

Katherine sunk to the floor and covered her face with her hands. She wept bitterly for the loss of her marriage, for the short time she had a marriage, for the absence of her brother and closest confidant, for the distance of her loving parents, and for everything else she had ever lost in her life, her dreams, her confidence, and probably her job at this rate.

She sobbed for a long time, five minutes, or maybe hours, she didn't know and didn't care. Then she dragged herself into the bedroom and changed into a dirty nightshirt and climbed into bed. After a short time, she slept.

When she awoke, it was close to four in the morning. Katherine got up and went to the bathroom to brush her teeth. Then she went to the kitchen to find something to eat. She laughed at the order in which she did things now. Nothing in her life made sense.

She made herself a bowl of ice cream. At least it looked like ice cream. It hadn't been touched since Mark was last there, and the ice crystals that formed on it took away most of the taste. She picked up a travel magazine that Mark must've brought home from the airport. Taking the magazine and ice cream to her room, she crawled back into bed.

Thumbing through the magazine, Katherine's mind wandered. The bed no longer smelled like Mark. The first thing she had done when she disconnected the call with his wife that day was rip the sheets off the bed and put them in the trash. She slept without sheets for a week before she went to the department store downtown and bought new ones. She couldn't bear to use any of the ones in the closet. Some nights she slept on the couch, unable to sleep peacefully in the bed they had shared.

Unable to think about sleep, Katherine looked down at the magazine under her empty ice cream bowl and saw a picture of a beautiful, tranquil beach. Children made sand castles next to umbrellas that were opened wide like flowers planted in the sand. 'Visit Chincoteague,' the ad said. 'We'll make you feel at home.'

Maybe that's just what I need, Katherine thought, a place that will do what this house no longer does – make me feel like I'm at home.

***

Katherine woke up to the beating of a drum, or was it her head still aching from the events of the past month? Outside, her neighbor's son was performing his annoying Saturday car-washing ritual and singing loudly with the song that was no doubt destroying his eardrums as it boomed from his car stereo. Didn't he have earbuds like all the other kids these days? Funny, how his obsession with washing his car early on Saturday mornings had never been annoying until now.

Sometimes Mark would play music on his phone out loud and dance to it in his underwear, reminiscent of Tom Cruise in his infamous home alone scene in Risky Business. Katherine would laugh until her side hurt, begging Mark to stop before her insides ruptured. More than once he ended the dance by ripping off whatever under garments he had on and jumping on top of Katherine in bed, on the couch, the kitchen table, wherever they happened to be at the time. They would make love right then and there, keeping in rhythm with the beat. Those times seemed so far away now, like they had themselves been part of a movie and hadn't taken place in the real world.

She rolled over and grabbed the clock off the nightstand and brought it to her face under the covers. The red digits seemed to jump out from the front of the clock - 11:05 a.m., not nearly as early as she thought it was. Katherine crawled out of the bed and slumped to the floor wondering how she would face another weekend without Mark. At least during the week, she could momentarily forget her predicament by concentrating on work. The weekends, however, were unbearable.

She let out a breath and opened her eyes. Lying on the floor next to her was the travel magazine still open to the ad reading 'Visit Chincoteague.' She looked at the picture of the serene beach, the sun's rays reaching across the ocean like outstretched arms beckoning her to follow them into the water.

Katherine picked up the magazine and read the web site of the local tourism center. She wondered if the site had information on rentals. She'd loved the beach as a child. She pictured herself building a sandcastle with Zach on the shores of Australia and New Zealand, running into the ocean and diving into the waves as they rose in front of her and then crashed down over her back as she swam through them. She did a little research and found that Chincoteague Island was voted '#1 Happiest Beach Town' by AOL in 2010, '#2 Best Island in the U.S.' by TripAdvisor in 2014, and 'Happiest Seaside Town' by Coastal Living. Happy was just what Kate was lacking right now.

It was an intriguing thought - leaving everything behind for a while, her house with its memories, her boring job, her married friends who had no time for her, and the people at work she called friends but were nothing more than people she filled her empty hours with on occasion.

Without thinking, Katherine rose from the floor and walked into the living room. She sat at her father's desk where he spent hours each day writing and re-writing the one book that defined his life and career. The few scholarly articles that he had published on the history of the world's indigenous peoples won critical acclaim; unfortunately, his only book never made it onto the bestseller lists. She supposed he was a man ahead of his time. Research on peoples and their relationships to each other and to the land were all the rage today, but her father lived a simple life now, one that took place mostly on the golf course. Katherine thought that was ironic considering how much he hated the acquisition of land for purely economic purposes.

Katherine brought her computer out of hibernation. Her email was up, but there was still no response from Zach. Navigating to a Web browser, she typed the URL from the magazine into the address block and waited for the page to come up on the screen. She explored the many links, checking out the island, researching its offerings in the ways of jobs and entertainment, perusing the rental ads.

An hour later, she impulsively picked up the phone and called a vacation rental company she located through links on the tourism site. She hoped she was making the right decision.

***

On Monday, Katherine gave her boss her two weeks' notice. He said he was sorry to see her go, but Katherine knew otherwise. He made no attempt to convince her to stay or assure her that everything would get better and that she shouldn't make such a rash decision. Instead he wished her luck and reminded her to clean whatever was hers out of the lunchroom.

Katherine didn't blame her boss for not wanting her to stay. She knew that she had not been the ideal employee since Mark left. She was late for work at least three times a week, and her efforts were sloppy at best. She hadn't brought in any ads in weeks, and her reports were often incomplete.

She didn't tell anyone at work that she was leaving, not even Megan. She didn't want anyone to make a big deal of it, throw a party, offer to take her out for dinner or a drink. More than that, she didn't want them to *not* make a big deal out of it, to act like her leaving was not important in any way. She was also afraid that if she told anyone of her plans, Mark would somehow find out where she was going.

There had been no sign of him since she took out the restraining order, but she was still worried that he might try to contact her. She hated the tingling in her belly that signaled fear. In just over a year, she had gone from a confident, happy, party girl to a stranger's wife, content with letting her life pass by unnoticed, to a sad and lonely and even frightened woman, grieving for the life she really never had and fearing the person she thought was her soul mate.

She worked quietly in her office for the next two weeks, making an honest attempt to reach her quota of ads. She talked to nobody, and her co-workers were either too busy to notice or not good enough friends to care. Even Megan eventually stopped asking her if she was okay. On her last day, she packed the last of her things in a cardboard box and carried it back to her Brownstone. She had the weekend to pack, which was more than enough time. There was so little of this life that she wanted to take with her.

***

He watched her as she emerged from the Metro and walked toward the home that they had shared. The smell of alcohol emanated from him, and he rubbed his bloodshot eyes to keep her in focus. She had ruined his life, yet he couldn't get her off his mind.

Why did you answer the damned phone? Why did you have to tell Marcie that we were married?

He took another swig of the whiskey that was wrapped in a brown paper bag and thought about Marcie. She had kicked him out just like Katherine had. She had already filed for divorce and was seeking full custody of their children. His children. And it was all because of Katherine. If she had never looked at him that way all those months ago in the pub. If she hadn't invited him back here, none of this would have happened. Sure, they were both drunk and not thinking straight, but she was so damned alluring. He just couldn't say no. And from that night on, he knew he had to have her, no matter the cost.

But he had never factored the costs. Once he knew all that he had to lose, he decided. Forget Marcie, who paid more attention to the kids and the house than she did to him. He was going to find a way to convince Katherine to take him back. If she would just listen to him, she would change her mind and take him back. She was so trusting, so gullible. It would be easy to convince her that she should let him back into her life. He just needed a plan.

He finished off the bottle before dragging himself back to the Metro. Stumbling on the stairs, he ignored the disgusted looks of the other people as they tried to avoid him. He made it onto the train in one piece, sat in the seat reserved for the disabled and elderly, and slumped over, his snores drawing repugnant stares from the other passengers.

Among Australian Indigenous Peoples, it is generally acceptable, and even encouraged, for widows to remarry immediately after the death of a spouse. The deceased person's name is never again spoken so as not to disturb the dead. The belief that life goes on is strong throughout these communities. Mourning periods are short after a death. The living must keep living.

From the *Studies of Indigenous Peoples*
by Walter Middleton

CHAPTER THREE

Kate never thought September would arrive, but when the day after Labor Day finally rolled around, she was ready. From the looks of the Mustang, one would never have guessed that Katherine planned on being away from home for six months. The few things she packed were tucked neatly into a large suitcase in the trunk. Her purse sat on the seat next to her. A tote bag on the floor of the passenger's side held a few personal items she felt needed to be close to her: a guide book about Maryland and Virginia's Eastern Shore, a map of the island, her laptop, information to give the postmaster to receive her P.O. Box key (which was so kindly set up over the phone with help from the real estate agent), and, of course, the keys to the beach house.

Before she pulled away, Katherine took one last look at the Brownstone. The stately house looked the same as it had for as long as she could remember, the Indian red bricks were still in perfect condition, as was the grey cone-shaped turret at the top which held a lightning rod that met the clouds as they floated carelessly by. As a child, Katherine imagined the clouds to be like puffy balloons that might pop if they floated too close to the rod.

The curtains were all closed, as was the storm door behind the screen door her mother installed years ago to welcome the breeze. Katherine plugged timers into the outlets in certain rooms throughout the house so that lights would turn on and off to give the sense that someone was there. It was a false security, she knew, but it worked as a backup plan in case the actual security system failed or was shut off. Her parents weren't thrilled that she was leaving the house uninhabited for six months, but they understood that she was in no state to be pressured.

When Katherine called, and told them about Mark, they did their best to be supportive and not sound judgmental. Katherine was grateful for that, but she knew that they were deeply disappointed in all the decisions that she had made as an adult so far. She always took the easy way out, and they let her, though they didn't hide their displeasure with her choices. Living in her family's home, still working at the dead-end job that her father arranged for her after college, partying all hours of the night, and wasting her expensive education, were all topics of conversation at family gatherings. At least she had never done drugs, not that it mattered to her parents. To them, she was still a major disappointment. It was finally time for Katherine to grow up, and they all knew it.

Katherine headed down M Street toward New York Avenue, which would turn into Route 50 once she entered Maryland. She skirted around the construction at 9th Street and caught a glimpse of the world-famous Capitol Building, its newly renovated dome a dazzling, almost blinding white in the morning light. The monuments and statues she drove by throughout the city were covered with glistening diamonds shining in the morning sun, the beads of water left from last night's rain. The day was cool for September, a cold front having moved in on the back of the Labor Day showers that tapped out a cadence on the roof during her last night in the Nation's Capital.

Forty-five minutes into her drive, the arches of the Bay Bridge came into view. Katherine stopped at the toll booth and paid to cross the Chesapeake Bay, the great expanse of water that divides the state of Maryland into Eastern and Western shores geographically, politically, and culturally. According to her father, the Algonquian Indians named the bay Chesepiooc, meaning 'Great Shellfish Bay.' The water gave no signs of pending change as she crossed the bridge, its sailboats and fishing boats dotting the waves between the two shores. But from the moment Katherine's car left the bridge and entered the land across the Bay, the landscape was transformed.

With the exception of the condos on the water's edge, and the few strip malls at the foot of the bridge, the scenery went from office buildings, traffic lights, and shopping malls to century-old farm houses and quilts of fields at various stages of harvest, some covered with gaggles of Canada Geese. Katherine knew that the birds migrated to the Chesapeake Bay region in the fall, but it seemed early for that. It was still pretty hot along the Eastern Seaboard. She had heard the term, 'resident geese' and wondered if that's what these were, geese that had lost their natural instinct to migrate.

Katherine watched as a flock of the beautiful black, white, and grey birds began to flap their wings and take off into the sky, following the leader of their V-shaped wedge, to their next stop. She continued on her own journey, both running away and toward something. She just wasn't sure what.

After another hour of driving, Kate stopped for a drink at a convenience store on the side of the road. Eyeing the choices in the case, she passed up her drinks of choice, rich with sugar and caffeine, and zeroed in on a bottle of crystal clear spring water. In that very instant, she made another decision to change something about her life. She would start drinking more water and less soda. Since she was planning on changing her mental health, she ought to also start paying attention to her physical health. No more ice cream dinners in the middle of the night or treating soda and alcohol as essential vitamins. She hadn't run since the morning Mark arrived, and her kayak was in the basement collecting dust.

Tasting the clear liquid as it slid past her tongue and down her throat, she decided that she actually liked the taste of the water. She placed the bottle in the cup holder between the front seats and consulted her phone's navigation app, another two and a half hours to go. She was glad she left home early that morning. It would be past lunchtime when she arrived at the beach house.

She put her sunglasses back on, started the car, and pressed the automatic window button. The air was still cool but a little warmer than it had been when she left the city, and the sun's rays poured through the windshield as it rose higher toward its pinnacle in the sky. She couldn't ever remember driving with the windows down except on the rare occasions she drove somewhere and needed to cool down her car while the air conditioning worked itself up to combat the summer's heat.

The wind rushed by as she drove down the highway, each mile taking her closer to the state line and the Eastern Shore of Virginia. Her blonde hair blew around her face, and she breathed in the fragrant, fresh air that only the combination of tall trees, fresh grass, and recently cut fields could produce.

When she finally reached the turnoff to Chincoteague Island, a prickle of excitement ran up her neck, and the flutter of butterflies awoke in her stomach. The drive down the causeway seemed to be endless even though the ride was just a few miles long. Passing Wallops Island, Kate knew she was getting close. Living in the DC area, she was familiar with the NASA rocket launching site and had even met someone once who worked there on occasion. As she neared the island, the roadsides became littered with billboard after billboard advertising hotels, restaurants, t-shirt shops, and other businesses promising to make one's stay on the island exciting and enjoyable.

As Katherine approached the bridge, her stomach fluttered with anticipation. She crossed the channel and noticed the blanket of rhinestones that covered the Bay as the mid-day's sunlight illuminated the water. Waterfowl flew in and out of the marshes on the shore of the island, and as she watched them, she felt like a child on Christmas morning waiting to open her first present.

Katherine Middleton crossed the small bridge to the island at the same time she crossed a much larger bridge in her life.

***

As she turned left toward the north side of the island, Katherine was pleased to see the stilted beach houses, marshes, trees, and waterways she had been hoping to find. It seemed that almost every house had a canal that sidled up next to it. She pulled up in front of the house and looked through her windshield at her home for the next six months. She climbed the tall stairway taking her up into the house. Each house rose off the ground, and most, if not all, had high porches, decks, and balconies, some that wrapped all the way around the house.

Katherine hesitated as she unlocked the door and went inside. The house was in Angler's Rest, a small beachside community on the island. The ad on the Internet described it as 'A luxury waterfront vacation home on the

Chincoteague Bay. Within walking distance of the downtown. Amenities include fabulous waterside deck with overhead balcony.' It was luxurious all right. The main floor was comprised of a comfortable living room, dining room, and kitchen with a small breakfast nook. A sunken level, just a few steps down from the kitchen, included a small TV room, a laundry room, two bedrooms and a bathroom. Next to the front door, a stairway led to an upper floor with a master suite and bathroom, another bedroom, and one more bathroom. In addition to the master bedroom balcony, which ran the length of the back of the house and could be accessed by both bedrooms, there was a long front porch and a large back deck.

It was much larger than Katherine needed, and the cost of the long-term rental, a hefty twenty grand, completely drained her bank account. It was probably the dumbest thing she had ever done, but she wasn't ready to buy anything, and the house came fully furnished. More importantly, it offered privacy as the last house in a row of ten that sat on the Chincoteague Bay. She knew she could dip into her trust fund if need be, but she always thought of that as her grandmother's money, and she hoped to use some of it for retirement and pass the rest on to her own children someday. She pushed that thought from her mind.

The natural colors and beach themed prints and furniture were soothing and welcomed her in after the three-and-a-half-hour drive. She looked out a window and watched gulls fly over the Chincoteague Bay. The closest house in the row was about forty yards down, a swath of green grasses separating them. Grass ran the length of the row and extended down to the water about thirty yards from the house. Katherine was surprised and a bit disappointed that there was no actual beach and was anxious to see what the other lots on the island were like.

She brought few things with her, so it took only a few minutes to haul her bags into the house. She lugged her heavy suitcase up the steps into the stilt-legged beach house, and then up the stairs to the master suite on the second floor. But the effort had been worth it. The view from the French doors that led onto the balcony was breath taking, and she was happy that this was the sight that she would be waking to for the next six months.

She eyed the phone on the nightstand and thought about checking in with her parents. There was no one else to call to say that she had arrived safely, that the house was beautiful, that they should come visit as soon as she was settled. Katherine hadn't kept in touch with any of her friends from high school, and her college friends were all married with children starting pre-school and even elementary school. She had stopped trying to fit into their schedules some time ago. She thought about Zach and wished he wasn't so out of reach. She longed to hear her brother's voice and tell him that the house was as perfect as she had imagined. He would be returning from the desert soon, and she hoped he would find time to come visit her at the beach.

With a sigh, she started to unpack. She hung her black and navy pants in the closet along with her jacket and winter coat. There was a cedar shelf built into one side of the closet where she gently piled her sweaters. She had packed just one dress and one skirt. She didn't plan on going out, and even if she did, this was a beach town. She planned on being very casual most of the time.

Her sweatshirts, long-sleeved Ts, jeans, socks, under garments, and the few shorts and t-shirts she brought fit nicely into the dresser. Her only pair of sandals sat alone on the floor of the closet while her tennis shoes remained on her feet. Should she have brought more winter clothes, she wondered. Did it snow at the beach? She didn't know. She had never been to the Atlantic in the winter, at least not in this part of the world. She had no idea what Chincoteague was like in winter. She supposed she would find out. She was sure it was a far cry from the sunny and humid winters her parents loved in their retirement village on San Marco Island.

She surveyed the room and noticed how little space her things claimed. She had so many clothes back in Georgetown. Had she really needed them all? She would know soon enough.

She walked through the house touching the furniture, looking closely at the beach scene prints on the walls. She stopped and stared at the print of the wild ponies on the beach and wondered if they ever walked on what was now her beach. She was fascinated by the thought that these animals had lived here for so long, still ran wild along the shores of nearby Assateague, and still claimed the area as their own. How different from the motorcycles, bicycles, roller blades, and skateboards that seemed to run wild in DC.

When her stomach growled, Katherine realized it was almost mid-afternoon. She remembered seeing a small grocery store when she drove through town earlier. She grabbed her keys from the kitchen counter and headed to her car. She had just enough money to get groceries for about a week. At least she hoped so. She planned on having some kind of job soon but hadn't bothered to secure anything before arriving. Her hope was that most seasonal families would be gone by now, and their jobs would be available. Of course, that was if those jobs even existed in the off-season.

Since she needed to be able to get her groceries home, she drove the short, walkable distance to the downtown. There were ponies everywhere, not the wild ones, but a pony ride in a small coral, stuffed ponies in store windows, and mechanical ponies on the sidewalks. She smiled at the thought of hundreds of out-of-town children clamoring to get a glimpse of a real, wild pony but being just as happy with these touristy stand-ins. What a delightful place this must be for young families, she thought.

By the time she got to the check out counter, her cart was filled with breakfast, lunch, dinner, and snack foods. She hoped her checking account could handle it. She refused to move any money from her trust fund.

"You must be staying for a while," the elderly gentleman asked as he scanned her groceries.

"A little while," she said. "I'm renting a house in Angler's Rest for the next six months." She watched the items add up on the register.

"Nice community," he said. "Are you a writer?"

"Excuse me?" she asked.

"A writer," he repeated. "Come out to work on a book during the quiet winter on the island. Happens quite often, you know."

"No, well, maybe," she hadn't thought about writing a book before, but according to her journalism professors she was a writer. She thought of her father and how he would feel about her following in his footsteps.

The man gave her a quizzical look. "Just looking for some privacy, I suppose," he said with a knowing look in his eyes.

She smiled. "I guess so. I really don't know what I'll do while I'm here. I majored in journalism and did work for a magazine in DC, but I don't have a job here yet. By the looks of that bill you're totaling up, I'd better get one fast," she laughed motioning to the register.

"Never shop when you're hungry," he told her. "People tend to spend the most when they're hungry, and you look like you could use a good meal."

"I'll remember that," she said nervously as she dug for her check card, a blush rising in her face. She looked down at her clothes and noticed for the first time how they hung on her neglected body.

"The Chincoteague Herald," he said, interrupting her thoughts. He was bagging her apples and oranges, and Kate wondered if she had imagined him speaking.

"Excuse me?" she said for the second time.

"The island newspaper," he motioned to the rack by the door. "They're looking for somebody to cover local events. Gus retired after all these years, and they haven't replaced him. Better grab it before someone else does."

"Thank you." She smiled and walked over to grab a copy. She handed it to him and waited for the amount then she ran her card through the reader on the counter.

"Happy to help. Welcome to the island." He smiled and handed her a receipt.

"Thanks, and it's Kate," she said. "Kate Middleton. I'm sure I'll see you again."

"Like the princess?" he asked.

Kate suddenly remembered why she had never warmed up to the name Kate. Too late now, she supposed.

"Yeah, like the princess," she admitted and avoided the man's gaze. She certainly didn't feel like a princess, and she knew she didn't look like one at the moment. When she made the decision to go back to her maiden name (not really a decision, apparently, she never was Katherine Leahy), she followed Megan's advice and decided that she might as well use a new name to go with her new life. It wasn't until that moment that she realized how ridiculous that notion was. What difference could a name make? And why on earth did it have to be such a recognizable one? Never anything but Katherine, she had never been compared to royalty of any kind. Now that the die was cast, she hoped she could live up to any expectations that the name brought her way.

"Have a nice day, Miss Middleton," the man said as Katherine picked up her groceries. She gave him a weak smile and went out to her car.

Kate looked up the address of the newspaper office and headed in that direction after loading her groceries into the backseat.

She parked in the only space in front of the office, checked her reflection in the rear-view mirror, and got out of the car.

Marge, the editor-in-chief, was impressed with her credentials from the Smithsonian even though Kate had never thought they were that impressive. She didn't ask for references or a resume before telling Kate that she was hired and could start the next day. Chalk that up to another difference between the small island and Washington, DC

"I guess Henry saw something in you, and your background sounds good," Marge said.

"Henry?" Kate asked.

"Over at the grocery store," Marge nodded toward the market down the street. Kate noticed a twinkle in her eye. "My hubby," she winked. "You'll find this is a very small town." Her smile was broad and genuine.

"I guess I'd better remember that when I'm talking to a stranger," Kate said, returning Marge's smile.

"They won't be strangers for long, especially with this job," Marge told her.

She would be covering small local events like Boy Scout ceremonies and school assemblies. She was encouraged to take pictures as well. Kate assumed this was an effort to keep down labor costs – no professional photographer for the community events.

Before leaving the newspaper office, she inquired about a local library. Marge directed her to the Island Library on Main Street. On the way to the library, Kate marveled at the irony of working for a newspaper when she hadn't even read one for almost two years.

The interior of the quaint little library drew her in as if she were at home. Kate sought out a librarian at the information desk and inquired about a card.

"I'm not actually a resident," she explained, "but I am renting a house on the island through the winter."

"That's not a problem," the librarian smiled. "Nowadays, our patrons can be anywhere in the country." She handed Kate a form that she filled out and returned.

"May I check out something today?" she asked.

"Yes, you may," the librarian told her. "Go ahead and pick out something while I enter your information into the computer."

"Can you recommend something new that will make me laugh?"

The librarian thought about it for a moment. "I believe the new Jennifer Cruise just came back in." She turned and looked at the cart of books behind her. "You're in luck," she said turning back around with a book in hand. "There are no more holds on this, and it's a delightful read."

Kate waited patiently while her information was entered and her new card scanned. Now she was ready to go home and get settled in.

By the time she got back to the house, she not only had a new name but a new job. Though it was just part-time, it would pay for her groceries and her utilities. Her bills from Georgetown would be minimal, and her cell phone bill was paid just before she left DC She planned on spending very little over the next few months, and she still had her trust fund, though she had gone eleven years without touching it and planned to keep it that way until she retired.

***

Kate had set her phone's alarm app for seven o'clock in the morning, but she woke up long before the app sounded. She wasn't sure if it was due to her body's internal clock, used to getting up at six, or the sunrise over the ocean, sending its welcoming rays through the French doors. Rising from the bed, she walked to the doors and pulled them open. She gasped at the beauty before her eyes.

The water was alive with colors. Kate couldn't tell where the horizon began or where the water ended and the sky began. At its farthest, the scene was a mixture of red and orange, a blaze of fire upon the water. The panorama was a palette of oranges and blues, creating a magnificent canvas of colors. Lazy white and blue waves rolled upon the shore stretching across the beach in a hue that matched the calm sea beyond the frothy tide. The orange, red, and pink clouds reached across the sky like puffs and strands of cotton candy as the yellow sun began to peek over the sea.

Kate had never called herself spoiled, but now she wondered what kind of lazy existence she had led that as an adult, she had never watched the sun rise to greet the day. Even when she and Mark had been in Mexico, they slept late in each other's arms, never leaving the bungalow to go to the beach. They hadn't known when the sun was high in the sky not to mention when it rose and set.

At the thought of Mark, Kate remembered what she had worked so hard to push from her mind. This date marked the day she thought would bring happy memories for the rest of her life. One year ago today, she and Mark said their vows to one another in front of the only sunset they managed to see while on the Mexican island. She closed her eyes and willed the thought away, as tears seeped through her lashes.

"No," she said, shaking her head from side to side as if it was an eraser on a chalkboard. She intended to erase all bad memories from her mind.

Kate forced herself to open her eyes, to once again look at the sun as it climbed further away from the water. A new day had begun, as had a new chapter in her life. There was to be no more crying, no more feeling sorry for herself. Somehow, she would survive the loss of her marriage. Her life was not over; like the day, it was just dawning, and she would stop mourning and get on with it.

***

When Kate walked into the cafeteria, the first thing she noticed was the long table stretched across the room with bowls containing treasures of every color. Along with an array of sprinkles, there was a bowl of M&Ms, one of gummi bears, mini marshmallows, maraschino cherries, and even a bowl of jellybeans. The toppings seemed endless, and the children happily piled as many as they could fit on top of the vanilla ice cream that the women at the head of the table scooped into their bowls. Kate wasn't sure whether to hold her stomach or grab a bowl. Who would've thought to put jellybeans on ice cream sundaes?

"Good afternoon, I'm Kate Middleton from the Chincoteague Herald," she said, walking to the table. She was met with friendly smiles from both ladies. It wasn't the kind of news she ever imagined she might be reporting, but then again, she never imagined she would be thirty-two and starting a new life on a tiny island.

"I'm Elaine Scofield, the principal," said the woman in the red dress. "This is Marian Grammer, our school librarian."

"Hello, Ms. Middleton," the librarian said with a raised eyebrow, no doubt recognizing the name of the Princess, "Thanks for coming over today."

"It's my pleasure, and please call me Kate. I'd like to start by taking some pictures if that's okay, and then you can give me all the details about the summer readers."

"That would be great," Elaine told her. "That way we can talk while they eat." She blew her bangs out of her face as a little boy pushed past Kate and reached for the bowl that the principal had just filled with ice cream. "No pushing, Bobby. Please apologize to Ms. Middleton."

"Sorry," he said with little remorse as he headed to the toppings. Kate took his picture as he scooped a mound of chocolate chips onto his sundae.

She took several pictures of children making and eating their treats as well as some of the ladies squirting whipped cream and chocolate syrup onto the dripping mountains of melting ice cream and candy.

"Will she eat all that?" Kate asked one of the women as a little girl walked away with a bowl filled with every topping and covered in whipped cream, chocolate syrup, and caramel sauce.

The woman laughed. "No, but she'll have fun trying!"

"Are you a teacher?" Kate asked, taking out her notebook.

"No, I'm Shannon Hill, President of the PTA. Tammi over there with the water jug is the Vice President, and Anne here is the Secretary."

"Hello," Anne said as she squirted the white foam into another bowl.

"I'm Kate Middleton, and I'm here doing a story for the Herald on the ice cream social. Did these kids really read over 100 books each during the summer?" She was amazed at the turnout. From everything she read and heard on the news, she assumed children didn't even know what books were anymore.

Shannon nodded. "Isn't it wonderful? Some of the older ones, who will be in here shortly, read twenty-some books on their own, and we're talking Harry Potter type books, over three or four hundred pages."

"That's really impressive, and what a fun way to start off the school year," Kate said as she took notes. "I wonder if we could get the entire group together for a picture."

After the ice cream had been eaten, they arranged the shot for the paper. Kate wondered about the ages of the women in the room. The principal didn't look a day over 40, and the librarian looked about the same age. The PTA moms were probably not much older than she was. She guessed that Anne was right around her own age although she obviously had school-aged children.

After Kate finished taking pictures and talking to Mrs. Scofield and Mrs. Grammer, she stayed and helped clean up. They insisted that was not necessary, but Kate felt the urge to stay in their presence, to be one of a group. She hadn't felt like she was part of a group since right after college when her friends started getting married, and her "group" dwindled to one. It was nice to imagine that she belonged with this one. Though some of the women in the room cast suspicious glances toward Kate, most of them were very welcoming and friendly.

When they were finished, she returned to the beach house to write her story. She emailed the article and pictures to the paper. She was instructed to let the editor decide which photos would go with the stories she wrote.

Marge called her right away to let her know that she was impressed with Kate's writing and that the pictures were great. Kate was thrilled that she had done well on her first assignment. Marge asked if she would cover the Boy Scout Eagle Scout ceremony the next evening, and Kate told her of course. Although the job was a far cry from writing for the Smithsonian Magazine or The Washington Post, Kate decided it was a great way to use her skills and get to know the island and its citizens. She looked forward to the Boy Scout event the next night.

Kate looked at the clock. It was just four in the afternoon. Though she felt hunger pangs, it seemed too early for dinner. Looking out the back door, her eyes scanned past the deck and onto the grassy area. The tide was high, and although the sun had yet to go down, the moon hung low over the water. She went upstairs and kicked off her tennis shoes, retrieved her sandals from the closet, and headed back downstairs. Halfway down, she ran back up for a sweatshirt as she remembered that she was along the Atlantic in early September and the evenings cooled off quickly as the cool wind whipped around the island.

She grabbed a banana, made sure the front door was locked, and headed out onto the porch, locking the sliding glass door with her key before she headed to the shoreline. Slipping the key ring into the pocket of her capris, she tied the sweatshirt around her waist as she headed to the water. She finished off the banana, rolled it into a ball, stuffed it into her pocket, and took off her sandals. She carried her shoes in her hand and stood in the grass. A thick marsh filled with tall grass separated her from the water's edge.

"I guess I won't be walking along the water," she said to herself. *Aren't islands supposed to be covered with sand and surrounded by crisp, clear water that dragged seashells onto the shoreline?*

Looking to the right, she saw that the blanket of grass rolled into marshland that continued all the way to the point. To the left, she saw that a grassy strip ran the length of the row of houses. She stood in the yard and watched as a solitary boat glided by and seabirds dove in and out of the gentle waves.

Further up the strip, behind the house closest to hers, she watched as two children raced through their yard flying a kite in the grass. A man sat on the deck and watched. Kate retreated to her deck and sat on the bottom step to watch them as well. Untying her shirt, she pulled it down over her head and rested her chin on her arms that were crossed over her knees. She thought about the plans she used to have for her future.

Would she ever sit on a deck or in a backyard and watch her own children play? Would she volunteer at school events and attend Boy Scout ceremonies for her son? A year ago, she was certain those things were just around the corner. Now she didn't even know where she wanted to live or what she wanted to do with her life.

As Kate watched, a woman came out of the house, and the two adults motioned to the boys, their words were carried away in the salty air and drowned out by the sound of the lapping waves. The children reeled in their kite and ran up the steps into the house, the older boy first, and the little one trailing behind.

Kate wasn't sure how long she sat there after that, but eventually she noticed that the moon shone a little brighter than it had when she started out, and the sun that dipped low behind her was casting small shards of light on the water. It was then that she realized she had sat and watched the children, thought about her future, seen the man and woman taking their family inside their cozy house, and she had not cried. It was a major breakthrough, she knew. Whether it was the town, the house, the job, or being around people all afternoon, she didn't know. But one thing was certain, Kate had re-entered the land of the living, and she was glad to be back.

***

Kate spent the next day browsing through the shops downtown. She especially loved the one with the handmade, glass blue crabs hanging on the wall and the balls made of seashells that decorated the windows. She decided that she would buy a couple of the crabs before her sojourn was over and take them back to hang in Georgetown. They would forever remind her of the time she spent on this beautiful island. She might even buy a couple for her mother for Christmas to remind her of being home in the Mid-Atlantic.

At the Chincoteague Island Museum, Kate learned about the history of the island. Just inside the museum was the famous pony of the stories, Misty, stuffed and on display for visitors to see but not touch. Kate learned that many of the original homes on the island actually were built on the neighboring Assateague Island. In the 1920s, when most of the island was bought up by one family, the other families were no longer welcome. Rather than abandoning their homes, they hoisted them onto carts and rolled them to water's edge where they transferred them onto boats and sailed them across the Channel to Chincoteague. Many of the island's original inhabitants were watermen who made their living fishing, crabbing, and tonging for oysters. That was still true today although tourism was now the main economy.

Unable to stop herself, despite her recent proclamation about eating healthier, Katherine made a stop at the island's giant candy store. She was never able to resist homemade peanut butter cups, and she bought a pound of dark chocolate and creamy peanut butter treats, which she was sure she would regret the next time she wore something tight fitting. A man came into the store just as she stopped to check out a display on her way out of the door. He greeted the woman behind the counter with a nod.

"Hi, Nick," the woman said. "Is Marian ready for the party this weekend?" she asked, coming from around the counter.

"She's more ready than I am," he replied. "I haven't even ordered the cake, and that's on my side of the to-do list. We've got her present, though. It's one of those American Girl Dolls. We had it delivered to my office so she wouldn't see it."

"She'll be thrilled, just thrilled. What can I do for you today?" the woman asked as she straightened some items on a display shelf.

Nick started to answer as Kate closed the door behind her, leaving the two to their business. She smiled as she recalled the story that Zach once told about buying an American Girl doll for the daughter of a fallen soldier he knew in Iraq. Kate admired her brother for his thoughtfulness and vowed to be more like him. Katherine may have thought more of herself than others, but Kate was going to be different.

***

The Boy Scout ceremony was to start at 6:00, and Kate arrived at 5:45 to introduce herself to the Scout Master and find out a little bit about what would take place. When she arrived, the first person she saw was Anne, the PTA secretary.

"Hello again," Kate smiled and waved as she walked toward the tall blonde setting out refreshments.

"Hi Kate," she said, putting down the tray of cookies and reaching out her hand, her broad smile brightening up the dimly lit corner of the room.

"You remembered my name," Kate said in surprise.

"It's not a hard one to remember," Anne smiled, and Kate blushed at her own stupidity. Of course, Anne remembered the name.

"You're Anne, right?" Kate said, taking the woman's hand as Anne nodded. "I haven't been to a Boy Scout ceremony since I was in high school and my brother made Eagle Scout. How many boys are being honored tonight?"

"Just one, Billy Hill. He worked hard all summer building new fences around the pony corral and finished just in time for the annual pony swim and penning. It was a huge project and a really big deal for the whole island. There aren't usually this many people here for an Eagle Scout ceremony, but what Billy did really affected so many in our community. Hi Mindy," she said as she reached for the tray of brownies another woman handed her. "This is Kate. She's covering the ceremony for the Herald. I assume that's why you're here?" she asked Kate.

"That's correct. Nice to meet you, Mindy," Kate said, extending her own hand this time.

"Hello," Mindy said, sizing up the newcomer. She shook Kate's hand quickly before turning to find a seat. Kate watched her leave.

Anne laughed, "Mindy's an islander since birth. It might take some time, but she's a real sweetheart once you get to know her."

Kate laughed nervously. "I'm getting used to those kinds of looks from people. It's so different in DC where practically everyone is from somewhere else. Oh, well, I guess I need to find a seat. Is there anything important I should know or anything special I should put in the article?"

Anne pointed to a tall boy in a crisp, clean uniform who was helping the other boys straighten out their uniforms and hold their flags correctly. "That's Billy Hill, the honoree. He's Shannon's son - the PTA President?" Kate nodded in acknowledgement. She remembered Shannon and how friendly she was. "He's such a great kid. In addition to earning his Eagle, he assists with the Webelo Twos. That's my Ben with the red hair. They're all here to support Billy. And over there," she said motioning to a man talking to another group of boys, "is Ted Arnold, the Pack

Leader. He's in charge of the show, so to speak. Just follow his cue, and you'll know everything you need to know."

Kate thanked her and found a seat. When it was time for the ceremony to begin, Anne sat next to her and leaned over.

"I'll help you with the names and spellings if you like," she whispered.

"That would be great, Anne," Kate said. "I'm new to the reporting business, so anything to help me along is greatly welcomed."

"You'd never know it by watching you. You did very well at the school yesterday."

"Thanks, I appreciate that," Kate said. She liked Anne and hoped to get to know her. She seemed honest and genuine, like someone who would jump in and help anyone in need – a true friend. It had been a long time since Kate had a real friend, and maybe that was part of her problem.

Anne and Kate left the ceremony at the same time. Anne stayed to help clean up after her husband took their kids, Ben and Lizzie, home to put them to bed. Kate stayed to talk to Billy and Ted to make sure she had all her details correct. The two women walked out together.

"So, what brings you to Chincoteague?" Anne asked as Kate helped her carry tablecloths and trays to her car.

Kate sighed. "It's a long, sad story. Let's just say, I'm finding myself."

"Fair enough," Anne said. "Are you here for good, or is this just a stop on the road to wherever you may find yourself?" she asked with a smile.

"I've rented a house on the beach for six months. After that, I plan on going home to Georgetown, but at this point, I'm open to any option," Kate said, realizing for the first time that maybe she wouldn't go back to the old Brownstone. Maybe she'd travel, move across the country, stay here. Who knows?

"Well, it'll be nice to have you here for six months, Kate. I hope we're able to make you feel at home." Anne shut the back of her Explorer and looked at Kate.

"We're having a cookout on Sunday after Mass. It's kind of a last hurrah before it gets cold. Would you like to come?"

"I'd like that a lot," Kate said.

"You're welcome to come to Mass, too, if you like. We attend St. Andrews on Church Street. Mass is at ten."

Kate pinched her lips between her teeth and thought for a moment. She hadn't been inside a church since she couldn't remember when. Her parents went when it suited them, so she never got into the habit of going even though she was baptized Catholic. But right now, she really didn't think she was in very good standing with the man upstairs.

"Um, thanks, but I think I'll just come by your house if that's okay." Kate blushed and looked away. She hoped she wasn't making a bad impression already.

"That would be fine," Anne smiled. "We're happy to have you come to the cookout." Anne reached into her purse and pulled out a business card and a pen. She wrote something on the back and handed it to Kate. "Here's the address. We'll see you around 11:30?"

Kate took the card and nodded. "Yes, that sounds good. Thank you." She smiled, and the two women said goodbye.

Kate started her car and watched Anne drive away as she thought about their conversation. She had a lot to think about over the next six months, but she was sure that the answers she was seeking couldn't be found in a church. She looked down at the card in her hand. Anne was a woman of many talents. In addition to being PTA Secretary and one of the Boy Scout volunteers, she ran her own travel agency. Kate thought it interesting that someone who lived in a tourist destination would be in the business of sending people on vacations to other places.

Kate began putting her car in gear when one last family emerged from the building in front of her. They were her neighbors, the man and woman and two little boys she had seen playing on the beach. She had noticed them at the ceremony but hadn't had time to introduce herself. She watched as the man and woman stood by a mid-sized SUV for a few moments and chatted while the boys climbed into the vehicle. Something seemed off about the scene, and Kate found herself putting her car back in park as her curiosity got the best of her. Once the boys were inside, and the woman checked to make sure they were buckled properly, she gave the man a quick, chaste hug and waved goodbye. He waved to the boys through the window and began walking to a truck across the lot. Kate sat back and watched as the man got into the truck, and the two vehicles drove off in separate directions. Perhaps they weren't such a happy family after all.

By the time both sets of headlights were out of sight, Kate was more than ready to go home. Though it hadn't been a very busy day, she was exhausted and was beginning to feel a little queasy. She realized that she hadn't been eating as well as she should be. A handful of chips and a cookie at the ceremony were all the food she had eaten since the sandwich she ate for lunch. Her stomach was certainly protesting its lack of good food. As she drove back to the house, she reminded herself of her vow to start eating healthier.

Within the Indigenous peoples of the Australian Outback, the sense of community and kinship is so strong, that all people are identified by their relation to others within the community. Even those from other hordes or outside of the Indigenous races, once adopted into the horde, are known as mother/father/sister/brother to the others in the horde. Nobody is alone once they are accepted into the community.

From the *Studies of Indigenous Peoples*
by Walter Middleton

CHAPTER FOUR

When Kate arrived at the cookout on Sunday, Anne was standing on the front porch, ushering another family into the house. She came down into the yard and welcomed Kate with outstretched arms and the same warm smile from the evening they first met.

"Kate, I'm so glad you came," Anne beamed, taking her hands and leading her to the backyard where a man was opening a large barbecue grill. A group of kids were playing on the swing set in the yard. "Kids, come here, please," Anne called. "Paul, you remember Kate? This is Lizzie and Ben."

"Yes, from the Boy Scout ceremony. Nice to see you again, Kate," Paul said, reaching out to shake her hand.

"Likewise," she replied. Lizzie and Ben both reached for Kate's hand and greeted her with nice, confident voices, "Nice to meet you, Ma'am." Kate was impressed with their manners and the way they spoke to her.

Anne introduced two other men standing by the grill, Sean and Lou.

"We're so glad you came," Anne said, "and what is this?" she asked, gesturing to the cake that Kate held in her hands.

"I'm afraid I'm not much of a cook, but I'm pretty good at opening cake mixes and following directions." Kate replied.

"How sweet of you," Anne said. "Why don't we take it inside and start getting things together for lunch?"

Kate followed Anne into the house which was situated near Memorial Park where several youngsters were playing. The house was typical of the island with a wraparound balcony as well as a wraparound porch, complete with a swing. Like many of the houses on the island, it was raised up several feet in case of flooding. The women went up the back steps into a screened-in-porch. The gardens surrounding the porch, with red, orange, and yellow roses along with gold and purple chrysanthemums, were exquisite even in September, and she wondered how long they would stay in bloom.

"I love your house," Kate told Anne as they walked inside.

"Thank you. It's a work in progress really. Has been since it was moved here in 1927."

Kate stopped and looked around. "Really? I would never have guessed that it was that old."

"We've renovated, upgraded, and added on, but the bones are still there. Of the house, I mean, not human bones. Though it's been here for so long that nothing we find surprises me."

"When you say 'moved,' do you mean it was actually moved? Was it one of the Assateague houses?" Kate asked, recalling what she had read at the museum. It made the house and Anne all that much more intriguing.

"Yes. A friend of mine lived here when I was growing up. It had been in her family since it was first built. I always loved it. Luckily, by the time Paul and I were looking for a bigger house, my friend decided to sell it. I'm sure it's a move she will someday regret."

"At least she knows it's being lived in by someone who loves it?"

"This is true," Anne said with a smile.

Inside the house, women whom Kate recognized from the school were already preparing food on the kitchen counter. Kate looked around the house as she placed her cake on the table. She caught a glimpse of what her life had almost been like. Family pictures hung on the walls, a large portrait of the four Parkers hung over the fireplace mantel—Anne seated with the children standing on each side of her, Paul's hand laying protectively and lovingly on her shoulder. Colorful drawings and photos of friends decorated the refrigerator while a ceramic bowl on the kitchen island held apples and bananas mixed in with granola bars.

Kate felt a knot form in her chest. Her head began to spin, and lightheadedness came over her. She reached for the top of a kitchen chair, its handmade, ruffled cushion standing out as if to point out to Kate how inadequate her life had been and still was.

"Kate, Kate, are you okay?"

"Kate, what's wrong?"

She could hear voices all around her, but the words weren't making sense. Bile rose into her throat, and she closed her eyes and swallowed it down, willing herself to take a deep breath through her nostrils.

"Get her to the couch," a voice said, "and bring her some water."

Kate felt hands leading her to the sofa in the living room where a glass of water was pressed into her hand and a cool cloth applied to her head. *Get a grip*, the voice in her head said from a distance. *You're making a fool out of yourself.*

After a few minutes, Kate opened her eyes and looked up into the worried and expectant faces above her, some she recognized, others she did not. Nick, the man from the candy store, Ted, the Scout Master and his wife and son, as well as Shannon and Tammi, the PTA President and Vice President, were mixed in among faces that she hadn't seen before like pieces of a puzzle that had been dumped out in front of her.

"Kate, are you okay?" Anne asked. "Should I call a doctor?"

Kate managed to shake her head. She swallowed again in an attempt to push down the taste in her mouth and find her voice. The emotion overcame her, and she started to cry.

"I'm sorry, so sorry," she told Anne who sat down and rubbed her hand on Kate's back. "I don't know what came over me." She shook her head and rolled her eyes, not believing that she had just had a total breakdown in front of all these people.

"Oh, Kate, honey," Anne soothed, "it's okay. Whatever it is, let us help."

"I wish you could," Kate smiled weakly. "It's just that, well, my life's a mess right now, and I thought leaving DC, coming here, being around strangers, living in a different house, getting a different job. I thought it would make a difference. But then, coming here, seeing this house—its pictures and lovely touches, the kids' things…" she stopped and took a breath. "It's what I thought my life would be someday."

Slowly, the onlookers dispersed leaving Anne and Kate alone.

Anne let Kate cry for a few minutes and then collect herself. "I'm so sorry," Kate said again. "I've ruined your barbecue."

"No, not at all," Anne smiled. "Everything is under control. Would you like to talk about what happened to you?'

Kate shook her head. "Maybe later." She tried to smile, and Anne patted her on the back.

"I'm here any time you'd like to talk." She stood and offered a hand to Kate. "Come on, let me show you where the bathroom is."

Closing the door, Kate splashed cold water on her face and stared at her reflection.

Great first impression.

She shook her head and swallowed several times to fight back her nausea. She wondered if she might be coming down with something but decided she was too hungry to be sick. She dried her face, straightened her clothes, and took a deep breath before opening the door.

When Kate walked back into the kitchen, everyone was laying out the food and chit-chatting in a friendly and easy manner. Kate quietly looked for something to do to help as she smeared some cheese on a cracker and tried to be inconspicuous while greedily shoving the whole thing into her mouth. She reached for a crab ball and popped it through her teeth on the heels of the cracker. There was certainly nothing wrong with her appetite.

"Unless you're interested in all the island gossip, the conversation isn't very interesting in here. How about helping me fill the cooler?"

Kate turned around and recognized the man from the beach and the Boy Scout ceremony. He was grinning at her with the most adorable dimples and a smile that said he was probably up to no good. He motioned with his head toward what Kate assumed was the garage door.

"Um, sure. I can help," she said and followed him to the door.

Once they were on the other side, he held out his hand. "Aaron Kelly."

Kate took his hand, "Kate Middleton."

"No way," he said. "Should I bow? Am I allowed to be touching you?" He did a mock curtsey as Kate rolled her eyes.

"For Heaven's sake, no. I am far from the princess my name suggests."

"More like your brother-in-law, Harry? A little on the wild side?"

Kate could see that he was teasing her, and she smiled. "Maybe in my younger years."

Aaron laughed. "Weren't we all," he said as he bent down and picked up a cooler. He headed to a refrigerator and began filling the cooler of ice with beer. "There's another cooler over there that has ice in it, too. Just start opening those cases of soda and put them in the ice."

Kate did as instructed, and the two worked together for several minutes in a comfortable silence. Kate glanced over at Aaron. He was devilishly handsome and extremely tall. She guessed he was at least 6'4" and was lean and trim. Though he had a shirt on, she could see the ripple of his tight abs when he moved. He had the legs of a runner which Kate appreciated. His hair was cut short in a military-type buzz cut, and he was clean-shaven.

"So," Aaron began. "You're not from around here, huh?"

"What gave me away? My royal demeanor or my British accent?"

His rich laugh once again filled the space between them, and Kate liked the sound of it. "I think it was the fact that I've lived on the island most of my life and would have remembered seeing you before."

Kate felt the heat rise to her cheeks as she tried to shove one more can into the packed cooler. Aaron reached in and put his hand on hers. "I think it's full," he said with his hand covering hers. Kate quickly pulled her hand away and dropped the can back into the cardboard box. She wiped her hands on her shorts.

"You're right. I guess we're done here." She didn't look at him, didn't know how to respond to his flirting.

Aaron was quiet for a moment and then turned and picked up the cooler of beer. "You're right. Just leave that, and I'll come back for it. Thanks for the help." His smile was genuine as he turned toward the open door at the back of the garage. Kate watched him go and took a deep breath.

It was fun for a while, she admitted, *but I'm not falling for a handsome face and a sexy laugh ever again, especially one who already has a wife, or ex-wife, and kids.* She hurried back into the house before Aaron returned.

Kate enjoyed the afternoon and found that she didn't feel as out of place as she feared. The other women were welcoming and fun, and the conversation ran from everything from a new teacher at school to trips that the local families had taken over the summer. It seemed that many of them left the island for most of the summer, renting their houses to beachcombers or just exploring tourist destinations other than this one which most of them just considered home. Kate shared bits and pieces of herself without going into too much detail. She noticed that Aaron and the boys' mother were friendly and playful, and she wondered again about their relationship.

"Time for some volleyball," Paul yelled after everyone had finished their lunch.

"Before dessert?" Lou asked. "I've got my eye on a blueberry pie in there."

"It will still be there when we get back," Paul assured him. "Who's in?"

"Count me in," Aaron called. "I'll captain the team that is going to whip your a-"

"Aaron!" The woman Kate had seen him with stopped Aaron as her boys looked on with large grins.

"Butt, I was going to say butt," Aaron protested.

"No you weren't, Uncle Aaron. You always say a-" His mother's hand was lightening fast as she clamped it over his mouth.

"See?" she glared at Aaron as everyone laughed.

Kate watched the exchange and wondered if he was the boy's real uncle or one of *those* 'uncles.'

"I pick the princess," Aaron called. Kate almost choked on her last bite of corn on the cob.

"Who?" Paul asked, looking around in confusion.

"Kate, I pick Kate."

"Okay, Kate, you're in," Paul said.

"Oh no, I haven't played volleyball in years." Kate protested, but the other women nudged and prodded her to get up from the picnic bench.

"Once you're tagged, you're it, Kate," said Tammi. Kate groaned and rose from the seat, wiping butter from her mouth.

Once both teams were established, all the adults and their children headed to the park where a volleyball net stood ready to be used. Kate stopped and admired the beauty of the view.

"Nice, isn't it?" Aaron said, coming up behind her.

"It's beautiful," she agreed.

"You're looking across the Chincoteague Channel to Assateague Island." He pointed. "See, that's the Assateague lighthouse over the trees." Kate nodded, and Aaron tugged on her arm. "Ready to kick butt?"

"You're going to regret this. I really haven't played since I was in high school."

Aaron shrugged. "Gotta get back to it some time. It's a rule on the island. Everyone plays beach volleyball." He winked and ran to the net. Kate followed and mentally crossed her fingers that she wouldn't further embarrass herself.

Most of the women wore t-shirts and shorts, even the ones who obviously had bathing suits on underneath, though the couple of teen girls who were present showed off their summer tans in bikinis. The men, however, all took off their shirts, pitching them to the side. Aaron's abs were indeed tight, the perfect six pack, and his arms glowed with a farmer's tan. He clearly spent a lot of the summer outside but with a shirt on, and Kate wondered what he did for a living.

After a bit of a rough start, Kate got into a groove. She even found herself having fun and laughing with the others. Aaron was quite the show-off and tried to make a big play with every volley. Some worked, and others made him the laughingstock of the crowd. He took it all in stride, and Kate had a sense that Aaron was one of those guys everyone liked and was drawn to. He was confident, fun, friendly, and sexy. He was a lot like her brother, Zach, and nothing like Mark. He also picked Kayla, his whatever relation she was, for their team, and they played well together, easily assisting each other's plays and often bringing their team a point. In the end, Paul's team beat them, but it was a very close game.

They returned to the backyard, and Kate collapsed into a hammock. Between the huge meal, the volleyball, and the still-hot September sun, she was ready for a nap. Luckily, she was feeling much better and guessed the queasiness was nothing but hunger and nerves.

"Not bad for someone who hasn't played since high school. When was that? Last week?"

Kate opened one eye and looked up at Aaron. "Do you ever leave a person alone?"

"Just trying to be welcoming," he said and winked at her again.

"You've made me feel quite at home. It's almost like being back at the palace with the court jester following me around."

That wonderful laugh filled the air. "Good one, Princess, good one," Aaron said as he walked away. Kate closed her eyes and took a deep breath, inhaling the smell of the grill, the salt air, and the roses. Without meaning to, Kate was soon sound asleep.

When she awoke, Kate was surprised and embarrassed to find that it was late afternoon. Why was she so tired lately? Emotional fatigue, she supposed as she looked around. The food had been cleaned up, and almost all the guests were gone. Shannon and Anne sat in Adirondack chairs and watched the kids run around in the yard. Kate hauled herself up from the hammock and grabbed a water from the cooler.

"Mind if I join you?"

"Not at all," Anne said. "Pull up a chair."

Kate dragged over another one of the massive chairs and sat down. "I'm so sorry about not helping to clean up. I truly didn't mean to fall asleep."

"It's the sign of a good day on the island," Anne said with a smile. "And you seemed to need a good rest."

Kate nodded. "It's been a long time," she said in response, and she wasn't sure if she meant a long time since she had had a good rest or just a good day. She shivered, and Anne called to her daughter.

"Lizzie, go grab one of Mommy's sweatshirts for Miss Kate." The little girls ran into the house without arguing. Kate realized that it had gotten quite a bit cooler while she was sleeping as the late afternoon sun made its descent toward the water.

"We were just discussing what's on our reading list for this winter," Shannon said. "Do you read, Kate?"

"I do." She laughed. "I was quite the party girl in college and didn't make much time for reading, but when I was growing up, I was quite the bookworm. My family traveled a lot when I was a child, so books were my best friends, along with my brother."

"What do you like to read?" Anne asked.

"Oh, everything." Kate lit up as she spoke. "I have a list of favorites a mile long, everything from timeless classics to little known contemporaries."

"Name a book that you loved that we probably haven't read." Shannon said. "I'm always looking for something new."

"Hmmm, let me think. Oh, I know. *The Thirteenth Tale* by… Gosh, I know the name. It will come to me."

"I've never heard of it," Shannon admitted. "What's it about?"

Anne and Shannon were completely enraptured by Kate's description of the book about a young woman who is hired to write the biography of a famous author whose tales seem older and taller than the woman herself. She thanked Lizzie as the little girl handed her a pink sweatshirt that read 'Shenandoah Mountains' and pulled the shirt over her head.

"Diane Setterfield." Kate snapped her fingers. "That's the author. She weaves this incredible story in which it's impossible to tell when or where the book takes place."

"What do you mean?" Anne asked.

"She describes things like, 'She received word that he wanted to see her, so she hurried to his home.' The reader has no idea how she received word, how she traveled, or to where she went, but it works."

"How intriguing," Shannon said.

"Have you ever read, *The Paradise Tree*?" Anne asked.

The other two women shook their heads.

"Oh, you must. It's written by a local Eastern Shore writer, Maria Elena Vidal, and it tells the story of her family's sojourn from Ireland to Canada. It has everything—murder, intrigue, romance, heartache. She's a wonderful writer who beautifully tells the story of how her family escaped their lives in Europe and began anew in the New World."

"I know exactly how they felt," Kate sighed.

"You know, Kate," Shannon said sympathetically, "we're all family here. We look out for each other. If there's ever anything you need, anything you want to talk about, we're here."

Kate smiled and took a sip of her water. She had noticed the stares of some of the other women and knew that they regarded her as an outsider, but Katherine could feel that Anne and Shannon were genuine with their offer of friendship. "Thanks, Shannon. I appreciate it."

The women were quiet as they sat and watched the kids play. Kate found herself looking around for Aaron, but she didn't see him or Kayla and the boys. Part of her wanted to ask about them, but she was afraid that her curiosity would be taken out of context. It wasn't Aaron she was interested in learning about. It was just the situation.

After a while, Shannon packed up their things and called to her kids. She and Lou left, and Kate asked Anne if she could help with the cleanup.

"No, it's all done, but thank you." She turned to look at Kate. "I'm really glad you came today. I hope you had fun."

"I really did, and I'm glad I came, too. It's been, well, I've been." Kate struggled with what to say. "I'm kind of messed up right now. I screwed up, and I don't know how to fix it. How to fix me." Kate thought she sounded like a child rather than the woman she was and blushed with embarrassment.

Then, taking a deep breath, and without even thinking, Kate began slowly telling Anne about her life in DC. Before she knew it, she found herself telling her new friend everything that led her to this moment – her parents' move, the absence of her brother, meeting the man she thought was her soul mate, and his ultimate betrayal of not only her but his wife and children.

Anne listened, never interrupting, and never offering pity or patronized understanding. Kate had never met anyone so easy to talk to, and she let herself reveal all her insecurities to the woman she had become acquainted with only a few days before.

When Kate was through, Anne remained in silent thought for a few minutes. Finally, she nodded her head and turned toward Kate. Without a single note of condescension in her voice, Anne looked Kate in the eyes and told her what to do.

"You're going to get over this, Kate. You've already started by coming and meeting new people and getting on with the next phase of your life."

Kate started to protest, "I don't think it's that easy."

"It is," Anne insisted. "You're stronger than you think you are, Kate. How else would you have been able to leave your life behind and come all the way out here to a strange place where you don't know a soul? And you're not alone, no matter how much it feels like you are right now. I'm here for you, and I think you'll find that others on the island will be, too. Like Shannon said, we're a family here. And now you're one of us. You're not the only one with a past or with secrets she doesn't want to share. You're going to fit in just fine here, and you're going to feel at home, I promise."

Looking into her eyes, Kate believed every word that Anne said. She felt inexplicably drawn to this woman, to this island. She felt a closeness that she had never even felt for Mark. For the first time since Zach said goodbye and left for some faraway desert, she felt like she had found just what she needed the most, a true friend.

***

Kate awoke the next morning to the screeching of seagulls flying over the water and the lurching of her stomach. She sprang from the bed and raced to the bathroom just in time. Sitting on the floor, a feeling of dread began to creep through her. She opened the bathroom cabinet and looked at the still-full box that she had bought just before leaving the city, figuring that she would need it almost as soon as she got to the island. But the box was still sealed, as Kate knew it would be. She closed the cabinet and sank back against the tub. Was this really happening? She couldn't think about it now. It was just too much on her already full plate.

Pulling herself off the floor, Kate rinsed her mouth and brushed her teeth. She wrapped herself in her light robe and walked downstairs to the deck at the back of the house. Pushing open the screen door, she inhaled the salty air. The sun hovered just over the bay, and the birds dove in and out of the water in search of breakfast. Kate went onto the deck and took in the fresh morning air. A cold front had come in during the night, and Kate shivered in the cool breeze. She closed her eyes and felt the rising sun on her face. She opened her eyes and turned toward the house next door. She tried to push her own predicament from her mind, and let her thoughts turn toward her neighbor. Was Kayla married? What was her actual relationship with Aaron?

Kate removed her gaze from the house and shook her head. Why did she even care? Was it because Aaron was everything that Mark was not? How could she even know that? He might have just as many secrets to hide as Mark did.

Mark. Thoughts of him brought the reality of her situation back to the forefront. Should she contact him. No. That was absolutely not going to happen. Was it wrong of her? Perhaps, but she didn't care. He could lay no claim to her, she wasn't going to let him lay claim to her. Or anyone else. Besides, she could be wrong, couldn't she? She decided not to dwell on it until she knew for sure.

Looking back at the other house, Kate realized that her real fascination was with Kayla. Not once did Kayla speak to her yesterday. In fact, she spoke very little. Was she painfully shy? She didn't seem shy with Aaron. Was she his sister or was she in love with him? If so, it certainly looked to be one-sided though they had an easy banter between them that seemed to come naturally. He seemed to be the only one with whom Kayla was completely comfortable. What was her story? Kate couldn't help but wonder. There was something about the woman that made Kate want to reach out to her. Somehow, Kate felt like Kayla might need a friend as much as Kate did. And boy, did she need a friend—now more than ever.

It was just past seven when, after a light run on the grassy strip, Kate heard the boys shouting goodbye. She went to the window and peeked out in time to see them climbing onto the school bus. Kate, already showered and dressed after her run, refilled her cup of decaf, luckily having sworn off caffeine as part of her healthy promise, and went outside, heading toward her neighbor's house. She walked to the back door of the cottage and knocked, calling through the closed door, "Kayla, are you home?"

Kayla came around the corner and saw Kate at the back door through the glass pane. She smiled, but her smile did not reach her eyes, and Kate wondered if this had been a bad idea. Kayla unlocked the door and opened it just a crack

"I'm sorry to bother you. I just thought that, since we're neighbors, we might share a cup of coffee." She held up her mug.

"Uh, sure," Kayla said uneasily. Gone was the woman who had laughed so easily with Aaron. She opened the door all the way and let Kate into the cozy kitchen. Kate was surprised that the house was shut up so tightly. The breeze was just beautiful.

"Can I get you anything?" Kayla asked.

"No thanks," Kate answered as she looked around the room. "I just thought it would be nice to get to know each other."

Kate noticed Kayla's hand shake a little as she poured herself a fresh cup of coffee. She seemed very nervous.

Kayla turned toward Kate and motioned to the kitchen table. "Would you like to sit? I was going to make myself some fruit and yogurt if you'd like some."

"Actually, that would be nice, thanks." Kate wondered if this had been a mistake. Kayla was clearly not thrilled with her being here.

"So, it looks like you have your hands full with those boys. My mom always said that I was a much easier child than my brother. It must be hard having two boys so close in age."

Kayla stopped slicing the strawberries and looked suspiciously at Kate. "Sometimes," was all she said.

Kate swallowed a mouth full of coffee and briefly considered making a run for the door.

"How old are they?"

Kayla looked at Kate for a moment before taking a deep breath. "They're seven and ten. They're good boys, but they've had a tough life."

"I know the feeling," Kate admitted. "My life hasn't been a bed of roses lately either."

At that, Kayla's shoulders fell, and her posture loosened. "I guess we all have our crosses to bear. I saw you crying at Anne's. I'm sorry for whatever happened to you."

"Thanks. It's water under the bridge, I guess. I thought I had met the perfect man, but he turned out to be a complete stranger."

Kayla nodded. "It happens. Sometimes even the perfect man can turn into a stranger." Their eyes met, and Kate saw something in Kayla's expression. She was guarded, on edge, and it was because of a man. Had she been abused? Was she hiding from the man she loved, the father of her children?

"I think you're right," Kate offered her. "It's hard to know who to trust." She held the other woman's gaze until Kayla blinked and looked away.

"It is," she said quietly, her eyes and attention returning to the berries. Kate watched her trembling hands as she cut the fruit and wondered who could have ever hurt this timid, beautiful woman.

Kayla placed the bowl of sliced strawberries, blueberries, and blackberries on the table and filled two small dessert bowls with yogurt. She placed honey and cinnamon on the table along with a couple of slices of bread.

"Banana bread," she said. "The boys won't eat them once they start to turn brown, and I can't stand the thought of throwing them away, so I bake a lot of banana bread." She smiled weakly at Kate.

"Well, I happen to love banana bread," Kate beamed at her. At that moment, she would be willing to eat anything that would placate her stomach, but she did love banana bread. "Feel free to share your excess loaves any time you find that you've baked too much." Kate reached for a slice of bread and put it on the plate that matched the dessert cup. "Are those chocolate chips in it?"

"Yep. It's the only way the boys will eat it."

"It's because they know you use the brown bananas," Kate said, and for the first time since Kate showed up at the door, Kayla laughed.

***

Sighing, Kayla watched Kate walk back across the grass. It was only a matter of time before Kate learned the truth. There were few secrets on the island, and there were no secrets online. A simple Google search would turn up everything Kate needed to know about Kayla's past. FOX News, CNN, and all the network programs had covered the story of her husband's murder. His association with the now disgraced, former Baltimore Mayor was the fodder for real news outlets and tabloids for months. *48 Hours* ran a documentary special on it, and she had heard that Lifetime had acquired the movie rights. She prayed that she and the boys would be left out of it. It had been five years, and they had moved on. Why couldn't the rest of the world?

Turning away from the window, Kayla sat at her desk and went over her notes from her meeting with Anne. The only thing she wanted to concentrate on was her new business venture, a catering service geared toward family meals rather than large events. If parents couldn't supply their own home-cooked family dinners, then Kayla was there to provide the meal. The families just had to supply the togetherness. Though her parents wanted to help, Kayla was determined to do this all on her own. She knew she could count on Aaron to help with the boys. He was always there for her and she couldn't imagine life without him. She knew that one day, another woman would come into his life and steal him away from her, but it would be impossible to undo their bond.

She looked back toward the window and thought about her mysterious new neighbor. Would she be the one? She was just the type that Aaron would be attracted to, someone who desperately needed a hero to rescue her from… from what? Kayla wondered what it was that Kate was hiding. Aaron was always the knight in shining armor, but even armor had weaknesses. She'd have to keep a close eye on Kate. Aaron might never admit it, but he was the one who needed rescuing, and Kayla wasn't going to let Kate or anyone else hurt the one man she loved and trusted more than anyone in the world.

There still exists a tremendous gap between indigenous and non-indigenous peoples when it comes to infant mortality. It's crucial that pregnant women get, not only the medical care that they need, but the support of their family and the greater community.

From the *Studies of Indigenous Peoples*
by Walter Middleton

CHAPTER FIVE

Kate had a busy week. She took a few pictures and took notes at the Girl Scouts Induction Ceremony, the annual oyster boat blessing, the Chincoteague Plein Air Art Show and Sale, and the Artful Flea community arts and crafts market and yard sale.

She didn't have to be at any of the events any longer than it took to snap a few pictures and write down what was happening, but she was trying to immerse herself in the community and get to know the people. She browsed the booths at the Artful Flea and purchased a jar of homemade Chincoteague Island Honey. She had no idea that honey looked and tasted different depending upon the time of year that it was harvested. She couldn't wait to make herself a piece of toast with the fresh, golden, spring honey.

She spent a fair amount of time soaking up the sun on her balcony, knowing that the autumn chill would settle in faster than she wanted it to. She regretted not spending more time outdoors when she lived in the city. Her only outdoor activities were running in Georgetown and kayaking on some of the waterways in the area. There were many places to go in the DC area where she could enjoy nature, most of them hidden gems that few people even knew about. She made herself a promise to begin exploring some of those places once she got back to the city, and then it hit her that her life in the city would never be the same again.

Earlier that week, a drugstore test confirmed what Kate's body already knew. At first, she cried, lamenting the life she always wanted and would now have but not in the way she imagined. Then she got angry. She was angry with Mark for putting her in this position, and then angry with herself for being so stupid. She hadn't even told Mark that she had stopped taking the pill. She assumed that he would be happy, but now she wondered why she had kept it from him. Somewhere in her subconscious, she must have known that something was off. Mark never talked about kids or wanting a family. Now she realized that he had his hands full with the family he already had.

The park was teeming with families as Kate walked around, snapping picture of the soccer games and taking down names of the kids making big plays. It was the island's annual soccer tournament, and teams from all over Maryland and Virginia's Eastern Shores were competing for trophies. Kate had been there all morning, enjoying seeing the people she had met at other events and meeting still more people. Knowing she needed to eat something, even if it wasn't the healthiest lunch in town, Kate bought a hot dog from the soccer league. As she was looking down and licking a drop off ketchup off her hand, she noticed a pair of shoes come to a stop in front of her. She looked up into the twinkling eyes of Aaron Kelly.

"It's dangerous not to pay attention to where you're going," he said with a smile. "Where are your bodyguards? Shouldn't they prevent you from running into people?"

"I didn't run into you," Kate said.

"No, because I was paying attention," he said with a slight smirk, his eyebrows rose as he looked own at her.

"Uh huh." Kate pointed to his shirt. "You're a coach?"

"I am the proud coach of the Chincoteague Ponies." He leaned in close to her face and whispered in her ear, "We're absolutely awful, but I will deny ever having said that." He pulled back and smiled down at her. Kate could smell the salt and sand on his skin even though they were standing on a grassy soccer field with no beach in sight.

"Do you have a son on the team?" she casually asked as she turned her attention back to her hot dog.

"No, just EJ and Todd. I do it for them." They began walking toward the game that was in progress.

"Kayla's boys?" Kate finished off her hot dog and took a swig of her water.

"Yeah, it's hard for them, not having a dad. I do what I can to help out."

"You and Kayla must be very close." Kate fiddled with the cap of her water bottle, intentionally not looking at Aaron. She didn't want him to think that she was digging into his personal life nor that she had more than a passing interest.

"Always have been. She says I'm her rock which I think is overkill. Whatever. I'll always be here for her, and she knows that."

Kate nodded. "That's nice. It's always good to have a friend like that." She hated the feeling of envy in the pit of her stomach. It was good that Kayla had someone like Aaron in her life. She seemed to need a rock, and Kate was more than happy to stand on her own two feet without support.

Aaron stopped and looked quizzically at Kate. "You do know that she's my sister, right? My twin sister?"

The look of shock must have shown on her face because Aaron began to laugh. "Did you think? No way. Really? Yuck!" He made a face of disgust but kept laughing.

"Well, I had no way of knowing. You don't look that much alike. Wait," she narrowed her eyes and looked at Aaron. "Are you pulling my leg?"

Aaron stood straight and held up three fingers. "Scout's honor. She got the looks. And the brains."

Kate felt stupid. Now that she thought about it, they did resemble each other, the same brown eyes and light brown hair. And those dimples. How had she missed those?

"Huh. I had no idea. You're much taller than she is."

"Yeah, I take after my dad. She has my mother's flare for the arts, whereas my dad and I have the same interests and abilities. But Kay's my best friend. I guess that sounds weird, but it's true."

"It doesn't sound weird to me at all. My brother and I aren't twins, but he's definitely my best friend. He's in Afghanistan, but he hopes to get home soon."

Aaron cast her a sidelong glance, and an unreadable expression crossed his face. Kate wondered what he was thinking, but the conversation was already more personal than she wanted, so she let it pass.

They continued walking and stopped on the sidelines to watch a couple of girls' teams play their first game of the season. Kate picked up her camera and took a picture. She'd have to ask for names, but she might as well make good use of her time while she was there.

"So, am I being too nosy if I ask what happened to the boys' father?"

Aaron was silent as he took a deep breath, held it for a moment and then slowly let it out. "It's messy," was all he said.

"Sorry," Kate answered as she nervously shuffled the camera back into its case. "I don't mean to pry."

"It's not that," Aaron said, shaking his head. "It's just that it's not my story to tell, and it's actually kind of a secret.

At least from the boys. Kayla doesn't want them to know the truth until they're older and can handle it better."

Kate watched the girls and waited to see if Aaron would say more. After a few minutes, he cracked his knuckles and took another breath. "Eddie Reynolds. He was Kayla's husband."

Kate searched her memory and had a vague recollection of the name. She wasn't sure why. She shrugged.

"I'm sorry. I guess I don't know that much about the island or its residents yet."

"He wasn't from around here. They met in college, Yale, actually. Kayla's a brain. Another way we're totally different." He looked at Kate and winked. The wink was beginning to grow on her. His expression turned somber, and he took off his baseball cap and wiped his forehead before replacing his hat. "Anyway, they lived in Baltimore. I thought that, being from the Western Shore, you might have heard about him. He was murdered a few years back."

Kate looked at Aaron. Had she heard him right? "Murdered?"

"Yeah, by his boss. I told you it was messy."

"Oh my gosh, I'm so sorry. And the boys don't know?"

"Nope. Kay didn't want them growing up with that knowledge."

They stood in silence after that, watching the girls play. Kate's heart broke for Kayla and her children, and her mind tried to put the name and the events together, to no avail. No wonder Kayla didn't talk much and seemed so timid and mistrusting. When the game was over, Aaron looked at Kate and smiled.

"Are you hungry? I know a great place for seafood."

Kate looked around for an excuse to say no and finally settled on the truth. She had had enough of lies. She smiled at Aaron but shook her head. "I'm so sorry. You seem like a great guy, but I'm just not looking for anything right now."

Aaron put his hands out in protest. "Whoa, I don't know what *you* had in mind, but *I* was just thinking about my stomach."

Laughing, Kate shook her head. "Thanks for the offer, but I really can't." She started to back away. "It was nice talking to you, Aaron."

As she started walking away, Aaron called to her, "How soon?"

Kate stopped and turned back. "Excuse me?" she asked in confusion.

"How soon until you get over whoever he was and say yes?"

"No, Aaron. It will always be no. I'm sorry." She lifted her shoulders as if to further apologize and walked away. She didn't turn back to see if he was staring, but she felt his eyes on her as she made her way toward Anne, Shannon, and Tammi who were cheering on their daughters.

***

On Sunday morning, Kate woke up as the sun peered over the bay. She grabbed the extra pillow on the bed and covered her head. She longed for those days of her youth when she didn't open her eyes until past noon. Late nights and even later mornings were the norm for her, but the older she got, the earlier she awoke.

"Jeez, I'm not even that old," she said out loud. "I'm not even close to forty yet. What's wrong with me?" *I'm talking to myself for one thing.*

She tossed the pillow aside and reached for her phone. She quickly sat up when she saw the notification with the little blue envelope beside it, "Middleton, Zach… Hey sis, I got your message."

That was as far as she got before her stomach began to roll. She held onto the phone as she raced to the bathroom. When the heaving subsided, she washed her face and hands and sat on the lid of the toilet, quickly tapped in her passcode, and waited for the message to fully load. The tears began before she even had a chance to begin reading.

Hey Sis, I got your message about finding Mark on Facebook. Sorry it took so long to write back. What a sonofabitch. I talked to Mom last night, and she said you were still taking it hard. I guess that's an understatement. She said you quit your job and went to the ocean for a while. Are you sure that was smart? Don't throw your whole life away for some jerk who threw you for a loop. And don't get any ideas about that ocean. I know how strong you are. Hell, you know how strong you are. Nothing gets in your way. I'll be home on leave soon, so your beach house, or whatever it is, better have an extra bed. I'll be there as soon as I can get out of this Godforsaken country.

I love you, Sis. I'll see you soon.

Zach

Kate wiped her tears and hugged her phone. She quickly typed a reply.

All is good here. I miss you. Hurry home.

Love,

Kate

She would tell Zach everything in due time. All that mattered was that he was coming home. She knew that it could be weeks, or even months, but he was coming.

Once dressed in her running attire, Kate made her way to the kitchen and picked up the running shoes that she left by the door. Sitting at the kitchen table, she laced up her shoes. She tapped the play button on her phone and plugged her earphones into her ears before grabbing an apple and heading out. She ate the apple in between stretches while Pit Bull encouraged her with the steady rhythm of his song. Though her mother would cringe at the lyrics, the beat was perfect for her daily run. Once Kate felt limber, she began her slow and steady run on the grass noting that she really needed to check out one of the trails on the island where she had learned that most people ran. Though she was hungry, she decided to eat breakfast when she got back. Running was a passion of hers, and she was going to enjoy it while she still could.

Kate looked up at Kayla's house as she ran by and thoughts of Aaron flooded her mind. How lucky they were, she and Kayla. They both had their hearts broken but had brothers who loved them and were there for them. And while Kayla's heartbreak was much worse than Kate's, at least Kayla's brother was nearby. Kate couldn't help but feel a little envious that her own brother was, for all intents and purposes, unreachable and so far away. But he was coming home. She didn't know when, but the thought of seeing him in the near future would sustain her.

She picked up the pace to keep up with the beat of her Pandora playlist and ran past a flock of ducks, scaring them out of the marsh. She ran harder and faster until she felt the pain in the back of her throat and her lungs caused her body to cry out for rest. Knowing that she shouldn't push herself any more, she turned around and headed back toward the house at a slow, easy pace. The sun rose above the water, and the breeze felt cool and salty on her skin. She ran to the wooden steps behind the house, and she braced herself against them, her head hanging down as she bent toward the grass, her breath heavy and uneven. She yanked loose her earphones and staved off a wave of dizziness.

"Good run?" Aaron called from Kayla's deck.

Kate could barely raise her head to look up at him. She nodded and then lowered her head back down, inhaling deeply to slow her breathing and alleviate the unusual pain in her chest. After a few minutes, she stood up and looked over at the house next door. The deck was empty, and Kate felt a pang of disappointment. Stretching a bit more, she trudged up the stairs, anxious for a shower and a cup of coffee.

Twenty minutes later, wearing yoga pants and a long-sleeved t-shirt that listed the tour dates from an In Sync concert season from years back, Kate settled down on her own back deck with a cup of coffee, a banana, and a bowl of Cheerios. She watched the sailboats several miles out in the ocean and enjoyed the peace and quiet, a far cry from the city streets of Washington. The days were numbered that she would be able to enjoy the back deck before the cold settled in, and Kate was determined to take advantage of every one of them.

"Mind if I join you?" Aaron stood on the grass below the deck, a cup of coffee and a doughnut in his hand. Kate had been so lost in her thoughts and in the beauty of the morning that she hadn't noticed him walking over.

"Only if you have another one of those with you?" She motioned, and he understood and smiled.

"Right here." He held up the hand that was holding the coffee and revealed a Dunkin' Donuts bag. "I came prepared just in case you said no. Who can resist a freshly baked Boston Cream doughnut?"

Healthy diet? Who cares?

"Certainly not me," Kate said as Aaron climbed the steps and took a seat in the chair next to Kate's. He was dressed in khakis and a long-sleeved button-down shirt.

Kate thought it was strange to see him somewhat dressed up, especially on a lazy Sunday morning.

"Who would have thought it would be so easy to slip past thy royal guards and onto the balcony of thou fairest castle with only a doughnut as a weapon."

"You know, that might have been funny the first fifty-seven times, but it is way past getting old."

"Aw, come on," Aaron said as he pulled another doughnut from the bag. "It's still funny, and you know it. My wit has no end."

"Yeah, you're a real Conan O'Brien." Kate closed her eyes as she bit into the Boston Cream. "Oh my gosh," she said as she licked her lips. "This is to die for."

Aaron smiled at the look of pure contentment that washed over Kate's face. "I'm glad I could make your morning."

Kate opened her eyes and looked at the man who sat across from her. "I had no idea that a doughnut could so easily make all of my cares go away."

"I'm here to please, your highness." Aaron bowed his head and Kate rolled her eyes.

"Do you run every day?" Aaron asked.

"I try to," Kate answered as it occurred to her that her morning runs would come to an end at some point over the next several months.

"There are a couple of great trails on the island. I could show them to you if you like. They're much better to run on than this marshy mess."

"Thanks for the offer. I'm sure I can find them on my own."

Aaron nodded and let the subject drop. Kate turned her gaze toward the ocean.

"What's it like here in the winter?"

"Lonely, but a good kind of lonely."

Kate continued to look at the water as she thought about his words. "I think I could stand a good kind of lonely."

Kate felt Aaron's stare and tried not to turn toward him. Then she felt a tear escape from her eye and trail down her cheek. Embarrassed, she quickly wiped it away and pretended it hadn't happened.

"I'm sorry," Aaron said quietly. "I didn't mean to make you sad."

Kate shook her head. "It's not you. It's," she blinked back another tear and leaned her head back on the chair, staring into the sky. "I've had a rough couple of months. I'm not usually like this—all weepy and emotional." She looked at Aaron with a small grin. "I was actually quite a hell raiser in my younger days."

"I knew it," Aaron yelled as he smacked his hand on the arm of the chair. "I had you pegged from the start."

"Yes, you did," she said, remembering their first conversation in the garage on the day of the cookout. "But those days are long gone," she said with a hint of sadness in her voice.

"Nah, they're never really gone. We outgrow them, but the wildness lives on. We just need to learn how to channel it into more adult-like behavior."

"Oh yeah?" Kate asked with genuine interest. "And how do we do that?"

"I could show you, but you've already made it quite clear that we aren't going to be seeing much of each other. Other than for doughnuts, of course."

Kate's curiosity got the better of her. "Well, perhaps just once, casually of course, I might be willing to go somewhere with you. Just to see how you've tamed your wild side, of course."

"Of course," Aaron agreed, nodding his head. He began cleaning up the trash from the doughnut shop. "Noon?" He asked as he stood.

"Noon?" Kate repeated the question.

"For the start of your lesson in migrating your wild side into adulthood. I'll be back here at noon to pick you up."

Kate hesitated but found herself smiling. "Okay, then, noon. What should I wear for this walk on the wild side?"

"You look good just the way you are," Aaron said with a wink as he walked down the steps. About halfway between her house and Kayla's, he turned around. "I'll see you at noon, Princess."

Kate smiled and shook her head as she watched him head toward Kayla's house. That man had a lot of confidence in himself, and somehow, she had played right into his hands. Oh, well, the least she could do was have a little fun. She had let him know that she wasn't interested in anything more than that, and soon, he would most likely not want anything to do with her anyway. She might as well enjoy her last few months before her life was no longer her own.

***

At 11:30, Kate heard Kayla's SUV turn into her gravel driveway. She put aside Harlan Coben's latest thriller, *Home*, and peeked out the window. She watched Kayla, the boys, and Aaron emerge from the vehicle, all dressed in nice clothes, the boys' outfits matching Aaron's khakis and dress shirt. Kate was intrigued by the sight of all of them in their nice clothes and assumed they had just returned from some kind of Sunday service. For the second time, since arriving on the island, she was reminded of the few times she had attended Mass as a child, and for the first time in her life, she felt a pang of guilt. Brushing it aside, she finished her granola bar and protein shake before going to brush her teeth one more time. She assumed that she and Aaron would get something to eat while they were out, but she didn't want to get sick or deprive the life that was growing inside of her of nourishment, so she made herself the light snack just to be safe.

At precisely twelve o'clock on the dot, Aaron knocked on the front door. Kate grabbed her wallet, phone, and a light jacket.

"Hi," she said as she opened the door. "Should I bring anything else with me?"

Aaron looked down at her sneakers, and shook his head. "Nope. Just an adventurous spirit."

Kate smiled. She was certainly intrigued. "Okay, then. Let's go." She locked the door and pulled it shut behind her.

Aaron opened the passenger door for her, waited for her to climb inside the truck, and then shut the door. Kate wondered if his manners were always so good, and she admitted that, from what she had observed, they seemed to be.

They drove in a comfortable silence, and Kate enjoyed the view of the island and the surrounding seashore. After a short time, Aaron spoke.

"We're crossing the Assateague Channel. It's where the ponies come ashore during the annual pony crossing."

"Like in *Misty*," Kate said as she craned her neck to look for the ponies.

Aaron laughed, "Yeah, that book single-handedly put our little island on the map."

"I actually just read it. I think I read it as a kid, but I don't remember for sure. I checked it out from the library when I first got here, and I saw Misty in the island museum. Truthfully, I checked out all the books. There are a lot of books in that series."

"There are. I didn't read them, but Kayla did. She wanted one of the ponies so badly when we were kids. But ponies aren't cheap to buy or to own. Most of them are sold to people who don't live here on the island."

Kate watched as they drove onto the Assateague National Wildlife Refuge. Aaron stopped at the gate and rolled down his window.

"Good afternoon, Commander Kelly," said the young man inside the booth. Kate was surprised at the greeting and even more surprised when she turned and saw that the young man was saluting Aaron.

"At ease, Ensign," Aaron said with a smile. "Lighthouse open?"

"Yes sir, it is, sir."

"Thank you, Brock. Ya'll have a good day."

"What was that about?" Kate asked as they drove through the gate.

Aaron shrugged. "Nothing. Just a friendly park ranger."

Kate looked at Aaron with suspicion but didn't pry. If she wasn't willing to open up to him about her personal life, then why should he? Still, she couldn't help but wonder.

They parked in a small parking lot, and Aaron asked her to hold on a minute. He leaped from his side of the truck, grabbed a backpack from the back seat, and hurried to her side where he opened the door and helped her out.

"Why, thank you," she said with a smile.

"Just trying to treat you in the manner to which you are accustom," Aaron said with a bow. "Ready for some adventure?"

Laughing, she pushed him gently, and he straightened up.

"Okay, let's go," he said as he headed down a dirt path that wound and bent through the trees. It was an uphill and Kate wondered where he was leading her. When they entered a clearing, Kate looked up and stared at the same red lighthouse Aaron had pointed out the day they met at the cookout. "Are we going up there?" she asked hesitantly.

"You said you wanted a walk on the adult wild side? Too much adventure for you?"

"No," she snapped at him with a look of reproach.

"Seriously," he grabbed her arm and turned her toward him. "It's 193 steps. I probably should have asked first. Do you think you can make it? I've seen you run and assumed you were in pretty good shape." His eyes made their way down her body and back, and Kate blushed as heat filled her belly.

Kate looked back up at the top of the lighthouse. She remembered walking up to the top of the bell tower of the Notre Dame Cathedral when she spent a mini-semester in France. It wasn't that difficult, but she couldn't remember off the top of her head how many steps it had. Her hand went instinctively to her stomach, and she swallowed.

"I'm in pretty good shape-"

"I'll say," Aaron chimed in, and her blush deepened.

"I've just been getting pretty tired lately. I guess it's the stress and the salty air. I'm not used to it..." Her voice trailed off as she stared at the tip of the structure. Then she nodded. "Sure, I can do it. Let's go."

"You're positive?"

"Yep, I'm in."

"Okay," Aaron said. "But if you get tired, just say the word. We can come down any time."

"I'm good," Kate assured him as she headed toward the door at the bottom of the lighthouse.

"It was built in 1830 when it was realized that there was no light between Cape Henlopen, Delaware and Cape Charles, Virginia. It's owned by the U.S Government and operated by the Coast Guard." Aaron stopped at the visitor's desk just inside the lighthouse.

"Good afternoon, Sir," Aaron said to the elderly gentleman giving directions to the visitors. "Do you mind if I stow this behind the desk?" he asked as he sat the backpack on the counter.

"Good afternoon, Commander. It would be my pleasure."

Kate shot Aaron a suspicious glance, but he ignored her as he handed the bag to the other man and thanked him for his assistance.

Without acknowledging the exchange, Aaron continued to talk as they climbed the stairs. Kate had questions, about both Aaron and the lighthouse, but she was unable to speak. Her heart pounded as they ascended, and she held onto the wall to keep her steady. She had calculated that she was almost eight weeks along. Every day, she noticed subtle changes in her body, and normal things seemed to be getting just a little more difficult to do. She should have been able to run twice as far this morning, and she shouldn't be feeling so winded now. A small part of her resented these changes, but she pushed the thoughts away in order to concentrate on the climb.

Once they reached the top, the view blindsided her.

"Oh my gosh, it's so beautiful," she said between heavy breaths. Beyond the tree line was a patchwork of sand and water. It was windy at the top of the building, and Kate's blonde hair whipped around her face as she went from one spot along the railing to another trying to take it all in. The green trees and marsh grasses showed no hint that October was just a few days away. The sun danced on the water between Assateague and Chincoteague, and a line of parked cars stretched along a strip of sand that ended at the crowded beach. Even from that distance, Kate could see crowds of people on the narrow piece of sand.

Moving around the catwalk, Kate gasped as she watched a white egret glide along the shiny surface of a small stretch of water to its resting place among a stand of reeds. She untied her jacket from her waist and slipped it on as she gazed out at the scene.

Aaron followed her around the structure. She came to a stop and stood looking out over the trees at the marshes. He placed his mouth close to her ear. "Was it worth the climb?"

"So worth the climb," Kate breathed, and her stomach gave a small tug as she felt the closeness of his body.

"It's where I come when I need to remind myself that there is still good in the world."

Kate turned to look at Aaron, their bodies almost touching. "Thank you. I needed to be reminded of that myself."

He gazed into her eyes for a moment. "I thought you might," he said quietly, and Kate noticed that his breathing was a little ragged as well. She didn't think it was from the climb.

Kate was sure he was going to kiss her, and she even thought she might let him, but instead, he raised his hand and pointed to something in the distance. "Relatives perhaps?"

Kate looked to where he motioned and took a deep breath. "Ponies," she breathed. "Misty's family."

They watched the wild ponies in the distance as the beautiful creatures grazed in a grassy area beyond the sand.

After a little while, Aaron motioned her back inside. She followed him down the circular staircase that wrapped around the inside of lighthouse, and once they were back on the ground, Kate found it hard to keep steady. Her legs felt like jelly. She surmised that she used completely different muscles for running than for climbing. Aaron led her to a nearby bench and took off his backpack. He sat it on the bench, unzipped it, and pulled out two sandwiches and two bottles of water.

"I thought a picnic would be nice after that climb."

Kate looked around at the few other visitors and felt self-conscious.

"Don't worry. People do it all the time." He handed her a sandwich. "I didn't know what you liked, but I figured I couldn't go wrong with turkey and cheese. And since I didn't know your condiment of choice," he reached in and took out a handful of mustard and mayonnaise packets, "I swiped these from the deli counter."

Kate laughed and took a packet of mustard. "I guess you thought of everything."

"I sure did," he said as he pulled out two Hershey bars. "Even dessert."

"Now that's what I like to see," Kate smiled as she took a bite of her sandwich.

"I saw the way you devoured that doughnut and hovered over the dessert table at the Boy Scout ceremony."

"Wait a minute, I wasn't hovering. I was helping."

"Helping yourself to the chocolate chip cookies," he teased.

Kate took a long swig of water and wondered exactly how much attention he had paid to her that night. She hadn't even noticed him until he and Kayla were leaving when she was sitting in her car.

"How are your legs?" Aaron asked casually, and Kate wondered if his were screaming as much as hers were.

"A little wobbly, but fine," she lied. To his credit, Aaron didn't challenge her, but she caught the smirk that he quickly hid.

After they finished eating and cleaned up their trash, Kate thanked Aaron for the trip.

"Are you asking me to take you home so soon? Where's your sense of adventure?"

"There's more?" Kate asked. The blood pounding through her legs was just beginning to return to normal.

"Only if you want there to be," he asked with genuine sincerity. Kate wasn't sure how to respond.

"I guess that depends upon what you have in mind. This was pretty cool, but tiring."

"How about a less taxing activity?"

"Well," Kate tried to decide what to do. She was certainly having a good time, and Aaron was a total gentleman, but she didn't want to lead him on. "What do you have in mind?"

"How about a quiet walk on the beach?"

Kate thought about it and decided that a walk on the beach couldn't hurt anything. "Okay, a walk would be nice."

They drove to the shore while Aaron told her a little more about the island. On their way, they stopped several times so that Kate could see, up close, herds of the famous ponies as they ate the grass along the road. Aaron parked and they joined the other onlookers on the side of the road, taking pictures of the island's famous inhabitants. Kate snapped pictures on her phone to send to Zach and their parents.

"Assateague is in both Maryland and Virginia. In Maryland, it's a state park, but in Virginia, it's federal land," Aaron told her as they continued their drive. He talked about the legend of the shipwreck that brought the ponies to the island, believed by many to be no more than a legend, and the annual fireman's carnival that rounds them up and sells them to raise money for the fire department.

"You have a great love and appreciation for the area, don't you?" Kate asked as they walked along the beach. The water was now cold, but they saw several kayakers and a few surfers braving the elements along with some small children who squealed and laughed as the water ran over their toes. Aaron and Kate followed the foamy, ocean waves along the shoreline.

"I do. I was away for a long time, but when I came back, it was like I never left. It has always been home."

"It's funny. I love DC. I still own and live in the house my family has lived in for over one hundred years, but I've never quite felt like that about the city. Maybe it was because we traveled and moved around so much when I was a kid. If I left it, I'm not sure I could go back and still feel like I'm at home."

"Military?"

"No, just the daughter of a nomadic researcher with hopes that his life's work would change the way people saw the world. It wasn't a bad life, but I don't think I ever really put down roots."

"Then what are you going to do when you leave here?"

"I don't know," Kate said, and she realized that she meant it. She really didn't know. "At first, I thought I could just come here for an extended vacation and then go back to life as I," she hesitated. "No, not life as I knew it. That life was over before I left." She shook her head and tightened her lips for a minute. "To whatever life I could salvage, I guess. I mean my house is still my home, but my job is gone. And my friends have all moved on. Literally. None of them stayed in the city once they had kids." Kate stopped suddenly. Kids. Did she want to go back to the city and raise her child there? What was she going to do?

"What is it?" Aaron asked. "Is everything okay?" He looked at her with genuine concern.

Kate took a deep breath. "I don't really know what I'm going to do. I guess I have a lot to think about."

"Well, you have plenty of time. Kayla says you're here for six months. Is that right?"

Kate calculated the time in her head. "I signed a six-month lease, but I don't know. I might need to leave sooner. Or later." She started walking again. "It's all too confusing right now. I'm just not sure."

Aaron took her hand. "Hey, Kate." He stopped her, and she turned toward him. "Let's just walk for now. You don't have to solve all of your problems in one afternoon."

Kate looked down at her hand in his. She started to pull away, but Aaron held tight. "Let's just walk," he repeated.

Trying not to let her emotions get the better of her again, Kate walked down the beach hand in hand with Aaron and enjoyed, if only for a brief time, the feeling of having someone care about her.

***

The trail was almost empty on Monday morning. Even at this hour, just barely past dawn, Aaron usually saw other runners. The island was home to many active and retired military, and many of them enjoyed a good run every morning before heading to work. Of course, the university and military academy students were gone, and they made up a good number of the health-conscious inhabitants in Chincoteague.

The air was cool, and a heavy breeze rustled the leaves and the grasses along the trail. Aaron preferred this paved trail to the gravel one and ran smoothly at a nice pace, letting his thoughts wander as he enjoyed his run. It was no surprise to him that no matter what crossed his mind, all trails seemed to lead back to Kate.

What was it about her that intrigued him so much? Kayla said it was because she seemed to be in need rescuing. He didn't take the bait on that one. Aaron had done his share of rescuing, and it didn't always feel like the accomplishment others thought it was. Not everyone could be rescued. There's nothing like watching a good man die to bring that reality home, especially when it was your fault that he was dead.

Aaron shook his head to clear his thoughts. He wasn't going to go there. He had been cleared, at least as far as everyone else was concerned. He had moved on, done his job and done it well, and was now an admired and respected person of authority. He couldn't change things now, and it was best to not dwell in the past. But what did he want for his future? It wasn't something he ever thought about. He had a good job, a close family, a nice house, and lots of friends. Not once in the past ten years, since the incident that had changed his life, had he considered his future. The road ahead was well paved, and he lived life as it came to him without needing or wanting more.

But suddenly that had changed. He watched his sister with her boys and wondered, just wondered, what his life would be like if he had taken a different path. His high school sweetheart, Debbie, went away to college and never came back. She wanted nothing more than to marry him and have a life together, but he wanted to set sail on the open sea. She cried in his arms the summer after graduation when he said goodbye. He was heading to Connecticut for R-Day and would begin Swab Summer, the most challenging summer of his life. Debbie was smart and popular, and he knew that she could take the world by storm if he let her go. And he was right. She came into her own once she went away to school and now managed her own private equity fund, traveling the world and turning heads everywhere she went. He was happy for her and knew that he had made the right decision. Not for a moment since then had he regretted concentrating on his career instead of looking for the right woman.

So, what was it that had him looking twice at the new gal in town? He let his thoughts continue to run around his mind as he circled back to the beginning of the trail. He couldn't stop thinking about her excitement at seeing the ponies, her sexy grin and warm laugh when he teased her,

her rolling eyes when he called her 'Princess,' and her apprehension when he even hinted at an interest in her. Maybe it was just the allure of the unknown, the mysterious way she blew into town and then fit right in as if she had been there her whole life. Whatever it was, Aaron was having a hard time fighting the feelings he had. He wanted to get to know her, to run his fingers through her smooth, blonde hair, to taste her pale, pink lips. He was a very patient man, and though she resisted his attempts to break through the shield that surrounded her, he was determined to learn her story. Perhaps her happy ending could also be his own.

It is often believed that the original inhabitants were afraid of and even tried to fend off European settlers in the New World. Historical accounts, however, tell us that this is far from true. Indigenous folk in North America accepted the strangers from across the Ocean with open arms from the very beginning, nursing them back to health and welcoming them into their homes and communities.

From the *Studies of Indigenous Peoples*
by Walter Middleton

CHAPTER SIX

That morning, Kate visited the island clinic. She had put it off long enough, but she knew that she couldn't keep denying what was going on. She didn't know whether she would tell her family and raise the baby on her own or give it up for adoption. She just knew that, despite her own lack of religion, she couldn't and wouldn't end its life. She had yet to begin thinking of this life inside of her as a 'baby,' but she knew that would soon change.

"Everything looks good," the doctor told her after her exam. "I agree with your guess that you're about eight weeks. The size and position verifies that assumption. I'm going to prescribe some prenatal vitamins. How are you feeling?"

"Tired. And nauseous in the mornings or if I don't eat when I feel hungry. And a little out of breath when I exercise or exert myself."

"That's normal. The morning sickness should go away, but it doesn't with everyone, so don't worry if yours seems to last past twelve weeks. You're probably going to feel more energetic in the second trimester and then tired again in the third. Do you have any questions?"

Kate sat on the table, wearing nothing but the paper gown, and looked at the older man. "About a million." He smiled.

"That's also perfectly normal. I can recommend some books for you to read if you like."

Kate nodded. "Please. I'd appreciate that." She hesitated. "I'm kind of in this alone, and I haven't told anyone, so I'd like to keep it to myself for a while."

"Of course. Anything that is said or done in this room is completely confidential."

Kate knew that already, but somehow, hearing it said out loud seemed to make it real.

"I do have a question," Kate wrung her hands as she thought about her night out with Megan and the afternoon of Anne's barbecue. "I'm not a big drinker, well not anymore, but I have had a few drinks in the past month or so." Kate blushed. "Before I knew I was pregnant, of course, but still…will that affect the baby?"

"At this stage, you shouldn't have anything to worry about. Stay away from all alcohol from here on out, and try to avoid caffeine."

"Hmm," she mused. "So much for my morning cup of Joe."

The doctor smiled. "It's a crutch that many of us rely on. One cup every now and then won't hurt. Now, about the father. Does he—"

"No," Kate cut him off. "There is no father. The man I married is dead." She hadn't meant to say it or to sound so blunt about it, but Kate had come to the realization that it was true. Mark was dead to her. In fact, the man she married really never existed to begin with.

"I'm so sorry." Doctor Louden stood and approached Kate. He put his hand on her shoulder. "Please call the office if you need anything. We are more than happy to assist you with whatever you need."

"Thank you," Kate said through tears. "It's been hard, but I'm going to be okay. We're going to be okay."

Kate left the office with several pamphlets, a prescription for vitamins, and a list of books that she intended to order on Amazon. She was grateful that she had a grace period with her insurance company, but she needed to fill out a slew of forms to apply for insurance once hers ran out. Her head swam with all the information, and she braced herself on her car before opening the door and getting inside. Across the street, from a café window, Kayla sipped her coffee and watched Kate drive away.

***

Shortly after lunch, there was a knock on the porch door. Kate was on the couch, halfway between sleep and consciousness, when she heard Kayla's voice call her name through the screen.

Peeling herself from the couch, she walked to the door. "Hi Kayla, what brings you over?"

Kayla looked unsure of herself. "Can I come in?"

"Sure," Kate said with uncertainty as she slid open the door. "Is everything okay?"

"That's what I'm here to find out."

Kate raised an eyebrow and waited for Kayla to say more.

"Look, I know it's none of my business, but," Kayla looked around the room. "Can we sit?"

"Sure, come in." Kate said, leading Kayla to the couch. "What's up?" she asked, though she wasn't sure she wanted to hear whatever this conversation was going to be about.

"Maybe I shouldn't have come over. It's just that you have seemed so, so lost, I guess, and sad. And when you came to the house the other morning, I sensed that you and

I have something in common. I'm thinking you've been through something pretty traumatic. Am I right?"

Kate slowly nodded her head.

"This morning, I was having a cup of coffee at the Island Café while waiting for Anne. She's helping me set up a business. She's good at that. Anyway, I was waiting for her, and I saw you."

Kate's stomach began to turn.

"Is everything okay? Are you sick? Is there something I can do to help?"

Tears welled up in Kate's eyes. "I don't even know where to begin. Did Anne tell you anything?"

"Anne has said nothing. You just looked like you had the weight of the world on your shoulders. I know that look. I've seen it in the mirror more times than I'd like to admit over the past five years."

Kate looked away. She wiped away the tears and took a deep breath. "Did you ever read *The Pilot's Wife*?"

Kayla nodded. "Years ago, when it first came out."

"You know how there was the pilot's real wife and then there was the *other* wife?" Kate let the question hang in the air long enough for Kayla to understand her meaning.

"Oh my God." Kayla grabbed Kate's hands. "And you are?"

"The *other* wife," Kate answered as she closed her eyes and lowered her head. She quickly looked back up at Kayla. "But I didn't know. I swear I didn't know."

"Of course, you didn't know. I would never have thought you did." Kayla pulled Kate into her arms and held her like she would have held one of her children.

"It gets worse," Kate said as she pulled away and looked at Kayla. "I'm, I don't even know how to say it." She looked up and began wringing her hands. Her tears turned into crying. "Oh, Kayla, I'm pregnant. I don't know what to do. I'm so scared."

Kayla wrapped her arms around Kate and let her cry. After a few minutes, her cries turned into sniffles, and soon she was wiping her eyes with the back of her hand and pulling herself together. She smiled weakly at Kayla.

"Thank you. I think I needed that."

"Nothing beats a good cry," Kayla said as she rubbed her hand on Kate's back. "So what's next? Does he know?"

"Oh God, no. And he's not going to." Kate stood up and began pacing. "Do you think I'm a horrible person for not telling him? No, don't answer that. I don't care. I'm not telling."

"I think you're incredibly brave, and I admire you."

"Really?" Kate stopped and stared at Kayla in disbelief. Kayla had to be the bravest person Kate had ever known, next to Zach.

"Really. It's not easy raising kids without a husband, but it can be done. And you're going to do it. And it's going to be okay."

Returning to the couch, Kate took Kayla's hands in hers. "Will you help me? I mean, at least for the next few months? I have no idea what to expect."

"Of course, I will. And so will Anne. And Shannon and Tammi. We're all going to be here for you. The guys, too. Everyone will be at your beck and call."

Kate was suddenly horrified. "Oh God, they're all going to know. I can't hide this. What will they all think?"

"That you're brave and admirable. And that we're all going to have a new baby to hold and ooh and ahh over."

"Your brother. He's been so nice to me."

"And he will still be nice to you. Everyone will. You're worrying over nothing. Do you think you're the only unmarried woman to ever be pregnant on Chincoteague? Come on. We all live in the 21st Century."

By the time Kayla's boys climbed off the school bus, Kayla and Kate had ordered three books from Amazon plus several, as Kayla called them, transitional outfits that would help Kate ease into her new body with style.

Marge called around four in the afternoon to ask Kate to cover the Chamber of Commerce meeting later that week, and Kate started to feel as if she would be able to handle things after all. That night, she called Anne and asked if they could get together the next morning. She might as well let her know. After all, according to everything she read online, her secret would be out within the next month.

***

"Go, Todd, run! Run!" Kate shouted for the little boy as he kicked the ball down the field. He tried passing it to another teammate, but the ball was intercepted by another player and kicked back toward the other end of the field. Without losing a beat, Todd turned and chased back after the ball.

"That kid can run," Kate said to Kayla.

"I know. He's not the best player on the team, but darn if he isn't the fastest."

They watched, screamed, moaned, and cheered as the Chincoteague Ponies lost, eight to nothing.

"Oh well," Kayla said. "They tried."

"Maybe they need a new coach," Kate teased.

"Bite your tongue. Aaron's the only person I know of with the patience and finesse to work with them and keep their hopes up."

They crossed the field and were greeted by a seven-year-old with a dirty face and bright grin. "Hi, Mommy, did you see me run? I almost made it to the net."

"I saw. Did you hear me cheering?" Kayla licked her thumb and wiped a stripe of dirt from Todd's cheek.

"Nah, I don't hear nuthin' when I'm running."

"I don't hear anything," she corrected him.

"Yeah, that," he said as he ran over to his friends to say goodbye.

"Hey," Aaron called. He finished packing his things and walked toward them. "I didn't know the paper was covering our game. Please don't make us look too bad to our devoted fans."

"This visit is strictly off the record," Kate laughed. "Kayla thought I needed a night out on the town, and this is her idea of a wild and crazy evening of fun and excitement."

Aaron's grin reached from one ear to the other. "I bet I could come up with a plan more to her Highness' liking."

"I'm sure you could, my liege, but I think that my carriage is about to turn back into a pumpkin."

"Come on, boys," Kayla called. "You've got school tomorrow."

"Why don't you take the boys home, and I'll give Kate a ride?" Aaron asked as Todd and EJ came bounding up beside them.

"Thanks for the offer, Aaron, but it makes more sense for me to ride with Kayla. I do need to turn in. I have a couple of appointments tomorrow." Kate noticed Kayla give her a sidelong glance, but she didn't say anything. Kate knew she wouldn't. Aaron might be her brother, but Kate took her as a person of her word. She promised not to tell him about the baby, and that was good enough for Kate.

"Another time?"

"Maybe. I've got a lot on my plate right now."

Disappointment was written all over his face, but to his credit, Aaron didn't push the matter.

"Okay, then. I'll see you around," he said as he walked toward his truck.

"You could have gone," Kayla said as they walked back across the field. "He's pretty harmless."

"I know, and I really do like him. As a friend, I mean. We had a good time the other afternoon. But I don't think it's a good idea. You know my situation. I couldn't involve him in that."

"Don't you think it's up to Aaron to decide whether he wants to be involved?" Kayla opened the door to the SUV and shuffled the boys in as Kate watched Aaron drive away. Closing the door, Kayla looked at her friend. "I'm going to be blunt."

Kate raised an eyebrow and looked at Kayla, waiting for her to continue.

"When we first met, I didn't trust you. I saw the way Aaron looked at you and how he flirted with you. He's a good guy, you know. He deserves a good woman. Maybe that's you, and maybe it's not, but I'm beginning to think that you'd be good for each other. There's no harm in at least giving it a try, figuring out if it will work. And before you protest that it won't work because of," she glanced in her rearview mirror and saw EJ pretending not to listen. "Well, you know." Kate nodded, and Kayla continued. "You should think about giving him the chance to say no himself. Just sayin'."

Kate was quiet on the ride home. She knew that Kayla meant well, but it was hard to figure what was fair, to let Aaron decide whether he was willing to date in her condition or to not make him have to decide at all.

***

Kate and Anne met the next morning at a local coffee shop. Anne was already there when Kate arrived, and she rose and met her new friend with open arms.

"You look absolutely wonderful. In fact, I think you're glowing. The ocean air must be good for you."

"I think it is," Kate told her, "but I'm glowing for another reason, a more traditional one."

The shock on Anne's face was fleeting before she broke into a smile. "Are you?"

"I am," Kate nodded. "I was totally shocked, but now, I'm feeling good about it."

"And your ex?"

"Is out of the picture and staying that way."

"Very well then. You'll just have to let all of your friends here take care of you."

"That's exactly what I was hoping," Kate grinned back at this wonderful, non-judgmental woman.

After a cup of decaf and a breakfast sandwich, Kate told Anne the few details she knew about the baby. Baby. The word was becoming more familiar to Kate, and she was beginning to wonder what her life with a child would be like. She spent the day wandering in and out of shops on the island looking at baby clothes and infant toys. It was all so unfamiliar to her, and she was grateful to have Anne and Kayla to help her and answer her questions.

Just as she was opening a package of chicken to cook for dinner, Kate heard a knock at the door. Island life was so different than life in the city where everything was scheduled, and people called to see if you were home or called to see if you wanted to go out. She put the chicken in the sink and looked around the corner to see who was there. Her stomach did a flip flop when she saw Aaron standing on the other side of the screen.

"Aaron, what a nice surprise. I was just getting ready to cook dinner. Would you like to join me?" She tried to appear casual, but her heart raced. Did he know? Was he coming to chastise her, or worse, pity her?

"Actually, I was wondering if you were up for another wild adult adventure."

Kate glanced at the clock. "Isn't it a little late for an adventure?"

"Late? It's barely five. What happened to the wild and crazy party girl? Surely you wouldn't have been planning on turning in at five when you lived in DC."

"Well, no, but—"

"No buts. Put the chicken away, grab your shoes and a sweatshirt, and come with me. We can pick up something to eat on the way. Hurry, we're running out of time."

Running out of time? Kate had to admit that, once again, she was intrigued by his offer. She re-wrapped the chicken, put it on a plate, and stuck it in the fridge. After washing her hands, she grabbed her favorite sweatshirt, a well-worn shirt she had owned since her Freshman year at George Washington University.

"Where are we going?" she asked as Aaron held open the truck door for her.

"It's a secret." He smiled as she shut the door. As he walked around the front of the truck, Kate noticed his own sweatshirt. It was royal blue and had the Coast Guard Academy insignia on it.

"No soccer practice tonight?" she asked after he sat and closed his door.

"Just ended. I try to have the kids done and home in time for dinner with their families."

"That's nice. Not all coaches are that considerate nowadays from what I hear and read."

"Family is important. That's why I spend so much time with Kay and the boys. They need to know that the rest of the family will always be there even if their dad is gone."

Kate looked at Aaron and was again struck by his sincerity and his attentiveness when it came to his sister and nephews.

"Nice shirt," she said. "Care to elaborate?"

He looked down at his shirt as if he didn't remember what he had on. "Oh, just an old shirt I had."

"So it has nothing to do with that kid the other day calling you 'Commander'?"

Aaron just shrugged and started the truck. "No big deal."

"So what is your deal, Aaron? I mean, you know what I do for a living. So, what do you do?"

"Actually, I know very little about you, Princess. So how about you go first?"

"That's not fair. I asked you," Kate protested.

"So we'll take turns. You first. What did you do in DC?"

That was an easy one. "I worked at the Smithsonian Magazine."

"Doing what?"

"Selling ads. It was such a glamorous career."

"But obviously not glamorous enough to keep you there."

"It definitely wasn't what I wanted to be doing."

"And what was that?" he asked, casually taking his eyes off of the road long enough to glance at her.

"I think it's your turn. I answered two questions already."

"Okay," he acquiesced. "Shoot."

"Where did you go to college?"

"That's too easy."

"Then confirm it for me."

"I went to the Academy. Hardest four years of my life but worth every minute."

"Where is that? I know it's not Annapolis."

"Nope, wrong seamen. Connecticut. Where the water's cold and the nights are even colder."

"Same deal, though, right? You had to be really smart and physically fit?"

"Basically. Same deal."

"So you were appointed to the Coast Guard Academy, and your sister went to Yale. Those are some pretty good genes." Kate absent-mindedly rubbed her belly and wondered about her baby's genes.

"I guess so. Mom's an artist, and Dad's a retired Vice Admiral. It's hard to go much further than that."

"Wow. He was career?"

"He was. Luckily, we didn't move around like most military kids. Most people don't think that Coast Guard families move a lot, but they do. We were just among the few lucky ones. My dad was aboard the Cuyahoga when it sunk in the Chesapeake Bay in 1978. He was hailed as a hero for helping to save the lives of the eighteen men who made it home. After that, he was pretty much given anything he asked for, and he asked for anything that was near his childhood home here on the island. He served at Virginia Beach, Wallops Island, Assateague, and finally retired here on Chincoteague. If fact, half the island consists of retired Coast Guardsmen. Anyway, none of Dad's appointments were glamorous, but they allowed us to live here while he commuted, and that's what he wanted. The only time he was ever away from us was during the first Gulf War. Again, he came home a hero."

"But you didn't stay in, did you?"

"What makes you think that?"

"I don't know. I'm just guessing that, at your age, you would be stationed somewhere, pretty high up in rank, and not spending your time playing beach volleyball and climbing lighthouses."

When Aaron stiffened but didn't answer, Kate apologized. "I'm so sorry. Did I say something wrong? I didn't mean to upset you."

"No worries. We're here." He turned off the truck's engine. They were at the end of a dirt road in a grove of trees.

"Where are we?" Kate asked.

"No time for questions. We've got to hurry." Aaron jumped out of the truck and ran around to the passenger side, opening Kate's door and urging her to quickly get out.

"It's down here," he said, taking her hand and leading her down a path through the trees.

The path opened into a clearing that housed four small boats tied to a small, very low to the water, dock.

"Kayaks? Really?" She could hardly contain her excitement.

"Yeah. I take it you've been in one."

"Oh my gosh, yes. Every chance I get."

Still holding her hand, he led her down to the dock.

"Where did you kayak in DC?"

"On the Potomac, the Tidal Basin, Great Falls, wherever I could, whenever I could."

"Ever paddle a tandem?"

"I don't think so."

"It's a kayak for two people. I'll take the back seat and do the steering. You just have to relax and enjoy yourself. We won't go out too far."

"I don't have a bathing suit on, and it's a little chilly, but I'm game."

"Don't worry. We won't get too wet."

"Promise?"

"Well, tandems are nicknamed 'divorce boats' for a reason, so I'm not making any promises I can't keep, but I'll do my best. The key with these babies is that we have to work together."

Kate watched Aaron as he opened a plastic tub at the end of the dock and pulled out two lifejackets.

"This is Kay's, so it should fit you," he said as he handed her the regulation personal flotation device. He strapped his on and then grabbed one of the kayaks and pulled it closer to the dock. Once she had her PFD buckled around her waist, he held the kayak steady so that she could climb inside.

"Oh my gosh, I can't wait. But," she looked out at the water. "I've never gone out in the dark. We'll be safe, right?"

"Wild and crazy, huh? You'll go to a bar in downtown DC, probably via the metro, surrounded by God knows who after dark, but you won't get in a kayak on a crystal-clear night in a small inlet?"

"You're right. Let's go."

Aaron helped her climb in, guiding her with instructions that would get her into the two-person boat without ending up in the water. Then he climbed in behind her. She held onto the boat as it bobbed from side to side while he got settled. Reaching onto the dock, Aaron grabbed the paddles and handed one to her.

"Where are we going?"

"Be patient," he laughed. "You'll see."

Kate tried to be patient while Aaron untied the kayak and eased them away from the dock. The thrill of being back in a kayak had her heart racing. She hadn't realized how much she missed it.

"We have to go a little bit fast to get there, but it will be worth it."

Kate followed Aaron's lead, paddling quickly in time with him, taking the little boat out into the water.

"Sorry for the rush, but there isn't much time."

"Time for what?"

"Time for that," Aaron said as the kayak made its way around a bend, and a magnificent kaleidoscope of colors filled the sky behind the setting sun. "The sun sets in the west, so you have to have just the right timing and the right place to see it from the east coast to really appreciate it. This is one of my favorite spots."

"Wow," was all Kate could manage.

"Yeah, it's pretty spectacular."

They drifted along as the sun set over the island, the sky a magnificent painting of purples and oranges spreading, not only across the sky, but across the water. Every cloud was perfectly reflected in the calm, still water, a brilliant collection of colors more splendid than Kate could ever have imagined.

After the sun disappeared, and dusk settled over the beaches and channels, Kate and Aaron paddled back to the dock. He tied the kayak to the dock and helped her up, guiding Kate back to his truck, his hand laid protectively on the small of her back.

"Dinner?" he asked as they approached the truck.

"Dinner sounds nice," Kate replied.

"Really?" Aaron was genuinely surprised.

"Yes, really. I'm starving."

"Oh, so you're just using me for food." Aaron stood by the passenger side door and smiled.

"Maybe," Kate said, "or maybe I'm actually having fun and enjoying the company."

"Good enough for me," he answered before closing the door.

Aaron took Kate to his favorite seafood restaurant and ordered a bottle of wine.

"Oh, no, none for me," she told the waiter with an uneasy smile. "I'm sorry," she said to Aaron. "I've decided to take a break from drinking. I need to be able to think clearly in order to figure out where my future is heading."

"No worries," Aaron said. He asked the waiter to switch their order to beer and water. "So, back to our game of twenty questions? I think it's my turn."

"Your turn? I don't think you finished answering my questions," Kate said though she recalled that he was somewhat hesitant to let her continue down that road earlier.

"Nope, you had way more than your allotted questions. Now it's my turn."

The waiter returned with their drinks, and they ordered a calamari appetizer before Aaron continued. "The Smithsonian wasn't your dream job. So, what is it you want to be doing?"

Kate took a sip of water and thought about it. "I guess I'm still trying to figure that out. I went to college with the desire to be a magazine reporter, but not a women's magazine or family publication. I wanted to write real news, and absolutely not travel logs, but my dad had connections, so I took the job at the Smithsonian. I would have been okay with writing for them, but all I was doing was selling ads. I had high hopes that I could work my way up the ladder, but I was just stuck in a job that was going nowhere."

"And now?" Aaron asked as he passed her the basket of rolls that the waiter placed on the table.

"That's a good question," she said as she chose a roll, broke off a piece, and buttered it. "I'm not sure any more. I like writing, and I'd still love to cover real news, but I don't know, maybe I'd rather just settle down." It wasn't entirely the truth, but it was now a necessary truth. Her life was going to change, and she needed to adjust her thinking and her goals. She became quiet as she took a bite of the bread.

"You still have time to travel," Aaron said as he swallowed his bite of bread.

"I guess. I'll have to see what happens. I traveled a lot as a child, so maybe it's time for me to stay in one place."

Kate told Aaron about all the places she lived as a child while her father did his research. It was fun and interesting some of the time, but she always longed to be back in her grandmother's Brownstone, going to a real school, making friends who spoke English. Sure, she could speak Spanish, Acadian French, Portuguese, and even some Swahili, but what she really wanted as a child was a stable home, in a nice place, with lots of friends.

"By the time I was in high school, my father was writing his book. It was great for a while, and we had a nice, normal life together, but then Zach headed off to college and afterward, enlisted in the Army." She shrugged. "And that's as interesting as my life gets."

"Wow," Aaron blew out a breath. "That's pretty darn interesting. I've seen many ports but never the parts of the world you've seen. It sounds like a pretty cool childhood to me."

Kate looked out the window at the star covered sky and its reflection on the water.

"Maybe, but I'm pretty content right here."

They ate the rest of their meal making small talk. Kate knew that she was on borrowed time. Kayla and Anne both knew, and it was only a matter of time before it became obvious. She needed to decide whether there was a reason to include Aaron in her secret.

When he dropped her off at the house, he walked her to the front door and made sure she could get inside.

Kate braced herself for Aaron to make a move. She admitted to herself that a kiss would feel right after their evening together, but it was not something that she was ready for, and she might not ever be ready. She wasn't going to let herself rush into something ever again, and there were still too many secrets between them.

"I had a really nice night, Aaron."

"But you're still not ready for more," he said with a hint of disappointment in his voice.

"No, but I will enjoy watching you walk away into the moonlight." Kate smiled, and Aaron laughed.

"I guess that's my cue then." He turned to leave. "But first," he turned back and leaned in, placing a kiss on Kate's cheek. "I'll walk into the moonlight tonight, but I'm not walking away, Princess." He winked at her, turned, and left.

Kate stood in the doorway and watched him drive away. She hated herself for trusting Mark, for losing the ability to trust herself, for not listening to her parents, for letting herself get pregnant. Mostly, she hated herself for letting Aaron walk away. But she knew she was doing the right thing. She still had so much to work out, and she wanted to be fair to Aaron, to herself, and to her baby.

***

For a time, Kate resisted the urge to google her new friends and neighbors, but her curiosity and her returning addiction to the news got the better of her. She decided to begin with Kayla and then move on to Aaron. It didn't take long to find Kayla's name and her tragic story. Her husband, Eddie Reynolds, had been working as an FBI informant when his boss, chief of staff to the Mayor of Baltimore, discovered that Eddie had been giving information to the Feds. Mayor Simpson was using the city of Baltimore as a front for his human trafficking ring, arranging government contracts with city hotels that would then 'employ' young women and girls who were kidnapped from the Caribbean. Kate read about the two little girls who witnessed Eddie's murder. As she read, the details of the case came back to her, and she recalled the story of how Alex Moore had killed the young man and hid his body. A small-town police detective and his girlfriend were protecting the children and solved the case. Kate remembered how it had rocked the city of Baltimore and was surprised that the mention of Eddie Reynold's name hadn't jarred her memory.

Without hesitation, Kate ran next door and frantically knocked on the glass door. As soon as Kayla saw Kate, she looked worried.

"Kate, are you okay? The baby?"

"No, yes. I mean I'm okay and so is the baby. Are you okay?"

Kayla searched Kate's face, and then it hit her.

"You know," Kayla said as she let Kate into the house.

"Oh, Kayla, I'm so sorry." The women embraced and then went into the living room to sit down.

"I knew it was only a matter of time before you found out. Aaron told me that he mentioned Eddie's murder to you."

"I should have remembered. The story was all over the news back then. I don't remember there being too much about you and the boys, though. How have you been able to deal with all of this?"

"It's been five years." Kayla shook her head as if in disbelief. "Jim, the detective, tried to keep us out of the story as much as possible, and everyone was pretty successful at keeping our whereabouts a secret. Oh, reporters stormed the island when I first moved back home, but everyone shielded us, and eventually they all left us alone. I'm still dealing with the fallout, but I'm okay. I have to be. I have two boys who count on me, and someday, I will have to find the strength and the right words to tell them about their father. He was a good man, and I believed the worst about him. I thought he was having an affair. It never even occurred to me that he might have a good reason for lying and keeping secrets from me. I made accusations based on my own fears and insecurities, and I left him. I was here on the island when he was killed."

"At least you knew that he loved you. You didn't waste your time on someone who was living a lie." As soon as the words were out of her mouth, Kate regretted them. "I'm sorry, what I meant was that he had a legitimate reason for lying to you. No, that still doesn't sound right." Kate sighed.

"Oh Kate, it's okay." Kayla grasped Kate's hands. "I know what you mean, and you're right. It's not the same. Eddie was a good man, and we loved each other very much. I will always have that. But you opened your heart to a man, thinking he was honest and good, and he abused it. I can only imagine how you feel, but I believe that you can bounce back from this."

"You're right. I know that, and being here, knowing you, meeting the wonderful people who are now a part of my life, has made me realize it even more. But what do I tell my own child? At least your husband died trying to do the right thing."

"You don't have to tell your child anything for a long time. And by the time he or she is ready to know, you will have moved so far along that it won't matter any more. You will have a new story to tell, and I'm willing to bet that this baby will have a better father than Mark could ever have been."

"But how can I trust someone again? How can I trust my own judgment?" She looked to Kayla for help while, at the same time, recognizing that Kayla hadn't learned to trust anyone either.

"Kate, you don't need to trust in yourself. Trust in God. He will lead you to the right person at the right time."

"Do you really believe that?" Kate was surprised to hear Kayla's words. This coming from someone who obviously still lived in fear.

"I do," Kayla said emphatically. "Just because I haven't found someone yet doesn't mean that I don't believe that I will. It's all in God's time."

Was it really that simple? Kate wasn't so sure. She had never trusted in God. It wasn't a conscious decision not to trust Him. It just wasn't something she had ever thought about before.

"How do I even start?" she asked.

Kayla stood and went to the kitchen counter where she had left her phone.

"Do you have your phone?"

Kate took her phone from her pocket.

"I'm sending you Father Darryl's contact card. Call him. Just talk to him. If he can't help you, then you can try something else. What have you got to lose?"

Kate accepted the incoming file on her phone and dropped the device back into her pocket.

"Why not?" she said to Kayla. "Like you said, what have I got to lose?"

***

Returning to the laundry room, Kayla piled the dry clothes into a basket and transferred the wet clothes into the dryer. As she stood in her bedroom and folded the clothes, she thought about Kate. Whatever suspicions Kayla had about her dissipated more and more each time they were together. Opening up to Kate had felt so natural. Why hadn't she done it before? They had both been happily married to men who hid things from them, and they both ended up single mothers. They each knew what the other was feeling and could lean on each other. The thought brought on a profound feeling of relief as Kayla acknowledged that she was glad to have Kate in her life.

More than ever, she could see Kate and Aaron building a life together. She hoped that this was the plan that God had in mind. Clutching EJ's favorite t-shirt to her chest, she closed her eyes and said a prayer. Never one to meddle in other people's affairs, she asked Saint Michael, the patron saint of the Coast Guard, and Saint Gerard, the patron saint of pregnant mothers, to watch over her brother and Kate and help them find their way to each other.

***

"How can I help you?" the young, red-bearded priest asked. Kate sat in a comfortable leather chair in Father Darryl's office and tried to relax.

"I'm afraid I haven't been to Mass in a very long time, Father. Actually, I haven't even thought about God in a very long time, most of my life really. But now, I'm wondering if it's time to start." She tried to hide her embarrassment.

"Well, it's never too late, and you're here now. So what brings you to this point?"

Without hesitation, Kate launched into the sordid details about her hasty wedding and her false marriage. It was easy to talk to Father Darryl. He had a quick wit and an easy-going style that allowed her to open up to him. When she finally ended her story with her recent discovery that she was pregnant, his face lit up.

"Oh, how lucky you are that God has blessed you with something good out of all of this tragedy."

"Really?" Kate was taken aback. "I would have guessed that you would have a problem with the circumstances. I mean, I'm not actually married."

"But you didn't know that at the time. You weren't willfully committing any sin. And all children are a blessing from God, no matter when or how they come to us. Do you plan on keeping the baby or giving it up for adoption?"

"At first, I wasn't sure what I was going to do, but the more I think about, the more I think I want to be a mom. I'm not saying I'm ready, but I want to try."

"Wonderful. However," his face turned serious. "I do have a question."

"Sure, what is it?"

"Have you contacted the father?"

Kate squirmed in her chair, and her face grew hot. She rolled her lips together. "No, Father, and I don't intend to."

The young priest sat back in his chair and crossed his fingers in front of him. It reminded Kate of the nursery rhyme she learned as a child about the church and the steeple with the fingers inside the hands as the people. She stared at Father's hands rather than looking up into his eyes.

"Kate, I strongly recommend that you tell him. As the father, he has a right to know. Not telling him would be a lie by omission."

Kate closed her eyes and felt tears forming. She took a deep breath and blinked them back before looking up.

"I'm so sorry, Father. I just don't know if I can do that. Can I at least think about it? Would that be a sin? To put it off?"

He thought about it for a few seconds, raising his index fingers into the proverbial steeple as if reading her thoughts. He tapped the tips of his fingers on his lips and then spoke. "How about this? Let's pray about it? I'll pray that you do the right thing, and you pray for guidance, reassurance, and confidence. Does that sound like a good place to start?"

"It does." Kate breathed a sigh of relief. She didn't want her first encounter with a priest after all these years to end on a bad note. She could, at the very least, do as he asked and pray.

"So Father, what do I do now, other than pray? How can I move on and figure out what the next step is for me? I don't mean to sound selfish, but how can I take care of a child when I don't know how to take care of myself?"

Father Darryl looked at Kate and smiled. His bright blue eyes twinkled as he nodded and spoke with confidence.

"Kate, you already are taking care of yourself. You are seeking answers, and in the right place. You left a poisonous situation and came to the beach to find rest and to make a new start. You chose to keep this gift from God when many in your situation would have made a different decision. You are doing exactly what God wants you to do. You just don't recognize it yet."

Kate sat back and thought about his words. She had done all those things on her own, or if Father was correct, with God's help.

"Okay, Father, so what now? What do I have to do next to continue down this path of righteousness that you have assured me that I'm on?"

"First, let's have ourselves an honest confession. Then, I'll see you at ten o'clock sharp on Sunday morning."

Twenty minutes later, Kate left the rectory feeling like a new woman. She wasn't entirely sure that she was ready to plunge headfirst back into Sunday Mass, Confession, and obeying all Ten Commandments, but she knew that she had to start somewhere.

The late September sun hung high over the island, and the salty breeze blew through her hair as she walked to her car. She headed to Anne's office with a smile on her face and a song in her heart.

"Good morning, Kate," Anne beamed and rose from her desk as Kate walked through the door. The two hugged, and Anne held Kate in her gaze for a moment.

"You look good. How do you feel?"

Kate nodded, "Pretty good. Hungry, tired, the norm."

"As to be expected," Anne said. "So what brings you here today?"

"I think I really need to see my parents. I'd love to have them come up for a visit and show them around the island. I have enough room in the house, but I was hoping you could help me with the travel details."

"I'd be happy to. Let's see what deals we can find."

It didn't take long for Anne to find Kate several reasonable airline fares into Norfolk, Virginia. They also looked at car rentals and the best upcoming travel dates. With all the info she needed in hand, Kate went back to the house and called her mother.

"Hello, darling. It's so good to hear from you." Her mother's warm and loving voice filled her ear and brought her right back to her childhood. "Walter, come here, Kate's on the phone. Hold on, dear, I'm putting you on speaker. Okay, so how's the beach?"

"It's nice, Mom, really nice. It's a great time of year to be here. It's just starting to get chilly during the day, and nights are pretty cool. Everything is still open, but the summer tourists and all the crowds are gone. It's the perfect time for a visit if you and dad are up to traveling. Please?"

"Oh, Katherine, you have no idea how much I've wanted to hear those words. We have been trying to give you your space, but I miss you so much and am so worried about you. How soon can we come?"

Kate loved her mother more than words could express. Why had she waited so long to invite her to come? She was so sure that it would show weakness if she called her parents, that she had completely shut them out.

Kate shared the information from Anne, and her mother consulted their calendars.

"Oh Kate, I'm so sorry that we can't come sooner. Your father is participating in a symposium at a nearby university in October. What about mid-November? We could stay through Thanksgiving if that's okay."

"Mom, that's perfect." Kate tried not to hide her disappointment. She wished she could see them sooner, but she understood.

"We're so happy that you called," her mother gushed into the phone.

"Me, too, Mom. I can't wait to see you and show you around the island."

"I guess it will be too cold to golf up there," her father's voice boomed through the phone, and Kate laughed.

"I don't know, Dad. It probably will be, but I'll see if there's a place nearby and check out whether it will be open when you're here."

When they hung up, Kate thought about how wonderful her parents were. Her condition was going to come as quite a shock to them, but she knew that they would be thrilled. Now, if only Zach would call. Then everything truly would be perfect.

Spirituality has played an intensely important role in the lives of indigenous peoples throughout history. To these groups of peoples the world over, religion and nature are intrinsically intertwined. The Métis and Inuit peoples of Canada believe in the two Transformers, one who created all good things such as the sun and moon, and one who created all obstacles to human health and happiness such as snakes, mountains, and disease. Praying to Glooscap, the good Transformer, inspired hope that a suffering person could overcome the obstacle placed before her by his brother, Malsum.

From the *Studies of Indigenous Peoples*
by Walter Middleton

CHAPTER SEVEN

October's Fall Art Festival was in full swing when Kate walked through the doors of the high school. She interviewed the chairwoman and several of the artists. There were a few pieces that she would have bought if she had the extra money. As she walked up and down the aisles, she was brought to a halt when she saw a painting of the sunset. The oranges and the purples spread across the sky and reflected on the water. A heron stood on one leg in the reeds as the sun hung low just above the horizon.

"Remind you of anything, Princess?" Kate, lost in her thoughts jumped at the sound of Aaron's voice.

"Is this from our spot?"

"It sure is."

"Did you do this?"

His beautiful laugh filled the room around her like it had on the day they met. "Absolutely not. I don't have the least bit of artistic talent. But my mother does."

Kate turned toward the woman in the booth. Until that moment, she hadn't even noticed her, and now she wondered how that had been possible. She was an older but just as beautiful version of Kayla with a touch of auburn in her hair.

"You must be Kate," the woman said. Her smile lit up the room, and she reached for Kate's hands just as Kayla had so many times. "I'm Ronnie. I've heard so much about you from both of my children."

Kate glanced at Aaron, but he looked away. "It's so nice to meet you. I adore Kayla. She has become the most wonderful friend."

"It seems to me that you have been just as much a friend to her since you arrived."

Kate blushed. "I don't know about that, but I'm happy if she thinks that's the case."

"So I take it Aaron showed you our little secret cove."

"He did, and I loved it."

"We don't go there often enough anymore," Ronnie said as she turned toward the painting. "Once the kids were grown, there just wasn't much time for such things." She turned back to Kate. "I'm so glad he took you there."

"Me, too. It was the most beautiful place to kayak. I'd love to go again."

"Any time you want, Princess. I'd be more than happy to take you."

"You know, your son lives in a delusional world," Kate pretended to whisper to Ronnie.

Ronnie laughed. "Yes, but he's earned the right."

What a strange comment, Kate mused. *I am definitely missing something.*

Aaron cleared his throat and pointed to one of his mother's paintings. "Mom, is that the view from the top of the lighthouse?"

Ronnie looked questioningly at Aaron and then turned her gaze toward the painting. "Yes, it is. I painted that last spring."

Kate looked from mother to son and wondered what their secret was. What was it about Aaron's past that he didn't want her to know? She realized that she had never gotten around to looking him up online, but for some reason, she didn't want to. She was going to trust him and let him tell her in his own way and in his own time. It was as big a step as she was ready to make at the moment.

***

Aaron and Kate walked around the high school, stopping at each of the booths to look at the art. At every booth that featured a local artist, Aaron was recognized. He introduced Kate to everyone he knew, and she was once again surprised at the closeness and familiarity of the small town. She could walk into every store within four blocks of her Brownstone and not see a single person she knew.

"Did you get enough info for your story?" Aaron asked once they had completed their walk around the room.

"I did, and I'm starving, so I hope you're offering to take me to lunch."

Aaron laughed. "Really? Well, how can I say no to that?"

"I really didn't mean for it to come out the way it did," Kate said. "I don't mean to twist your arm."

"You're not twisting my arm in the least. What are you in the mood for?"

"Spinach pizza," she said out without even stopping to think.

"Are you kidding? What the hell kind of food is that? Pepperoni belongs on pizza, or sausage or mushrooms. Spinach?"

"Uh huh. I'm dying for spinach pizza."

"Is that a fancy city thing?" he asked as he opened the door to his truck and held it for her.

"Um, maybe, but…" was she really going to do this now? She thought about it just briefly and then plowed ahead before she could change her mind. There would be no more secrets on her end. "For me, it might be a craving thing." She bit her lip and looked at Aaron waiting for him to process the meaning of her words.

Aaron looked perplexed as he stared at Kate. Finally, she looked down and placed a hand on her belly. She raised her eyes toward his and bit her lip a little harder. A silent "Oh" formed on his mouth.

"Yeah, I wasn't sure how to tell you."

"Well, I guess the cat's out of the bag. Spinach pizza it is." He closed the door and walked to the other side of the truck with an unreadable expression on his face. He climbed into the truck, slammed his door, and started the engine.

"Aaron, I-"

"Stop. You don't have to explain anything to me. Let's get lunch, and then I'll take you back to the school to get your car. You probably need to rest after all of that walking around." His tone wasn't exactly cold or chastising, but it certainly wasn't friendly.

"Aaron, that's not fair. It's not like I was under any obligation—"

"You're right," he said, never taking his eyes from the road. "You have no obligation to me at all. I'm just some guy who's around to show you a good time while whoever he is sits back in DC and waits for you to get over your mid-life crisis."

"Aaron Kelly, you can stop this truck right now and let me walk back to my car if that's how you're going to treat me. I expected more from you."

"Well, maybe I expected more from you," he snapped back.

Kate sat in silence while Aaron drove to the pizza place. Without a word, Aaron put the truck in park, slammed the door, and stalked around to Kate's side. She opened the door before he got there and started to climb out, but Aaron stopped her. He stood in the open door and shook his head, a multitude of emotions playing across his face. One particular emotion stood out as she looked into his eyes. He wasn't angry. He was hurt.

"Look, I'm sorry. I was just surprised. You caught me off guard, and I'm usually better at reading the signs than that. You've been telling me from day one that you aren't interested and that we're just friends. I guess, in my mind, I kept hoping I could change your mind."

"Aaron, it's not you, or anybody else for that matter. Look, I really am starving." She put her hand on his arm that was draped across the opening between the door and the truck. "Can we get that pizza to go and find some place to talk? There are things that you don't know, and I'd like to explain. Please."

With his jaw set and his expression unreadable, Aaron looked away for a moment before turning back to Kate. He sighed.

"Yeah, sure. You can wait here, and I'll run inside and order. Water?"

"Yes, please," she said as she pulled her legs back into the truck so that he could close the door. She blew out her breath, unaware until then that she had even been holding it, and closed her eyes. She was not looking forward to this.

Thirty minutes later, they pulled up to the dock where the kayaks were tied. Aaron opened the door and took the pizza from Kate before helping her down. His constant attention to chivalry amazed her. They made their way down onto the dock and sat with the pizza box between them. Kate opened the box and saw a half spinach and half pepperoni and mushroom pizza. She smiled.

"Weren't willing to try?"

"Not on your life," Aaron told her as he scooped up a piece of pizza from his side of the box.

Kate slowly ate a slice, and they watched the heron glide across the inlet. Before starting her second piece, Kate took a long drink of water.

"I was married," she began, "to the man of my dreams, or so I thought." She played with the cap of her water and resisted looking at Aaron as she spoke. "We met at a bar and were married, just three months later, on a beach in Mexico. I thought it was the most romantic thing that could ever happen to me." She stopped and took a bite, chewed it slowly, and then went on. "I was an idiot, and I know it. My parents hated him. Zach wrote to me and told me he hoped I wasn't making a mistake."

"You're pretty close, you and Zach."

"Extremely. For most of our childhood, we only had each other as playmates and whatever kids lived in the village wherever we were at the time. I miss him now. A lot."

"I get that," he said. "It's hard for the family back home, and for the one serving."

"It is," she said, shooting him a look that she hoped conveyed a warning that his turn was next. She was curious about his military background but needed to get her history out of the way first. "Anyway, everything seemed perfect, despite my family's warnings. But then, in one instant, everything changed."

Aaron stiffened, and a look of anger crossed his face. "Did he hurt you?"

Kate shook her head. "Not physically, but he may as well have punched me in the gut. He was a pilot. He was in DC for a few days at a time every other week. I didn't mind because it was what he did. That's how it always was, even though he promised me that he was working on getting a transfer so that DC would be his main hub. It never happened, and I never questioned it. I was so stupid."

She stopped talking and looked at the water. Aaron waited for her to continue.

"Then one day, he forgot his phone. At first, I thought it was someone else's phone, but then, the things she said, the coincidences. Nothing added up, and then everything added up."

"Hold on, slow down. Who is 'she'?"

Kate looked at Aaron and took a deep breath. "His wife. His real wife. The one in California with three kids and a mortgage and a real marriage license." She ripped up a slice of pizza and put a small piece in her mouth.

"Damn," Aaron said as he exhaled in disgust.

"You can say that again," Kate smirked.

"What did you do?"

"I cried. A lot. Then I called my dad and asked him to help me to fix the mess I was in. He made some calls and figured out the marriage thing. There wasn't one, as it turns out. The man who married us wasn't even licensed."

Kate looked back at the water and took a deep breath. "Then Mark started showing up at the house." She felt Aaron's body tense beside her and rushed to put him at ease. "He didn't do anything. He said he just wanted to talk, but there was something about him; something had changed. The police told me that he'd been drinking. I was surprised. Mark liked to drink as much as anyone, but he was a pilot, so he tended to be careful about how much he had. Anyway, I knew that he'd changed. Or maybe I just saw him for who he was for the first time. I don't know. Either way, I was scared."

Their eyes met, and Katherine saw Aaron's anger toward the man he had never met turn to empathy for the woman he barely knew. He reached for her hand.

"Did he ever try to do anything? To hurt you in some way?"

She shook her head. "He tried to get into the house, but it wasn't like he was breaking in. I'd changed the locks, so he pounded on the door and yelled a lot. I called the police after the third time he showed up and wouldn't leave. They took me to the station and had me get a restraining order. Twenty-four hours later, I decided I needed to get out of there. So I ran. I quit my job, locked up my grandmother's house, and threw caution to the wind."

"And you ended up here."

"And I ended up here. And then I found out that I didn't come alone." She gave him a half-hearted smile and let go of his hand. She finished off her water.

"It's not quite the fairy tale ending you expected."

"Nope." She gave him a questioning look. "Funny, Zach said something like that, too. Anyway, your sister and Father Darryl have both assured me that it's not over. They've convinced me that my life is just beginning, or they've tried. I guess we'll have to see about that."

"Kayla knows? And Father Darryl?"

"Yeah, I told Kayla about a week ago, and I saw Father the other day. And it was amazing. When I left, I felt like I was starting over again. Except for one thing."

"What's that?"

"He says I have to tell Mark. About the baby, I mean." She picked at the label of the water bottle as she thought about her promise to pray for guidance. She was trying, but praying was hard when she hadn't done it for a while, especially when she didn't want to hear the answer.

"I see." Aaron was quiet as he looked out over the still water. After a little while, he spoke. "I can be there, if you want. If you want to call or go see him. I can't imagine how hard it might be to face him alone."

Kate looked over at this remarkable man. He hardly knew her, had no real connection to her, yet here he was, offering to be there for the hardest conversation that she might ever have in her life.

"You're really something, you know that?" she said to him.

"Why? I'm just offering my support."

"No, it's more than that. You're offering to be there for a complete stranger, to help her through a very difficult time, not having any idea whether or not you'll ever get something in return. In six months, I could be gone, and you'd never see me again, but you'd do it anyway, wouldn't you? You'd help me out without ever asking for anything."

Aaron held her gaze with confidence. "I may be crazy, and you may not like me saying it, but I don't think you'll be gone in six months. You're right. I'd help you without ever asking anything in return or expecting anything from you, but I don't think I'm wasting my time, Princess. You're here for a reason. I've known that since I first saw you."

A chill ran down her back, but at the same time, she felt a warmth in her belly. Kate had never met anyone like Aaron, so willing to do the right thing and so full of faith that everything in life worked out the way it was meant to. They might still be little more than strangers, but he looked at her with such intensity, like he could see into her soul. It was both unnerving and wonderful at the same time.

"Thank you, Aaron," she said with sincerity. "I really appreciate that. I honestly have no idea what I'm going to do, but you'll be the first to know when I make up my mind." She put the bottle down and stretched out on the dock, leaning back on her elbows.

"Now, it's your turn. No getting out of it this time. Tell me about yourself, who you are, what you do. Tell me anything. Just don't keep leaving me in the dark. You now know all there is to know about me."

"There's not much to tell. I served my time on one ship or another, commanded a couple." He looked away, a pained expression on his face. "After that, they let me choose my own station, and I chose home. I command the Chincoteague Coast Guard Station. It's not glamorous, but I like it. It keeps me home but allows me to still serve in the Guard." He shrugged. "That's pretty much all there is to tell."

Kate sensed that there was more. There was something under the surface that he still refused to talk about, but she was satisfied for now. Aaron was real, and he was honest. Whatever it was that he wasn't ready to talk about could wait.

***

It was Kate's first time in church in many years, not counting all the weddings she attended after college, and she had to admit that she was nervous. She had been wrestling with misgivings for the past couple days and wondered if this was what she really wanted. Katherine would have gone through the motions until something better came along, but Kate wanted more than that. If she was truly going to return to the Church, then she wanted to do it right. The question was, did she want to? As she listened to the readings, she recognized a quote from back in her days of Catholic school. "Come unto me, ye who are weary and overburdened, and I will give you rest." Kate certainly felt weary and overburdened, but there was something about this island that strengthened her. Though she had been there just over a month, she had come to think of it as home. Maybe that was just what God had in mind.

Kate looked down the row and smiled. She sat next to EJ who was comfortably sandwiched between her and his mother. Next to Kayla was Todd, and beside him was

Aaron. Aaron must have sensed her looking his way because he leaned forward and looked at her, winking before turning back toward Father Darryl. After their talk the day before, they took the kayak out for a slow, easy paddle, soaking up the early October sun on what was forecast to be the last warm Saturday of the season. They didn't talk at all, and Kate felt relaxed and at peace in Aaron's presence as the light breeze caused the water to gently rock the boat.

After Mass, Anne greeted Kate with a hug. "Welcome back," she said as if she had known all along that opening up to God was all Kate needed.

"Thanks. It was Kayla who suggested I talk to Father Darryl. He helped a lot."

"How are you feeling?" Anne asked. "Tired?"

"Not so much," Kate said as they walked toward the parking lot. "I don't work that many hours, so it's not like I'm running around all day. In fact, I guess I should be looking for something a little more stable."

"How are you with computers?" Anne stopped at the edge of the sidewalk and put her hand over her eyes to block the sun as she looked at Kate.

"Um, well, I can do photo editing, typing, the normal stuff."

"If I teach you how to use web design software, could you update my site? It's not as much computer knowledge as it is the ability to write, and you've got that. Your articles in the Herald are great."

"Sure, I could do that. I used lots of design and layout software in college. When do you want me to start?"

"Are you covering anything tomorrow?"

"Nope, my whole day can be yours if you want."

"That would be great." Anne smiled and nodded. "I'll only take up your morning. Nine o'clock?"

"Sounds good," Kate said with a smile.

"Nine o'clock for what?" Aaron asked as he and Todd came up beside them.

"A job," Kate said. "Anne wants me to update the copy on her website."

"Awesome," Aaron said. "Right, Todd?"

"Awesome," Todd repeated. "Now can we go have lunch?" Aaron laughed.

"We're heading to the café for brunch. Care to join us, Anne? Paul can be back home before kickoff."

"Thanks, Aaron, you all go. I'd love to join you, but the kids have homework to do, and my parents are coming for dinner. I'll see you in the morning, Kate." Anne hugged Kate again and headed to her car.

"You're right. That was awesome," Kate said as she watched her friend close the door and say something to Paul.

"The job?"

"Everything," Kate replied. "I'm not sure my life could get more awesome, and under the circumstances, I can't believe I'm even saying that. But it's true. You have no idea how happy I feel here."

"I think I do," Aaron said as he smiled at Kate.

"I'm hungry," Todd said as he pulled on Aaron's arm. "Mommy's already in the car."

Kate and Aaron looked at each other and smiled. They each took one of Todd's hands and walked to the car. Kate had no idea what she was doing next month or next year, but she was going to bask in the happiness she felt right at this moment. And she was going to enjoy eating crepes for two.

***

Later that afternoon, the low-sitting sun cast an orange glow through the sunroom at Aaron's house. After brunch,

Kate had gone back home and settled in front of the TV to watch a movie. A couple hours later, the sound of her phone awoke her. Kayla called to extend an invitation from her parents to join them for an end-of-the-season crab feast at Aaron's.

"I had no idea you could still get crabs in October," Kate marveled.

The table was covered with brown paper, paper towels, bowls, knives, and a large pile of the biggest steamed crabs Kate had ever seen. Aaron's screened-in deck was the perfect size for the crab feast. His boat was docked in the canal that ran between his yard and his neighbor's behind him. Trevor and Ronnie had taken out the boat early that morning to catch enough crabs for everyone. They preferred going to Mass on Saturday evenings and enjoyed doing things together on Sunday mornings.

"October is the absolute best time of the year for crabs," Ronnie said as she helped Kate carry trays of drinks onto the deck. "Everyone thinks of Memorial Day as the best time, but the crabs are small and lean at the beginning of the summer. This time of year, they're large and fat."

"I'll say," Kate agreed, eyeing the jumbo sized, red crabs with gigantic claws.

"You know what always gets me," Kayla joined them on the deck. "Why do artists, or whoever makes souvenir junk, always paint live crabs red? Why do they think they're called 'Maryland Blue Crabs' if they're red? Come on."

"Not all artists." Ronnie pretended to be insulted.

"Not you, Mom. But you know what I mean."

"You're totally right, Kayla," Kate agreed. "Even in DC and Baltimore, you see red crabs everywhere. It's insane. You would think that locals would know that they're only red once they're cooked."

"Enough talk about what color they are. Let's eat," said Trevor, taking his seat at the head of the table.

"I'm with Dad," Aaron chimed in as he popped open a bottle of beer and took a seat.

Everyone sat down and joined hands to say the blessing before diving in.

"We're so happy you could join us, Kate," Ronnie said, reaching for a nice, fat crab with extra-long claws.

"I'm happy to be included. It's a rare treat for me to have crabs this time of year, or any time of year really. Crabs are expensive in restaurants."

"You'll have to go out with us to catch them sometime. It's a lot of fun," Trevor remarked.

"I'd love that," Kate said, using her knife to crack open a claw.

"Uncle Aaron, you were wrong," Todd nudged Aaron and waved his knife toward Kate. "She doesn't bang the crab with a hammer. You owe me a dollar."

"Bite your tongue, Todd," Kate scolded. "I might be a city girl, but I know how to pick a crab. No hammers allowed." She cast a glare in Aaron's direction to let him know that she didn't appreciate his doubting her. "That will teach you to bet against me."

"Hey, sorry." He waved his hands in front of him. "I've seen lots of city slickers, who claim to know how to pick crabs, completely destroy them with those wooden hammers. I just thought,"

"You just thought I didn't know a hammer from a crab knife. Give me a little credit. And give Todd a dollar."

Todd held his hand out with a smug look on his face.

"Later, buddy," Aaron said as he took a swig of beer.

The conversation dwindled as they enjoyed their catch, perhaps the last of the season as the weather was starting to turn colder. Kate ate until she couldn't eat another bite. She looked around the table at the Kelly family. She could get used to this—crabs in October, the salty breeze blowing through the screens, and a happy family enjoying each other's company. Aaron caught her eye and flashed her a smile. When he winked, she felt her insides begin to melt.

***

"I feel like my writing is so bland. It's dry and boring," Anne said to Kate on Monday morning as they looked over the website. "How can I entice people to travel to places they've never heard of if I can't put into words what those places are like?"

"Most of it is just spicing up your language, making it appealing." Kate scrolled through some of the pages. "Lucky for you, I've done quite a bit of traveling. My father wrote about exotic places, and my mother liked to be with my dad, so we spent most of my youth traveling to the most remote locations on the earth."

"Not the normal family vacations to Disney World?" Anne asked.

"No, my parents were more of the far-away lands, untouched by modern man, type. We lived in a lot of places like New Zealand and Brazil. It helped that we didn't own a house and lived with my grandparents when we were in the States, so there was never a mortgage; and dad taught history and anthropology in the winter and made money writing for academic journals and travel guides during the summer. He published a book on indigenous peoples that he worked on for most of my childhood." Kate felt the stare of the older woman working at a desk in the back and glanced up at her. The woman eyed her suspiciously for just a few seconds before looking away. Kate, recognizing that she was still a newcomer in town, tried to ignore the woman and turned back to Anne.

"Wait," Anne said as she straightened up and looked at Kate. "Is your father Walter Middleton? The historian?"

"You've heard of him?" Kate was amazed. "How can that be?"

"I was a history and anthropology major, and I run a travel agency. Of course, I've heard of him. No wonder you're such a gifted writer. What were you doing stuck in an office selling magazine ads?"

"I wanted to do it on my own. I wanted my merits and my writing to stand out. Dad did help me get the job," Kate admitted, "but I refused to let him use any of his influence to help me advance or move into the writing department. I thought I could make it there myself, but it's so much harder than I thought it would be, and I got lazy. All my friends were getting married and having kids, and I was alone. I lost all ambition to do anything else. For ten years, I worked at a job that I hated because I didn't have the desire, or maybe the guts, to try and move on. And then Mark came along, and I thought, why worry about it? I mean, he was a pilot, so I could party when he was gone, and together we could travel if we wanted. If I was low man on the totem pole, nobody would care if I wasn't around all the time."

"But you never traveled with him, did you?"

Kate shook her head. "Never. Maybe he traveled with his wife and their kids, but it wasn't even an option for us. He always said that it was impossible to get seats to any place worth going, and having been all over the world I accepted that. Now I know that he just couldn't be seen with me in an airport." Kate sighed and blinked back a tear. "I can't believe I'm crying. I really am so over him."

Anne put her arm around Kate. "It's not just him, it's the idea of him and the whole future you lost. It's normal."

"Nothing about this is normal. But thanks. I appreciate you letting me act like an idiot on my first day on the job." She managed a weak smile.

"Yes, but only the first day and just because your hormones are going crazy right now. But you have work to do, and a whole new life to enjoy."

Kate picked up her cup of decaf. "To a whole new life," she said.

Anne picked up her mug and clinked it against Kate's. "I'll drink to that."

The morning went by quickly, and Kate was pleased with her work. So was Anne.

"It's wonderful," she said as she read the copy on the site. "Your father would be so proud."

"Did I tell you that they're coming?" Kate asked as she stood.

"Only about ten times," Anne laughed. "You seem just a little bit excited."

"Oh my gosh, I can't tell you how excited I am. I just wish they could come sooner." Suddenly the room began to spin, and Kate reached for the chair to steady herself.

"Kate, are you okay?" Anne grabbed Kate's arm.

"Um, yeah, I think so. Phew," she blinked a few times. "I just got really dizzy. I guess I stood up too fast."

"When do you see Dr. Louden again?"

"Not until later this month." Kate took a deep breath and let go of the chair. "It's okay. I'm fine now."

"Are you sure?" Anne looked unconvinced, but Kate smiled reassuringly at her.

"I'm sure. It's been several hours since I ate something. I'll go home and make myself some lunch and rest for a while."

"Do you have to go back out this evening?"

"No," Kate answered as she walked to the door. "I have to interview someone about the upcoming autumn festival tomorrow, but my schedule is clear for the rest of today."

"Okay," Anne said as she held the door open for Kate. "But call me later, will you?"

"Sure," Kate assured her. "And thanks again for the job. I really appreciate it."

"No need to thank me. You're really the one coming to my rescue."

The women hugged, and Anne watched Kate walk to her car. Once inside, Kate closed the door and started the engine. She cranked up the air conditioner and leaned her head back waiting for the cool air to help her to feel better. It wasn't hot outside. In fact, it was quite cool today, but she was sweating, and her chest hurt. She took several deep gulps of the cool air before turning down the fan and putting the car in drive. Sometimes, when she ran, Kate had chest pains but never had she experienced them when just standing or walking. She had read that being pregnant put extra strain on one's heart, and she supposed that she would need to start getting more rest. Her late night reading or TV watching and her early morning runs would have to cease for a while.

The Aumaga, based in each village of American Samoa, have deep rooted traditions that have proven essential in times of emergency. Their reaction to natural disasters serve as models for modern day response teams. Their timing in sounding alarms throughout the villages in the face of impending disaster, often save thousands of lives. Furthermore, their disaster management systems and relief shelters give aid to vulnerable victims without government assistance.

From the *Studies of Indigenous Peoples*
by Walter Middleton

CHAPTER EIGHT

Kate had been following the news for the past few days. A tropical storm had formed, and the weathermen were watching it closely. Overnight, the storm had increased in size and intensity. The local news station was warning residents of Norfolk, Chincoteague, and the Maryland and Delaware beaches to be prepared. Kate had an assembly to cover at the school that morning, and by the time it ended, everyone was on high alert. The students were dismissed early, and frantic parents hurried their children into cars that zoomed out of the lot in an effort to get home and batten down the hatches. Hurricane Tara had been named and was barreling toward the Eastern Seaboard with Chincoteague directly in its headlights.

Having lived through many hurricanes, Kate wasn't worried when she first heard the news. But then she recalled the pictures on the news of places like Maryland's Eastern Shore after Isabel and the Jersey Shore after Sandy. It hit her that she was now living on the coast, and she needed to be prepared for whatever havoc this storm was going to create for herself and her neighbors.

She called Aaron, who was at work at the Coast Guard station, but he wasn't able to take her call. He sent her a quick text asking if everything was okay, and she replied that it was. She felt bad for bothering him. Of course, he'd have his hands full for the next twenty-four hours or so. She called Kayla and was grateful that she picked up right away.

"I was thinking about you," Kayla said. "Are you prepared for the storm?"

"That's why I'm calling. I have no idea what to do to even begin to prepare. We're right on the water. That's dangerous, right?"

"Well, we're elevated, so flooding shouldn't be a problem. We haven't been told to evacuate, so that's a good sign."

"Evacuate?" Kate's heart beat heavy in her chest. Evacuation was not something she had even considered.

"Don't worry. We might have to leave the waterfront, but we rarely have to leave the island entirely. Whatever happens, we won't leave without you."

"What about Aaron? He'd have to stay, wouldn't he?"

"He would. I'm not any happier about it than you are, but it's his job. You'll get used to it. You won't ever like it, and you'll be overjoyed when he returns safely home, but you'll get used to it."

Kate wondered if she was reading too much into Kayla's words. "Um, I don't think Aaron and I—"

"Not yet, I know. But you're the only woman he's been remotely interested in since high school, and I keep telling you that you're good for each other. At some point, you'll see it."

Uncomfortable with the topic, Kate steered back to the issue at hand. "I can't think about that right now, Kay. Let's focus on the hurricane. What do I need to do?"

"Shopping for one. But it's a little late. The stores are probably out of everything. On second thought, I have enough here for a small army. Bring anything you might need and whatever food you do have and come on over."

"Kayla, I don't want to intrude." Kate looked out the back door at the waves as they swelled to enormous heights and crashed against the marshes, drowning the reeds and grasses.

"Are you kidding? I'll be stranded with EJ and Todd, completely outnumbered. I need you here."

Kate laughed. "Fine, but what about my house? What should I do before I head over there?"

"Hold on, someone's calling."

Kayla put Kate on hold and answered the other call. Within minutes she was back.

"Forget Plan A. We're going to plan B."

"What does that mean?"

"It means that the storm surge is predicted to be at least twenty feet high. We have to get off of the waterfront, and fast. Most of the island doesn't have to worry about the surge, but we do because we're so close to where the Channel meets the Ocean. My parents are on their way over to help. Grab whatever you need and anything valuable and put them near the front door. Then bring in the furniture on your deck and balcony. I'll see if Paul and Lou can come board up the windows once they're settled at their own places."

Before Kate could respond, Kayla was gone. Kate stared at the phone in her hand and tried to remember everything that Kayla had said.

She gathered a bag of clothes, some toiletries, an extra blanket and pillow, her cell phone charger, the Herald's camera, her laptop, and some food. She didn't have anything of value with her, and she hoped the owner of the house didn't have anything there that they wanted her to take with her. Kate was about to go out onto the back deck when she heard a knock at the front door. She was surprised when she opened it and saw two young men in uniform standing on the front porch.

"Are you here to evacuate me?"

The men looked at each other and then back at Kate.

"Seaman Tate, Ma'am, and Seaman Rollings. We're here to help you batten down the house. We were told that you had somewhere safe to go when you leave here."

"Oh," Kate said with surprise. "I didn't know you all did things like that, helped residents, I mean."

"We do whatever our CO commands us to do, Ma'am. But we need to be quick, Ma'am, in case there's an emergency at the station."

The station. Of course. Probably risking his own career, Aaron had sent these young men to help her.

"I'm so sorry. I'll get out of your way. What do you need from me?"

"Not a thing, Ma'am. We've got it under control."

The men turned before she could thank them and quickly ran around to the back of the house. Emerging from underneath the deck a few minutes later, she saw them hauling out large boards. Kate went onto the deck and picked up a chair, maneuvering it into the house.

"Excuse us, Ma'am. We should have gotten those for you."

The young men took just minutes to bring in all the furniture from the deck before asking permission to get the few pieces of furniture from the balcony. Within an hour, they had every window on the house boarded up, and Ronnie was at the door helping Kate with her bags.

"Trevor and the boys are just finishing up at Kayla's. Let's get y'all back to the house before conditions worsen."

Without a word, the seamen left and headed back toward the station while Kate locked the doors and followed Ronnie outside.

"Just follow us. No sense leaving your car here to get flooded, and you never know when we might need extra vehicles."

"You don't have to leave your house?"

"Nope, we're on higher ground. That little cove you've been to will most likely flood, but it won't come up far enough to get to the house."

Ronnie climbed in with Kate, and the two women watched as Kayla and EJ climbed into her car while her father and Todd climbed into his. Then the three of them followed each other out of Angler's Rest and down the windy road that led to the cove. Before reaching the cove, they turned and ended up in a small opening where a lovely, stilted house stood, welcoming them with its cheery flower boxes along the deck railings and a waving American flag.

"Trevor forgot to take the flag down. Can you manage your things while I take it down?"

"No problem," Kate told her. She made one trip, and then Ronnie was back to help her with the rest. It wasn't a lot, but it was haphazardly thrown together into more bags than necessary. By the time they were finished, everyone was inside and ready to start thinking about dinner. Kate's cell phone sounded while the three women were talking about what to make.

"Hey, sorry I couldn't take your call earlier." Aaron's voice was a soothing balm to Kate's nerves. Her adrenalin rush was starting to wear off, and fear about the coming storm was setting in. "Everything good there?"

"Yes, I'm at your mom's. They insisted I come. We're all good. We're figuring out dinner." She left the room and searched for a place to talk in private. This was her first time in Aaron's childhood home, and she wasn't sure where to go. She finally opted for the front porch where a white swing blew in the wind.

"Hey, did you send those guys to help me?"

"Yeah, I couldn't get away myself, probably won't get away until long after Tara passes. Even when it's over, there may be ships that need help, people to be rescued who were too stupid to stay indoors or leave their homes in flood regions, or damage to be assessed and fixed. I just wanted to make sure that you're okay."

"I am, but I'm worried about you. Can't you get into trouble for sending them to help me? Aren't there ships lost on the sea or something like that they needed to find?"

"It's all good. They're young recruits who need to be kept busy doing whatever we need them to do. Helping the residents is part of the job. Once the storm hits, though, it will be all hands on deck. Gotta go. Stay safe, Princess. I'll text you if I can. Tell Mom I'll call her. See you soon."

With that, he was gone. Kate looked up at the beautiful, clear blue sky that made it hard to believe that any kind of storm was on the way. If not for the trees that bent sideways and the surf she witnessed earlier, she would never have guessed that there was any danger. But isn't that just the way life goes? One minute you think everything is fine, and the next, you're hurrying to take shelter from a sudden storm. An inexplicable feeling of dread crept up Kate's neck, causing her to shudder.

***

"A horse, a donkey, a giraffe?" Kate called one animal after another attempting to identify whatever it was that EJ was trying to draw.

"Times up," Kayla called.

"A gorilla, it was a gorilla," EJ said in exasperation. Everyone laughed, and his grandfather reached over tussled EJ's hair as the young boy took his seat. The storm raged outside. With each flash of lightning, the trees in the yard could be seen bending toward the earth from the violent gusts of wine. Inside, Kate felt warm and safe among Aaron's family.

"A gorilla?" Ronnie said. "Seriously?"

"Our turn," Todd yelled as Kayla pulled a card from the box.

"Who's turn is it? Dad?"

"I'll give it a try, but you know this game isn't my best."

"It's probably your worst, Granddad," EJ said. "That's why I'm on Grandma's team."

Trevor gave EJ a stern look that sent the little boy into a fit of giggles instead of fear.

Before Trevor could begin drawing, the lights flickered, and then, there was darkness.

"Aw man, no fair," said Todd. "I didn't get to draw yet."

"Good thing we filled the bathtub with water, I know I'm gonna have to flush the toilet soon."

"EJ," Kayla admonished him.

"What? I can't help it. It's just a fact of life."

Kate watched with a grin. This would be her life in a few years. School, and board games, and nights with grandparents. Well, at least one set of grandparents. How would Mark's parents feel if they knew they had another grandchild out there somewhere? Mark's story that his parents were deceased may or may not have been true, but Kate would probably never know, just as they would never know, if they were alive, that this baby existed. She still couldn't decide whether it was right or wrong to keep the baby a secret from Mark, and for now, she had other things to keep her mind occupied.

"I guess this means it's bedtime," Kayla said as she rose from the couch.

"No," both boys chorused.

"Yep, time for bed. The adults have had a long, busy day. Now don't argue with your mom. Come, give Grandma a hug and kiss." Ronnie lit a candle and set it on the side table as she reached her arms out to her grandsons.

"We want Granddad to tuck us in bed," Todd said, pouting his lip.

"Granddad? If Granddad puts you to bed, you'll never go to sleep," Kayla said with a twinkle in her eye.

"We know," Todd giggled. "That's the idea."

"Okay, who wants a story?" Trevor stood and stretched.

"Me."

"Me, too."

Each boy grabbed a hand and led their grandfather down the hall and up the stairs.

"He's as bad as they are," Kayla said.

"It's hard to believe that he was a rough and tough Vice Admiral," Kate said, shaking her head.

"He was the toughest around," Ronnie told her. "Now he's just an old teddy bear."

Kate wondered how her own father would be as a grandfather. He was always so preoccupied as a father. He worked long hours, either teaching and grading papers or researching, interviewing, and writing, re-writing, publishing. Her entire childhood was spent watching her father's back, not figuratively but literally. She watched him leave the house, sit at a desk, observe a village, all from behind his back. She didn't ever remember sitting on his lap or having him tuck her into bed. But now… Now her father read and golfed and enjoyed a leisurely lifestyle. Being a grandfather could be the highlight of his life.

"Kate? Dear, are you all right?"

"I'm sorry," Kate realized that both Ronnie and Kayla were staring at her. "Did you say something?"

"I asked if you're tired. I'm sure it's been an exhausting day for you in your condition."

Kate looked from Ronnie to Kayla and saw the color rise in her friend's cheeks.

"I'm sorry. I figured since Aaron knew,"

"It's okay," Kate said. "I'm fine; thanks, Ronnie. It has been a long day. Maybe I will turn in."

"Please don't be embarrassed, Kate. Kayla told me everything. What he did to you was dreadful. Nobody blames you."

"Thanks, Ronnie. I appreciate that. But the truth is, I blame myself. I allowed myself to get swept off my feet, and I learned the hard way that the world just doesn't work like that."

"Oh, on the contrary, my dear, the world most certainly does work like that. Just because he wasn't honest, and your heart was broken, doesn't mean that you can't be swept off your feet again. Trust in your heart, and in God, and everything will be fine."

"Now I know where Kayla gets it from," Kate said with a smile.

"Faith is strong in our family. It has to be. We've seen the worst in the world and the best. You must have one to see and appreciate the other. In time, you'll see that, too. Sometimes, we find ourselves in the darkest hole, one so deep that we can't see the light above us, and we don't believe we will ever be able to climb to the top. It is at those times that we must trust that we will be lifted out from the deep well of fear and darkness and into the light of a new day where we can start again. For every dark night, there is a dawn. Your dawn is here. You just have to open your eyes and face the glory of the new day."

Kate was silent as she let Ronnie's words wash over her. She had been in that well and had indeed climbed out of it. She could see the light and was almost ready to embrace it with open arms.

***

In the dark of night, Kate was awakened by an earth-shaking roar of thunder. Lying in bed, she heard an unfamiliar noise and sat up, trying to remember where she was. Pitch blackness engulfed her. She fumbled around for a light and found her phone on the nightstand beside her, but it was dead. She felt her way across the table to a lamp, but it wouldn't turn on. Then she recalled the electricity going out, her talk with Kayla and Ronnie, and using one of Trevor's heavy duty flashlights to find her way down the hall and get ready for bed.

Rising from bed, she heard voices down the hall. She reached for the flashlight and panned the room with the light, searching for something to put on, and managed to find her sweatshirt on the floor. Pulling it over her head, she opened the door and followed the voices as they got louder. There was crackling and popping, and it took her back to her childhood days when the only form of communication was an old transistor radio that played out-of-date music and gave news about the faraway land she called home.

"This is Coast Guard Vessel 25385. Repeat, this is Coast Guard Vessel 25385. We are at longitude 38.151837, latitude 73.693542. Vessel Lunar Ride is in sight. Over."

"This is Sector Field Office Chincoteague. Repeat, this is Sector Field Office Chincoteague. Coast Guard Vessel 25385, Copy that. Over." Aaron's voice broadcast over the crackling noises.

"This is Vessel 25385. Repeat, this is Vessel 25385. We are attempting to secure and board the ship. Over."

"This is SFO Chincoteague. Repeat, this is SFO Chincoteague. Copy that, Vessel 25385. Over."

The men shouted over the radio while wind and waves competed to be heard. Suddenly, the voices became urgent.

"This is Vessel 25385. Repeat, this is Vessel 25385. Mayday, mayday. Vessel 25385 has been struck. I repeat, Vessel 25385 has been struck. We're going down. Over."

The voice was frantic, and Kate felt her heart start to race as she heard Aaron's voice answer back.

"This is SFO Chincoteague. Repeat, this is SFO Chincoteague. Vessel 25385, do you read? I repeat, do you read?"

Silence engulfed the room save for the crackling of the open airways.

"This is SFO Chincoteague. Repeat, this is SFO Chincoteague. Vessel 25385, can you answer?" Aaron's voice rose with a fevered pitch.

"Someone will get to them, right?" Ronnie asked, fear radiating from her as she wrung her hands.

Trevor stood over the kitchen table, his hands braced on the polished wood, his face close to the radio.

"Someone will get them, right?" Ronnie repeated, her voice rising in panic.

"They'll try, Ronnie," Trevor said as he concentrated on the radio.

"But someone from Norfolk, certainly they will go."

"There's not time, Ronnie."

Ronnie braced herself on a chair and sunk down into it, laying her head on her arms on the table.

Kate gripped the doorjamb, fear welling up inside of her, her legs shaking.

"This is SFO Chincoteague. Repeat, this is SFO Chincoteague. Vessel 25385, Motor Lifeboat 45 is on the way. Repeat, Motor Lifeboat 45 is on the way. Seaman Tate, do you copy? Over."

"This is Motorboat Lifeboat 45. Repeat, this is Motorboat Lifeboat 45. We're en route to Vessel 25385. Over."

"Oh God, no. Those poor people." Ronnie cried. Trevor placed one hand on her back and used his other hand to steady himself on the back of another chair.

"Ronnie, what's happening?" Kate's voice shook as she tried to fight her fear. She was so confused about what she was hearing and couldn't figure out what was taking place.

Trevor turned toward Kate and pulled out the chair next to Ronnie. "Come, sit. We'll know more soon."

Kate nodded and took a seat. Her eyes had adjusted, but the room was still eerily dark. The crackling of the radio and the lack of any light, mixed with the occasional flash of lightning, sonic booms of thunder, and howling wind, created a surreal feeling. It was like being in a horror movie.

Kate remembered seeing the movie, *The Finest Hours,* with Chris Pine and Kasey Affleck. The movie itself hadn't been that great, but the true story was gripping. In that situation, the Coast Guard sent a couple of young men, boys really, with little to no experience, to save a crew of sailors on a sinking ship during a Nor'easter. She remembered holding her breath as the crew faced sixty to seventy foot waves that tossed their ship around like a toy in a bathtub.

"Seaman Tate, he was at my house today. He's just a boy, barely out of school." Kate said.

"The storm was pretty bad farther south. Most of the ships are down that way. It was expected to move out to sea and decrease, but it didn't. It hit land sooner than expected which is good for us."

"Aaron, he won't go out in this, will he?"

"He won't. His place is at the station. And that's the problem."

"I don't understand." Kate looked at him in question.

"He's responsible for those boys. If he loses them, it will weigh him down for years. Just like…" his voice trailed off.

Kate continued to look at Trevor for answers.

"Just like what?" She looked at Aaron's mother, but Ronnie refused to face her. "Like what?" Kate repeated. "What is it that I'm not supposed to know."

"This is Vessel 25385 on board the Lunar Ride. Repeat, this is Vessel 25385 on board the Lunar Ride. This is PO Warren. Everyone on the ship is safe and secure. Over."

"This is SFO Chincoteague. Repeat, this is SFO Chincoteague. Copy that, Vessel 25385. Motor Lifeboat 45, do you copy? Over."

"This is Motor Lifeboat 45. Repeat, this is Motor Lifeboat 45. Copy that, LC Kelly. Over. We're headed back in. Over."

A collective sigh of relief blew through in the dining room.

"Go back to bed, ladies. I'll stand guard. Hopefully this is the only rescue of the night."

Ronnie stood and hugged her husband, bidding goodnight to Kate. After she was gone, Kate faced Trevor.

"Why won't anyone level with me? I know that Aaron is holding something back. What won't he tell me?"

"It's not 'won't.' It's 'can't.' Someday, maybe you'll understand. For now, Kate, go to bed. We don't know what tomorrow will bring."

***

When Kate woke up the next morning, it was light, but rain continued to fall, and the house was still without electricity. The rest of her night had been restless, and what little sleep she managed to get was punctuated with dreams about storm surges that washed boats into the beach house, and Mayday calls, and frantic screams. Kate was more tired now than she was when she went to bed.

She opened the door and heard voices echo from down the hall. After using the bathroom to clean herself up as much as she could, using the water that was saved in a bucket the day before, she changed and headed to the kitchen where Kayla and the boys were eating cereal and doughnuts.

"Hey, Kate, we're eating doughnuts." Todd enthusiastically held his chocolate frosted doughnut up for her to see. Frosting was smeared around his entire mouth, and his gap-toothed grin showed brown teeth.

"Miss Kate to you, buster," Kayla said as she covered his mouth with a wet paper towel and rubbed off the frosting while he pushed her away.

"I can see that." Kate said with a grin. "Did any of that frosting make it into your mouth?"

"Mom says that the hurricane is still here, so we won't have school today, and maybe not tomorrow," EJ said, his mouth full of what Kate guessed to be a powdered jelly doughnut.

"Boys," Kayla said in exasperation. "Don't you have any manners at all? Close your mouths and eat."

Kate stifled a chuckle as Kayla rolled her eyes and held up her hands as if to say, 'Boys, what can you do?'

"Do you want one, Aunt Kate?" Todd asked, lifting the box for her to see the contents.

Kate looked at Kayla with a raised brow. "How did I get to be 'Aunt Kate' all of a sudden?"

The little boy shrugged as he polished off his doughnut. "You're Uncle Aaron's girlfriend, and he's never had a girlfriend, so I think that means you'll get married."

"Oh, is that your logic?"

"Huh? What's lo-gic?" He gave her a lopsided look, his nose crinkled up, and Kate thought she could just scoop him up and hug him forever.

"It's a way of thinking. And while it might make sense to you, I'm pretty sure that Uncle Aaron and I are just friends."

"If you say so." He shrugged and reached for another doughnut. Kayla's lightning fast hand closed the box just in time.

"No more, young man. We don't have the water to hose you off. Now go, get dressed."

Without a word, Todd padded off down the hall.

"I am amazed at how obedient your boys are. Over the past several weeks, I have never seen them argue with you or disobey you. How do you do that?"

"She locks us in the basement and beats us within an inch of our lives if we try to argue. I've had bruises from here to," EJ pointed to his head and then bent down to his toes, "to here."

"Enough, EJ. That's not even remotely funny. Go."

With a wink at Kate, EJ put his dishes in the sink and followed his brother down the hall.

"He's Aaron all over," Kate said.

"That he is," Kayla agreed as she handed Kate a warm, steaming mug. "We don't have any instant coffee, but we do have a gas stove. It's decaf tea. I hope you like it."

"It's fine, thanks. Seriously, how do you do it? I'm going to take notes."

"I honestly don't know. EJ was only five when Eddie died. Todd was just a baby. But somehow, his death and my parenting them alone had a profound effect on all of us. I'm sure that will change once they're teenagers. It's too good to last forever."

"I hope you're wrong."

"I think Aaron has a lot to do with it. I don't know what he says to them, but I know that he has a lot of influence over them. He has a way with them that even I don't have. He's always been good with kids and brings out the best in them. When we were teens, he babysat more than I did. I guess it's a gift. Special K?"

"Sure," Kate said, sitting down at the table. "Aaron seems to have a lot of gifts. It's nice but kind of intimidating at the same time."

"Try sharing a womb with him. And every class up through high school. He was always Mr. Popularity. I was always the class bookworm."

"What was he like back then?"

"The same as he is now. Everyone's friend and savior. He had everyone's back. Going into the military was a natural move for him although I always thought he'd branch out after the Academy. Once they graduate, they can choose any branch of the service they want to, and I pictured him as a Seal or a Green Beret, something that always had him saving someone. Then again… well, anyway, he seems to have made the right choice. He's happy, and he's been saving me for years."

Kate looked across the table at her friend, Aaron's sister, Trevor's daughter, and wondered once again what more there was to Aaron's story.

"Good morning, girls," Trevor said as he entered the room. "Why don't I smell coffee?"

"I guess we all forgot to get instant."

"Huh. Did you check the freezer?"

"The freezer?"

"Yeah, your mother usually keeps a stash in there." He opened the door and poked around for a few minutes, shifting this and that, until he called out, "Ah-hah. Coffee. Who wants some?"

"I'm good with tea. Kate?"

"No thanks, I can't have the caffeine."

"Dad, I have a question for you. Why have you never invested in a generator? You know, they sell them right downtown at Herb's Hardware."

"Generators are for p-, uh, wimps. I don't need a generator. We can make do with what we have."

Kayla grinned at Kate and shook her head. Just then, the phone rang.

"Kelly, here. Uh huh. Yep, we're all fine." He looked at Kate. "Yep, she looks fine to me." He winked, and Kate could see his son in him. "Only two, that's good. No deaths? Good, good. I see. Okay, I'll let them know. You, too, son. Bye."

Trevor picked up the whistling teakettle and poured the boiling water into two mugs. He stirred them and placed them both on the table. Taking a seat, he called, "Ronnie, are you coming?"

"I'm here," Ronnie said as she came into the kitchen. She sat down and poured a little milk into her mug. "Was that Aaron?"

"Yep. He says that the hurricane has stalled off the coast. The rain will continue today, and we may have a few more showers tomorrow as it wraps back around before heading out to sea. Conditions aren't horrible. They expect quite a bit of flooding, though. You girls won't be able to go back to your houses for a couple more days. The waves are at sixteen feet right now, and it's not even high tide yet."

"Will our houses be okay?" Kate asked. While the beach house technically wasn't hers, she was concerned for Kayla.

"They should be. They're both sturdy and high up off the ground. They're also far back enough from the surf that the surge shouldn't reach them. Evacuating is just a precaution. Emergency vehicles would have a hard time getting to you if something did happen. Aaron said that two ships went down, but they were able to save all of the passengers. No deaths reported so far, which is good, more than good. A tornado was spawned down in North Carolina, but nothing like that here. Other than the flooding and the storm surge, we've seen the worst of it."

"That's what you think," Kayla said. "Just wait until you've been locked up in this house for another 48 hours with those two down the hall. You'll be praying for this to all be over with."

***

All in all, the stay at Ronnie and Trevor's wasn't too bad. The boys did indeed get restless, and everyone tired of playing board games, but Trevor's quick thinking saved the day. Introducing a ten-year-old and seven-year-old to poker may not have been the smartest move, but it saved everyone's sanity. By the third night, though, Kate was more than anxious to be back in her own place. She had finished reading the book she brought with her, a light and fun romance in Susan Mallery's *Fool's Gold* series, and was already almost finished James Patterson's latest Michael Bennett book that she borrowed from Ronnie. She abandoned her reading to help with the dinner preparations. They were just sitting at the table when they heard the front door open.

"Anybody home?" Aaron's voice rang through the hall.

"In the dining room," Ronnie called. "You're just in time for dinner."

"Granddad made steaks on the grill inside the garage. And last night he made chicken and vegetables on the grill even though grandma has a gas stove. He said they'd taste better, and he was right, and he taught us to play poker, and-"

"Jeez, buddy, slow down. You don't have to tell me everything at once."

Todd sat back down and picked up his fork.

Aaron leaned down and gave his mother a kiss on the cheek. "Grab yourself a plate and get a chair from the kitchen," Ronnie told him.

He squeezed Kate's shoulder as he passed by.

"This looks great," he said as he got out a plate. "It's much better than the chow I've been living on. Things should be better by tomorrow. Hopefully the power will be back on soon, but the winds and moisture are still bringing down trees."

Once Aaron was seated, they said grace and began passing the food.

"I hope the power's back on soon. We've eaten just about everything in the freezer," Ronnie said as she passed the instant potatoes to Aaron. "And these contain the last of the milk."

"I can get you some supplies, but I take it you've got nowhere to keep them cold."

"Not unless you've finally talked Dad into a generator," Kayla said.

"Why don't you all go to my house? I haven't even been home to turn the generator on. It should have plenty of power."

Everyone groaned. "Now you tell us," EJ said. "I could have been watching TV all day."

"Not likely, my man," Aaron said between bites. "The cable is out for sure."

At that moment, the lights flickered, once, twice, and then, as everyone held their breath, everything came back to life. A cheer went up around the table.

"Can I see if the cable is working?" EJ asked.

"Not until you've eaten every bite on your plate," Kayla said, and EJ proceeded to plow one bite after another into his mouth. "Slow down, EJ. The TV will be there when you're done."

"Does this mean we can go home?" Todd asked. Kayla and Kate both looked at Aaron.

"Let's see if it stays on, buddy. I think it would be a good idea to stay here tonight, and then I'll go over and check out things in the morning and let you know. Deal?"

"Deal," Todd agreed.

They finished their meal while Aaron told them more news about the storm and its destruction. Kate continued to worry about their houses on the waterfront but tried to follow Ronnie's advice and put her trust in God that everything would be okay.

When Aaron left, he promised to be in touch the next morning. Though they weren't a couple by any stretch of the imagination, Kate noticed an emptiness with his absence. It made the last night feel even longer than the first two combined.

In the morning, Aaron called to say that their neighborhood was a mess, but the houses were fine. Kate, Kayla, and the boys returned to find debris scattered along the shoreline, through the marshes, and all the way up the stilted buildings; but the houses stood firm, and the boarded-up windows were still intact. It took another week for them to get everything cleaned up, but they were home, and Kate had survived her first hurricane. She prayed that it would be the last one she would encounter during her stay.

***

By the time the week was over, Kate was exhausted. She met Anne for lunch, and they talked about the work that Kate had managed to get done little by little over the past week.

"I don't know how you managed to do all of this with everything that was going on all week."

"I had to take a lot of breaks from cleaning up. I didn't realize how exhausting a pregnancy could be. Every time I started making real progress on cleaning up the yard or taking down the boards from the windows, I had to stop and take a break. I've never felt so winded in my life."

"It must be all of the excitement combined with your hormones and everything. Still, I'd have it checked out if I were you. You can never be too careful."

"I guess so," Kate said as worry crept in. "Do you think something's wrong?"

"Probably not," Anne waved off the notion. "It was a trying week for everyone. I would just make sure that you don't need some kind of supplements or something to keep up your energy."

They finished their lunch, and Kate went home, but their conversation stuck with her. She'd look in her books and see if they gave her any clue as to what to do to boost her energy. She hadn't told Anne about her shortness of breath, and Kate wondered if Anne was right that she should call Dr. Louden. For the time being, though, she was too tired to think about it.

***

Katherine was in bed in their bungalow in the Amazon coloring in her favorite coloring book. There was a tray on her lap that held the coloring book and crayons. She concentrated on the pony on the paper. It was pink. The grass around it was green, and the sky was blue, just as they should be, but she wanted the pony to be pink. She leaned closer to the page as she pressed the crayon down to make the pink a darker shade. When she was satisfied, she reached for the box to put the crayon away and to look for the purple one for the mane and tail. She'd been sick for a few days, and as she colored, she became sleepy, and her head began to pound. Mommy, she wanted Mommy.

She pushed away the tray and crawled out of the bed. The house was small, only a few steps separated her bedroom and the kitchen where her mother was making dinner. Katherine tried to call for her mother, but she felt dizzy and unable to make a sound. She reached for her mother and felt herself falling, grabbing onto a nearby chair. Katherine and the chair crashed to the floor, and in her dream, the chair bounced on the floor, creating a knocking sound. Katherine's eyes followed the movement of the chair as it went up and down. From a distance, she heard her father's voice calling her name.

It was then that Kate opened her eyes with a start. Her heart raced, and she was bathed in sweat. The dimness of the room made her think that it was late in the afternoon.

"Kate, are you okay?" Aaron's voice rang out from the patio door.

"Coming," Kate called as she sat up and took a deep breath to calm her heart. Flashes of the dream came back to her, but most of it was lost, and she couldn't make sense of it. Something about a pony, her mother, and a chair falling.

She walked to the door and waved to Aaron when he came into view through the glass.

"I'm sorry," she said as she opened the sliding door. "I was asleep."

"I've texted you a hundred times. I tried calling, but you didn't answer," Aaron said as he entered the house. "And your door was locked."

"So? I was out today. I never unlocked it this morning." She checked her phone and had seven texts and two missed calls from Aaron. "The sound on my phone was off for my meeting with Anne. I guess I forgot to switch it back on."

"You actually lock the doors? I thought only Kay did that," Aaron said, and at first Kate thought he was kidding.

As she studied his expression, she realized that he was serious.

"Of course, I lock the doors. Don't you?"

Aaron shook his head. "Most people around here don't, at least not after the summer season ends."

"Hmm," Kate thought this was odd but didn't comment. She couldn't imagine ever leaving a door unlocked.

"Anne told Kay that you were a little dizzy earlier when you left the café." Aaron said as he looked around the kitchen. "Have you eaten anything today?"

Kate looked at Aaron in surprise. "Anne told Kayla?"

"Well. It's not like she called her up the second you left. They ran into each other at the grocery store a little while ago. Kay mentioned it just now when I dropped off the boys. I picked them up after school so that Kay could run some errands. She's been so busy with the cleanup and getting the house back in order that she's behind in everything. I told her I'd stop by and check on you. How are you holding up? I'm sorry I couldn't be of much help with the cleanup. We've been swamped at the station. Tara may have ended days ago, but the aftermath takes longer to deal with than the actual storm."

"I guess so," Kate said. "It was quite a storm."

"That it was. So, are you okay?"

Kate blinked and looked up at Aaron. "Um, yeah, I'm okay. I was just really tired. I took a long nap, maybe too long. I hope I can sleep tonight." She furrowed her brow and tried to remember what time it was when she laid down on the couch.

"You haven't answered me," Aaron said. "Have you eaten?"

Kate shook her head and looked around the kitchen. "I think so. I honestly haven't had time to do any real shopping either. I had planned on going while I was out, but I was just so tired."

"You think so?" Aaron raised his eyebrows. "I don't think I've ever not been sure about whether I ate something."

"I ate," Kate said as she pushed him out of the way. "I just can't remember what I ate." She walked to the fridge and opened it. "Oh yeah, I had some leftover salad, some grapes, and an apple. I do have a few things that I picked up the other day after we left your mom's."

"That's not food," Aaron said. "That's what food eats. Come on." He gently led her away from the refrigerator and closed the door. "We're going to get some real food."

"You don't have to do that," Kate protested. "I'm sure I can find something to whip up." She reached for the handle again, but Aaron grabbed her hand. She looked up into his brown eyes.

"Kay is making homemade spaghetti, and she always makes way more than she needs. She would be thrilled if you joined us."

"I don't want to—"

"Don't even say it. You're not a bother or intruding or inviting yourself or any other excuse you can come up with. You've practically been indoctrinated into the family after spending three nights at Mom's and surviving all that chaos. Just put on your shoes, and let's get going."

Kate's stomach began to growl, and she realized just how wonderful homemade spaghetti sounded. She nodded, went to retrieve her shoes from beside the couch, and joined Aaron at the back door.

"Oh, wait, I need to get the key." She turned, but Aaron put out his arm.

"It's fine. We're right next door. Let's go."

She hesitated for a moment and then shrugged. Aaron closed the door behind them and put his arm protectively around her back as he led her across the beach to Kayla's house.

A little more than an hour later, Kate was fully satisfied as she sat at the table and watched Kayla and Aaron do the dishes. She wanted to help, but they insisted that she stay put. Aaron even made her elevate her feet on one of the kitchen chairs. She had to admit that it felt good. Her whole body just seemed so worn out, and that nagging pain in her chest wouldn't go away. She had an appointment with Dr. Louden in two days and planned to mention it.

Kate peered around the corner to the study room that Kayla had created in what should have been a dining room. EJ and Todd sat at their own little desks and worked on their homework. Two posters hung on the wall behind them, one of the United States and one of the World. A bookcase full of all sorts of books stood on one wall, and a computer desk with a laptop and printer stood on another. It occurred to Kate that she might need a room like this one day, or at least a child's desk, some books, toys. Her mind began to think about all the things that she didn't have and was going to need to get over the next few years.

Indigenous Peoples from various countries share the belief that the whole community is responsible for each other. Children, the elderly, and the infirm are taken care of, not just by extended family, but by the entire village. Social connections and relationships ensure that every individual plays a vital role within the community. All members of the community are bound together in a great support system that should be the envy of all Western Civilization.

From the *Studies of Indigenous Peoples*
by Walter Middleton

CHAPTER NINE

Once everything was cleaned up, business on the island returned to normal. Kate had an appointment at the Chamber of Commerce to write an article about this year's Christmas bazaar. Even though it was not yet November, the Christmas bazaar was just around the corner. It took place the weekend after Thanksgiving, and there was a lot of work to be done before then. She woke without morning sickness, but her breathing was labored, and her chest hurt. She was seeing Dr. Louden that afternoon and was anxious for him to assure her that everything was okay.

She made herself an omelet with spinach and mushrooms and a piece of toast to go with her fruit and yogurt, hoping that she just needed a boost of protein and some carbs. She hesitated at the door when it was time to leave but ended up locking it on her way out. You can take the girl out of the city… she thought with a smile.

Kate had a hard time concentrating on the interview with the bazaar chair, Shannon Hill, also the PTA President. They hadn't spoken since before Tara blew through and spent the first several minutes catching up on how everyone fared and how the community rallied around those who needed shelter, clothing, and food. Shannon moved to

Chincoteague with her family five years earlier, a lifelong dream to live at the beach thus fulfilled; and she felt at home from the beginning. She wasn't at all surprised that Kate felt the same. Once they began talking about the bazaar, though, Shannon was all business.

"The local merchants donate bushel baskets of prizes worth hundreds of dollars for the live auction. It's the highlight of the weekend," Shannon was saying when Kate stopped writing. She felt herself being propelled into darkness as Shannon's voice grew distant.

***

"Kate, Kate, are you okay?"

Shannon caught Kate just as she fell forward. She tried to settle the unconscious woman back into her chair and reached for the phone on the desk. Her fingers felt disjointed, and her dialing was clumsy. Shannon trembled as she held the receiver to her ear.

"I need an ambulance at the Chamber office. Kate Middleton, she's pregnant and just passed out. She's unresponsive. Oh, please hurry."

Shannon punched the speaker button and listened to the instructions from the dispatcher. She did as she was told, and eased Kate onto the floor, feeling for a pulse.

"It's weak, and her breathing is shallow."

The dispatcher continued to talk to Shannon after alerting the EMTs. Shannon gently removed Kate's sweater and unbuttoned her oxford shirt. She could hear sirens getting closer and said a quick prayer that they could get her to the hospital on time. She ran to the door and waved to the paramedics.

"In here. She's in here. Hurry," she frantically called.

Moving out of their way, Shannon let Tori and Jimmy into the office and retreated to a corner as they examined her and lifted her onto a stretcher. As they carried her outside toward the ambulance, a black truck screeched to a halt in the street, and Aaron leaped out of the vehicle looking every bit as white as Kate.

"Tori, what's wrong? I heard the call on the scanner. Is she okay?" He looked from Kate to Tori with a pained expression.

"We're taking her to the mainland."

"I'm going with you." Aaron put his polished shoe on the back of the ambulance and reached for a hold to lift himself inside, but Jimmy grabbed his arm and pushed him away.

"You can't go, man, I'm sorry. It's against the rules. You'll have to follow."

"The hell I won't. Get out of the way, Jimmy." Aaron braced himself for a fight, but Shannon's voice rang out from behind him.

"You're holding them up, Aaron. Paul's on his way. He'll take you. Now move."

Aaron looked defeated when he backed away and watched as they hoisted Kate into the back of the vehicle and closed the doors. As they pulled away, Paul's cruiser came to a stop behind Aaron's truck.

"Are your keys inside?" he motioned to the truck.

"Yeah," Aaron answered despondently as the ambulance drove away, lights flashing and sirens wailing.

"Shannon, move his truck off the street. Aaron, get in. We're wasting time." Aaron stood, watching Kate being driven away. "Aaron," Paul shouted. "Get a move on. Now!"

As if pulled out of a dream, Aaron shook his head and focused on Paul. Without further hesitation, he started to run toward the police cruiser, stopped, ran back and retrieved his hat from his truck, placed it on his head, and ran to the cruiser and jumped inside. Paul hit the gas, and they sped away after the ambulance.

***

A dim light peeked out from beneath the shade on the window. Beeping and pulsing sounds filled the air, and an antiseptic smell wrapped itself around Kate's head as she looked around the sterile room. She tried to move her arm and felt the tug of an IV. At the same time, she became aware of the pads that were sticking to various parts of her chest, ribs, and sides, their wires snaking out from under the blanket and stretching up to one of the machines that pulsed beside her. An oxygen tube clung to her nostrils, and she heard the hissing of the pump that pushed the oxygen into her.

Slowly reaching for the control that she spied next to her on the bed, she pressed the red button and closed her eyes as she waited for someone to appear. After a few moments, the door opened, and someone, a nurse she presumed, entered the room. She checked the machines and leaned over the bed with a smile.

"Good morning, Kate, how are you feeling?"

"Where am I," she asked, her voice weak and low.

"You're at Norfolk General Hospital. You were taken to Pocomoke Hospital by ambulance yesterday morning and then transferred here. Do you remember anything?"

Kate tried hard to remember. Various pictures flowed through her mind: being with Aaron's family, the beach cleanup, dinner with Aaron, Kayla, and the boys; a pink pony; Shannon's face; her mother cooking dinner; a chair falling. She closed her eyes and took a deep breath, but there was pain, and she winced. Nothing made sense. Everything was fuzzy, a jumble of images.

"It's okay. Don't force it. You need to rest."

Suddenly Kate remembered something. She grabbed the nurse's arm. "The baby. Is the baby-"

The nurse smiled. "The baby is fine, strong and healthy. Dr. Sprance will be in shortly to talk to you. And there's a man who's been here all night who wants to see you."

A feeling of alarm passed over Kate. Her eyes widened. How did he find out? How did he find her?

"He's quite the handsome one, he is, in that Coast Guard uniform of his."

A calm washed over her. She swallowed and breathed his name, "Aaron." She felt better just hearing it on her lips.

"Should I show him in?"

"Please," Kate said as she exhaled in relief.

Within less than five minutes, the door opened, and Aaron walked into the room, his uniform wrinkled and his face lined with worry. He paled when he saw her hooked up to so many machines with oxygen being pumped into her body, but he rallied and rushed to her side. Grabbing her hand, he gently pushed her hair from her forehead and leaned over her, brushing a light kiss on her soft skin.

"Kate, Princess, are you okay?"

"I was hoping you could tell me that," she said quietly. "Why am I here?"

"They won't tell me anything," he said, frustration evident in his tone. "Shannon said you passed out and wouldn't regain consciousness. She called 911, and Tori and Jimmy took you to the closest hospital, and then they sent you here."

"Who?" Confusion crossed her face.

"The paramedics. They took good care of you, according to the doctor. They saved your life. Your heart almost stopped beating. I don't know why." He shook his head and looked down at the wires leading from her chest to the beeping machines. "I got that out of Tori, but nobody here will give me any more information. Damn HIPPA laws."

"The baby," Kate breathed. "She said the baby is okay."

"Thank God," Aaron said, resisting the urge to place his hand on her stomach.

"Have I really been out for twenty-four hours?"

"Yeah, they gave you something. They needed to run tests and do a sonogram and had to keep you calm, your heart rate even."

"Why?" Kate was desperate to know what was happening.

"I wish I knew, Princess. I wish I could tell you something."

When she closed her eyes, a tear escaped and trailed toward her ear. "I'm scared."

Aaron squeezed her hand tighter. "Me, too." He lifted her hand to his lips and lightly kissed her fingers. "But it's going to be okay. No matter what. I promise."

Keeping her eyes closed, Kate nodded and sniffled, another tear following the trail of the first one.

***

Aaron's own heart ached. He watched Kate and wished he could kiss away her tears. The hour-long drive to the hospital had been the longest hour of his life; and once she was stable, they sent her to a hospital even farther away. The day seemed longer than… well longer than the day that he thought would mark the worse day of his life. He never thought he would see the world the same again. He went through the motions of having a normal life, told his therapist that he was fine, that he was over it, but that wasn't true.

Shouts still haunted his sleep. The sound of gunfire, the smell of blood, sweat, and fear. Yes, fear has a smell, and it surrounded him in his bed until his eyes opened, his heart racing in panic. Sometimes he could smell fear in his own room. He sheltered everyone from his feelings of guilt, even Kayla, and put on the face of a guy who was carefree enough to have fun but responsible enough to lead a normal life. He had no future plans and no desire to actually get married and live a 'normal' life. Until the day he first saw her. From the moment he spotted her, taking pictures at the Boy Scout ceremony, his heart was no longer his own. Thoughts of her consumed him. Who was she? Where did she come from? What was her story? Once they spoke, in the garage at the cookout, he couldn't get enough of her.

Aaron looked at Kate and realized she had drifted back off to sleep. He had no idea what they were giving her, whether her sleep was medicinally induced or the sign of a life-threatening problem. The thought made his stomach roll, and he said a prayer that she was going to be okay as he had promised. That was the one thing that had saved him—his faith, his belief that God could make all things better, could turn all bad into good. She was the sign he had been waiting for.

Refusing to leave her alone, he gently let go of her hand and pulled the hospital chair closer to the bed. He reached for her again and settled in to watch her sleep. It was then that he realized how his life paralleled his work. He had been a ship in distress, lost at sea, unable to cross the waves and see through the fog until the day he first saw her smile, shining like a beacon on the distant shore leading him home.

***

The door to the room opened, jarring both Aaron and Kate. A bright overhead light momentarily blinded Kate when she opened her eyes, and she blinked until she could focus on the man standing over the bed. Her fingers felt naked without Aaron's strong hand holding onto them.

"Katherine Middleton? I'm Dr. Sprance. I'd say it's nice to meet you, but I prefer to meet my patients under better circumstances than this." His words might have worried her if not for his broad smile and reassuring demeanor. He looked at Aaron and held out his hand. "Dr. Sprance."

"Nice to meet you," Aaron shook his hand. "Aaron Kelly."

"Are you related to the patient?"

Aaron looked at Kate. "No, sir. We're, uh, friends."

"Then I need to ask you to leave while I examine her and talk to her about her possible diagnosis."

"No problem. Kate, I'll be right outside." Kate nodded and tried to swallow her fear. She felt very alone as she watched Aaron leave.

"What's wrong with me?" Kate's voice cracked as she looked back at the doctor. She felt bad that she didn't have a friendlier greeting for this tall, handsome, bearded doctor with sparkling blue eyes and gentle hands that squeezed her shoulder.

"Do you prefer Katherine or Kate?"

"Kate, I guess."

"Okay, then. Kate, let me have a listen."

He placed his stethoscope just inside her gown and listened. He felt her glands, looked into her eyes and throat, all of the normal things she would have expected. Then he stood back and asked the unexpected, "Kate, have you ever heard of mitral stenosis?"

Kate shook her head and furrowed her brow. "I don't think so. I don't know anyone who has it. I don't think I do anyway." Her voice trailed off as she tried to think.

"Were you ever very sick as a child? Do you remember suffering from rheumatic fever?"

"I don't know," Visions of reaching for the chair and falling to the floor came flooding back. "I think, maybe, when we lived in the jungle in Brazil, I got very sick. I was in the hospital." Memories came pouring into her mind, images and feelings she had forgotten about. "I was so young, and it's all fuzzy, more like a dream, but I remember being sick, nothing abnormal, and then, I was suddenly very sick. I don't remember why." She shook her head and tried to recall more.

"It's okay, Kate. I just have a few more questions. Have you ever had any heart problems before?"

"No. I mean, not that I know of. Sometimes I get short of breath or have mild chest pains when I'm running, but I've always been athletic and in good shape. I played volleyball and tennis in high school. No, I've never had an issue. I really don't understand why this is happening."

Dr. Sprance laid his hand on Kate's arm. "That's what we're here to find out. Now, you say you've had shortness of breath. Has that gotten worse since you've been pregnant?"

"Yes, as a matter of fact, it has." Kate was getting worried. Had her pregnancy triggered something, or had she always suffered from something unknown?

"Kate, What about your parents? Are they reachable?"

"Yes. They live in Florida, but they're both alive, if that's what you mean."

"May I have permission to call them? To let them know what's happening and to discuss your medical history?"

She nodded and anxiously looked at the doctor. "Yes, please call. They're supposed to be coming to visit next month. Will I be okay? Will the baby? Do we know for sure that's what wrong with me?" Alarm covered her face.

"That is certainly what the tests indicate. I had hoped that it might be mitral-valve prolapse, but that doesn't appear to be the case. Mitral stenosis is extremely rare in patients who have not had rheumatic fever. If that's what you suffered from when you were younger, it changes everything."

"What do you mean?"

"If we are dealing with mitral stenosis, you're going to have to wear a heart monitor, at least until we have a better handle on what the heart is doing. You're going to be on medication, but it's not something that will affect the baby. In fact, it's necessary for both of you. We'll have to monitor you throughout your pregnancy, and your labor will be riskier than the average pregnancy."

"That all sounds pretty scary," Kate admitted. "I've never been pregnant and never had health issues. This is all pretty big news to me."

"I understand, but we're going to take good care of you and your baby. I promise. Now, I have that you're twelve weeks, is that right?"

"Yes, that's about right. Oh, God, I should have called Dr. Louden sooner. I had an appointment," she had to think about what day it was. "Yesterday, I think. I should have listened to my gut that something was wrong and not waited." She began to cry, and Dr. Sprance patted her arm.

"You didn't know, Kate. You had no way of knowing anything was wrong. It sounds like you've been asymptomatic, and that's not unusual. As you said, you're healthy and fit. You've taken good care of your heart and your body. As soon as I talk to your parents, we can confirm the diagnosis and go from there. But know that you didn't cause this."

"I'll try," she said, wiping her tears and reaching for the standard hospital tissue box on the nightstand next to her.

"One more question," Dr. Sprance began. "Is there a father who should be notified? I see on the chart that you're unmarried."

"There is no father," Kate said, shaking her head. "Am I being punished? Is this what I get for marrying him, for hurting his real family, for leaving and not telling him about the baby? Oh, God, what have I done? I should have listened to Father Darryl." Kate's tears flowed, and she covered her face with her hands.

"I'm sure you're not being punished for anything. This is something that most likely dates back to your childhood. As soon as I speak with your parents and run a few more tests, we'll have answers." Dr. Sprance patted her arm again. "I'll send in Nurse Lloyd to help you calm down. You're going to be okay, Kate."

"Thank you, Doctor. Thank you," Kate managed to say through her tears.

As the doctor was leaving the room, Kate stopped him. "Dr. Sprance?"

"Yes, Kate, what do you need?" he asked kindly.

"The man outside, Aaron, would you mind talking to him? I feel the need to explain my situation, but I'm not really in the right frame of mind. He can tell you. Is that okay?"

"It's fine, Kate, but it's your business. I'll take care of you and the baby, no matter what the situation is."

Kate was already half in love with the doctor. His demeanor, his kind voice and reassuring way, his bedside manner; she wished all men could be like him.

"Please, it would mean a lot to me for you to know, to understand."

"Okay, Kate. You rest now. I'll be back later."

Kate needed the doctor to know what happened, but she couldn't tell him, couldn't bear to face him as he heard what she had done. She much preferred for Aaron to tell him. She was still crying when Nurse Lloyd entered the room. She smiled at Kate as she placed the needle into the IV line. The last thing Kate remembered before falling back to sleep was Aaron kissing her on the forehead and taking her hand as he settled back into the chair by her side.

***

"You're awake," Aaron smiled as he walked in and saw Kate sitting up in bed, the oxygen tubes gone and her coloring back. After two nights in the hospital, Kate was anxious to be released.

"Where were you?" She asked as he leaned over to give her a hug and a kiss on the cheek. He was dressed in casual clothes that looked new, and Kate wondered if he had been home at all since she had been admitted.

"I had to do some shopping. I called Anne and Kayla to give them an update. Everyone has been real worried about you."

"You just missed Dr. Sprance. He said I can go home today. Thank Heaven. I can't wait to be in my own bed. It's hard to believe, but he doesn't seem to be judging me at all."

"Kate, it wasn't you. You need to remember that. Let's concentrate on you and the baby and your future and forget about the past."

"I'll try," she forced a smile. "Mom and Dad should be landing in any minute. How long is the drive from the airport?"

"About a half hour if traffic isn't bad. I guess you'll want to ride home with them." Aaron tried to hide his disappointment, but Kate caught it.

"Yes, but I'd like you to be here when they arrive. This has come as quite a shock to them as you can imagine. I still can't believe that they had to hear about the baby from Dr. Sprance while I was asleep and couldn't even soften the blow."

"I'm sure they'll be happy. It's not like you're in high school."

"I know, but I'm still their little girl. And to be honest, I haven't tried very hard to change that view. Now is my chance to show them that I'm an adult, and they don't have to worry about me."

Aaron laughed. "I don't know about that. My mother still calls me every day to make sure I'm okay, and I live a mile away from her. I think it comes with the job."

"I guess so. I have to admit that this little one isn't even close to being out yet, and I worry about him or her all the time." She rubbed her stomach and noticed for the first time that she had more than just a bump pushing up from under the blanket. "Do you think I'll be all right? As a mom, I mean?"

Taking her hand, Aaron kissed her fingers and looked her in the eye. "Princess, you're going to be a wonderful mom, the very best."

***

Just as Kate signed the final release form, the door swung open. Her mother, as stunningly beautiful as always, in black slacks and a cream-colored cashmere sweater, her dark brown hair pulled elegantly pulled back from her face, rushed into the room. She was followed by Kate's father, tan and bald, wearing crisp khaki pants, navy blazer, and an unbuttoned blue and white striped shirt.

"Katherine, darling, why didn't tell us?" Mitzi Middleton folded her daughter in her arms and hugged her fiercely.

"Walter Middleton. You're Aaron?" Walter reached his hand out and took Aaron's hand in a strong but friendly handshake.

"Yes, sir." Aaron put on his best military face and looked sure of himself as he shook Walter's hand.

"Thank you for taking care of our little girl. She tells us that you haven't left her side."

"I didn't want her to be alone, sir."

"I appreciate that. We've got it from here, Aaron, but thank you."

"Yes, sir."

Kate watched as Aaron nodded in her direction and took his dismissal in stride. Part of her couldn't believe that he would just turn and leave like that, but she saw his stance, the tightening of his jaw, the flexing of muscle, and she knew that he was just obeying a command. He was leaving, but he wouldn't be gone.

"I'm so sorry, Mom," Kate turned her attention back to her mother. "I wanted to tell you when you came next month. I was in shock for a while and wasn't sure what to do, but now, I just can't imagine not having this little one with me."

"What about Mark? Does he know?'

Kate blushed and looked away, shaking her head. "He doesn't, and I don't want him to know." She looked back at her mother. "Does that make me a horrible person?"

"Absolutely not," her father said. "That man has no claim to you or your child. I didn't like him from the start. I don't know what you were th—"

"Walter," her mother stood and put her foot down, literally and figuratively. "It's over and done. We will not go back there. Katherine has learned from her mistakes and is in no state to argue with you about it. You and I both know that this is going to be a rough few months for her, and you will not make it harder."

"Mom, why didn't you tell me? Why didn't I know that I almost died as a child? I barely remember it."

"It's not something I ever wanted to remember. I see now that it was wrong of me. I should have warned you, told you to have yourself checked before, well, before you found yourself in this predicament. We were in that village, and the doctors were good, but not the best. They told us that you would be fine, and we believed them. When you never had any other symptoms, and regained your strength, we assumed that it was over, that you didn't have any long-lasting effects."

"I remember it, Mom. I remember trying to call out to you and falling, taking a chair with me. I starting dreaming about it maybe a week or so ago. I thought that's all it was, just a dream, but then I started to remember. I remember feeling like I was dying, but I don't remember anything else."

"You were always so healthy, so athletic. The doctors checked when we got home, but nothing showed up. After a while, I convinced myself that we had nothing to worry about." She looked back at Kate. "I'm so sorry."

"Mom, it's not your fault. And I'm okay. Dr. Sprance says I need to keep seeing him, and I'll have to wear this monitor," she lifted her shirt. "I'll need to take medicine and be careful not to push myself, but I'm going to be okay." Mitzi nodded and wiped her tears.

"There is just one small problem," Kate said, biting her lips and feeling embarrassed. "When I left the magazine, I extended my benefits, but they're not going to last very long. I was going to look into getting new healthcare, but it wasn't my top priority. Getting myself together and forgetting Mark was my priority, and then," she looked down at her stomach, "this happened."

"I'll call my agent and see what we can do," Walter said. "How are you paying for the hospital bills?"

"Hopefully, they'll be covered. If not, I guess I'll have to dip into my trust fund."

"Absolutely not." Walter took out his phone and left the room. "I will figure this out."

"Mom, I'm sorry. I really wanted you to believe that I was being responsible."

Mitzi patted her daughter's leg. "Let's let your father deal with this. It will give him something to do. You are not to worry about it."

And with that, Kate was relegated back to being a child in her parents' care. When would she ever grow up and prove to them that she was an adult, more than an adult? She was thirty-two years old and was going to be a mother. They made her feel like she had spent her entire youth making one bad decision after another, and that's what they expected from her. The way her father treated Aaron showed that they had dismissed him as just another mistake. But what was he? Kate wasn't sure herself. She just knew that she wasn't that much different than most of the other people she had gone to school with, and being with Aaron didn't make her feel like a failure. But watching him walk out of the door several minutes earlier was like watching her heart exit her chest and go with him.

***

Balloons flew from the railing by the front steps, and the house smelled wonderful when Kate opened the door. Flowers were everywhere, their fragrance filling the air, and mixed in with the heavenly bouquet was the scent of an array of foods. Walking into the kitchen, Kate saw chocolate cake, a pie, a fresh loaf of banana bread, and an oven that was turned on to a low setting; she opened the door and peeked, yes, a homemade chicken pot pie. A note on the counter was signed by Kayla.

Dinner is ready and being kept warm in the oven. Aaron called me when you left the hospital and told me your ETA. Anne dropped off a sweet potato pie, and Shannon left the cake. We're all anxious to see you, but take your time. Enjoy being home and with your parents. Call me when you're ready.

Love,
Kayla

Tears flowed down Kate's cheeks. Never in her life had she had friends like Kayla and Anne. Even Shannon had pitched in to take care of her. And Aaron, dear sweet Aaron. Kate had noticed the truck when they left the hospital. He had waited to be sure that she was okay and heading home, and then he trailed behind them the entire way back to the island. He texted her when he got home to say that he would call her later. Kate knew that, of all the things she had done wrong lately, Aaron was not one of them. Whatever he was or might become, he would never be a mistake.

Over dinner, Kate brought up the subject that had been on her mind all afternoon.

"Mom, Dad, I'm not sure I'm going to go back to DC." She took a long drink of water as she let her words sink in. Her parents looked at each other, neither sure of what to say. Finally, her mother spoke.

"Katherine, dear," she said as she laid down her fork and wiped her mouth with her napkin before replacing it in her lap. "We know that you've had quite a shock, several actually. First Mark, and then the baby, and now the heart condition. I'm not sure that this is the best time to make such a rash decision."

Fully expecting this response, Kate was ready with her rebuttal. "It's not a rash decision, Mom. It's something that I've thought about a lot since I arrived, and especially since I found out about the baby."

"Katherine," her father pointed at her with his fork. "If this is about that Aaron who was at the hospital-"

"No, Dad, this is not about 'that Aaron,' but he has contributed to my decision. Not in the way you think," she hastened to add. "He is kind and considerate, and he genuinely cares about people, his friends, his parents, his sister, and me. But so does everybody else around here. I'm closer to people I've only known for two months than to people back home who I've known my whole life. And just look around, the air is cleaner, the crime rate is a heck of a lot lower, non-existent, in fact. I don't have to look over my shoulder when I walk down the street. The medics who took me to the hospital? Aaron knew them by name. When does that happen in DC?"

Walter and Mitzi exchanged looks. "And what will you do for a living?" her father asked.

"I actually have two jobs. They're both part-time, but that's perfect for me under the circumstances. I'm writing for the local paper, just covering low-level events around the island, but it's fun, and it's how I've gotten to know people. And my friend, Anne, has a tourist agency downtown, and I'm writing copy for her website. It's something I'm able to do at home. She's a big fan of yours by the way." She looked at her father.

"How are you going to make enough money to support yourself and a child? Do you have any idea how expensive children are? And where will he or she go to school? I doubt there's a private school on this island. What kind of education will he get here? How far will that take him?"

Kate's ire rose, and she took a deep breath before answering. "As a matter of fact, the schools here are very good." Kate had no idea how the schools were. She hadn't even thought about any of the things about which her father inquired, but she was sure that she right. She had proof. "That Aaron, as you called him, is a graduate of the Coast Guard Academy, and his sister, Kayla, attended Yale. Apparently, their education paid off."

Her father was speechless, a rare phenomenon, and Kate relaxed a bit and continued to eat Kayla's scrumptious chicken pot pie. Savoring the bite, she thought about her father's concerns. She was certain that she could find a way to make things work for herself and her baby on this island. And she was determined to prove to her father that she was finally ready to become the adult she should have become ten years ago.

For the Torres Strait Islanders, family means more than simply being related to someone. There is an unbreakable bond of kindship that extends beyond the immediate family. The Aboriginals rarely use names when speaking to and of family members, referring to them instead as brother, sister, mother, father, or cousin. There is a strong sense of belonging, and people often identify themselves by their familial relationships.

From the *Studies of Indigenous Peoples*
by Walter Middleton

CHAPTER TEN

It was amazing to Kate that for the entire time she was at the Kellys' house, without electricity or the ability to go anywhere, she never felt trapped. After just twenty-four hours with her parents, however, she was feeling claustrophobic. It wasn't that she didn't love them and appreciate them being there. She just wished they would let her do something, anything. Just about the only thing they let her do on her own was brush her teeth. She prayed that it wouldn't be like this for the next few weeks, especially since they would be there longer than planned.

They ate leftover pot pie in silence, each lost in his or her own thoughts and trying not to up the existing tension. Kate wondered what Aaron was up to and when she would see him again. He called late the night before and texted her several times that day to check on her, but she was hoping he would drop by.

Just as Kate stood to begin clearing the dishes, she saw headlights shining through the front window. To her disappointment, she could tell by the height of the vehicle that it wasn't Aaron's truck, and she wondered who it could be. Kayla perhaps? Anne? The car came to a stop and then reversed out of the driveway. Perhaps it was just someone turning around in her driveway. As she reached the sink to rinse her dishes, a loud knock sounded on the front door.

"I'll get it," Mitzi said, placing her napkin beside her plate and rising from the table.

Before opening the door, Mitzi peeked through the window and gasped in surprise. "Oh my God," she cried out as she unlocked the door and swung it open. A very tall, muscular man with a crew cut and wearing Army fatigues burst through the door and took her in his arms, lifting her into the air and spinning her around the room.

Kate ran to her brother, leaping into his arms just as he put their mother down. "You're here! I knew you were coming, but I didn't expect it to be so soon. I can't believe you're here." Zach released his sister, giving her a final squeeze before turning to their father who had gotten up from the table and was waiting his turn. The two exchanged a manly, but warm hug, and Kate noticed tears in her father's eyes.

"I thought I'd hear back from you when you were on the way," Kate said as they stood in the living room taking him in. His dark hair was shaved close, and his bright green eyes that matched his sister's sparkled with excitement but also concern.

"I don't know how she did it, or who she called, but Mom's message that you were in the hospital made it to right person. They let me leave earlier than planned. I've been given a month's leave to take care of my family."

Kate reached up and gave Zach another hug. "You're just the medicine I needed."

"What's the wonderful smell? It sure isn't Army chow or an MRE."

"You must be starving. Come have some of this delicious chicken pot pie that Katherine's friend cooked for us. Even as leftovers, I've never tasted anything so good."

Mitzi led him to the table, and Kate prepared a plate and put it in the microwave.

"Kayla is the best cook I've ever known. No offense, Mom."

"None taken. This truly is the best pot pie I've ever had."

"Bathroom?"

"Oh, down the hall, Zach. On the left."

"Kayla's trying to open her own business," Kate explained while the food heated. "Not a full-service restaurant, but a place where busy families can order a meal to be done by a certain time and then picked up and taken home. With two little boys, she knows how hard it is for families to have a sit-down meal together every night, and she believes in the importance of eating together. Her meals will be made from scratch with all healthy ingredients and offered at a price that any family can afford. She'll even offer dessert, and wait until you taste her desserts."

"It doesn't sound very lucrative," her father said as Zach came back into the room and took his seat at the table. "How does she intend to make money?"

"She has a business degree from Yale, so she knows what she's doing. And Anne is helping her to find investors. Everyone seems to think that it's going to be a huge business." She placed the food in front of Zach and was surprised to see him bow his head in prayer before picking up his fork. She had never known him to pray.

"What does her husband do?" Kate's mother interrupted her thoughts.

"Um, she doesn't have one. It's really tragic." Kate began clearing dishes. "Do you remember the scandal a few years back involving the Mayor of Baltimore?"

"Let me do those, honey," Mitzi said, shooing Kate out of the way.

"Was he the one who had some kind of human trafficking ring being financed by the state?" Walter asked.

"Yep. He had several people killed in order to protect his side business, and Kayla's husband was one of them."

"Oh my God," her mother breathed. "How horrible."

"Yes, they had two small children. Kayla moved back here to the island where she grew up and where her family still lives. They helped her to get through it. They're very close. In fact," she nonchalantly mentioned, "Aaron is her brother."

"Back to him again," her father growled.

Zach devoured his serving of chicken pot pie while he listened to their conversation. "This is awesome. Is there more?" He handed his plate to Kate. "Who's Aaron?" he said as he reached for his glass and drank the entire thing down in one long gulp.

The air hung heavy with silence as Kate and her father stared each other down.

"Well? Is anybody going to clue me in?"

Kate handed her brother the rest of the pot pie and then cut four slices of Anne's sweet potato pie and set them in front of each person before sitting back down.

"Aaron is a friend, that's all. Dad has already decided that he's not worth getting to know."

"I never said that."

"You didn't have to."

"Whoa, slow down. Is there something I'm missing?"

"Dad thinks it's too soon or that I'm too emotional or hormonal or that someone from the island is not good enough. I don't know. Maybe he can explain it." She shoved a piece of pie in her mouth and tried to enjoy the sweet taste.

"That's not fair, Katherine. I only want what's best for you."

"And how do you know that's not Aaron?" Kate's outburst surprised everyone, including herself. She blushed and tears came to her eyes. She put her head in her hands and tried to get a handle on her emotions. Her family looked around the table unsure of what to say.

Exhaling, Kate looked up. "I'm sorry, Dad. I didn't mean to do that to you. I'm tired, and I'm not sure how I feel about anyone or anything. But to be honest, so far this island, these people, and yes, Aaron, are the best things that have happened to me in a long time." She looked at Zach. "And having you here. That just takes the cake. So now it's your turn to talk. Where have you been? What can you tell us?"

"Honey, it's been a rough few days, a rough few months." Her mother went to her and wrapped her arms around her daughter. "I think you need some rest, and I'm sure Zach does, too."

Kate shook her head. "No, I really need some time with Zach. With all of you. Let's clean up and sit in the living room. I want to hear everything that Zach can tell us about his life."

"I'd like to shower and change first, if that's okay," Zach said as he stood.

"No problem. I'll get you a towel." Kate stood, anxious to do something that didn't put her under her parents' feet and equally anxious to be alone with her brother.

They walked down the short hall arm in arm. "Mom's message was vague," Zach said. "I'm missing something big. What's not being said?"

"Well, I guess you're the last to know." Kate gave him a weak smile. "Mark took everything from me, but he left me with something, something unexpected."

"Oh damn," Zach said, stopping outside the bathroom door and turning her in his arms. "Are you sick? Did he give you a-"

"No, gosh no." She took his hand and placed it on her stomach with a smile. "He gave me this."

Zach felt the bulge, and his eyes widened. "You're pregnant? I just thought you'd gotten fat." Kate punched him in the arm, and he laughed before turning serious. "Is this good news or bad?" His concern warmed her heart.

"I wasn't sure at first, but now, I think it was meant to be."

"Does he know?" His expression hardened, and his jaw twitched.

"No," she shook her head. "And I don't want him to. This is my baby, not his, and I don't intend to share it. But honestly, I'm still working on what to do about Mark."

"And this Aaron guy, where does he fit in?"

"I truly don't know, but I'd like you to meet him."

"Just say the word," Zach said. "I'd do anything for you."

Kate hugged her brother and then left him to his business. When she returned to the kitchen, her parents had almost everything cleaned up and put away.

"Let's go sit," Kate said after they had put away the last of the food and turned on the dishwasher. "We need to reconnect, and I need some time with my family."

***

The next morning, Zach and Kate were both up early. With a cup of strong black coffee and a cup of decaf with cream, and clothed in sweats, they went for a walk on the beach.

"So, tell me about this Aaron guy."

"I'd rather hear about you. What's going on with you these days? We never hear anything about your life or what you're doing. You were so vague last night."

Zach shrugged. "Not much to tell. Half of it, I can't talk about, and the other half I don't want to talk about."

"But are you happy?" Kate asked, stopping to really look at her brother for the first time in years. Zach shrugged.

"I'm not sure what real happiness is, Sis. I've seen so much hate and destruction. I don't think I could ever make anyone happy, and I'm not sure how to feel it myself."

To hear her brother talk like that broke Kate's heart. She reached out and lovingly touched his arm. She didn't see the curtain move in the house behind them as they walked up the beach, his arm around her waist.

After breakfast as a family, Kate suggested they head downtown so that she could show them around. Her mother protested, but Kate assured her that she felt fine.

The first place they visited was Around the World. Anne jumped up and greeted Kate with open arms.

"Kate, I'm so glad you're home. How are you feeling? Kayla told me everything." It was the first time Kate's parents had heard her called anything but 'Katherine,' and she noticed their surprise when Anne said her name.

"I feel fine. Just knowing what was wrong helps a lot. Now I know what I can and can't do and what signs to look for. Hopefully that won't ever happen again. Labor might be hard, but we'll deal with that when the times comes."

"And we'll pray," Anne said before turning toward Mitzi. "You must be Kate's mom. It's so nice to meet you."

Mitzi took Anne's hands in her own. "Thank you, Anne, for taking care of Katherine. Your friendship means a lot to her, and your kindness means a lot to me."

"It has been my pleasure. We've all fallen in love with your daughter."

Kate blushed, but she felt a swelling of love for Anne and for everyone she had met on the island.

"And you're Walter Middleton," Anne said, reaching her hand out to shake his. "It is both a pleasure and an honor to meet you."

"Thank you. Kate tells me that you're familiar with my work. It's nice to know that somebody has read at least one thing that I've written."

Anne laughed, and Kate could see that she was star struck. It felt strange to Kate to think of her father as someone's idol.

"I've read many of your writings. I am a great admirer of your research on the history of indigenous peoples."

Kate watched her father puff out with pride. That had been his self-proclaimed greatest accomplishment, and she knew that Anne's accolades meant the world to him. She beamed with pride for her father as he and Anne discussed the articles that consumed much of Kate's childhood and took them to places most people only dream of – Alaska, Australia, Thailand, New Zealand, and the remote reaches of the Amazon.

"Kate is a wonderful writer. Your influence certainly shows," Anne said, and Kate cocked her head in surprise. Her father looked equally perplexed.

"Really? Katherine has never shown me any of her writings."

Embarrassed, Kate looked at her dad. "I guess I never thought you had the time or the desire to read anything I've ever written."

"Well, you'll have your chance today," Anne said, moving them further in the conversation. "The local paper came out this morning, and Kate has several nice pieces in it. Her coverage of the aftermath of Tara is genuinely moving."

"They're just local coverage pieces. Nothing like what you write," Kate said, looking away.

"I can't wait to read them," her father said. "I'm sure they're wonderful."

Kate smiled and hoped that she lived up to her father's expectations. No matter how old she was, his opinion was so important to her. Unfortunately, she never felt like she was good enough for him. Somehow, she would change that.

After a quick stop at Shannon's and the newspaper office to see Marge and pick up a few copies of the day's news, they went to the deli for lunch.

"I'd love to show you all the lighthouse on Assateague. Maybe tomorrow. I think I need to take a nap today if that's okay."

"Of course it is, Katherine. We're here to take care of you, not have you entertain us and be our tour guide."

"I know, Mom, but that's what I wanted to do. Originally. I wanted you all to come for Thanksgiving so that I could show you around, introduce you to everyone, and show you the cooking skills I'm developing. Well, attempting to develop. I do admit that I really miss all of the carry-out options I used to have."

"Does that mean you're having second thoughts?" Mitzi asked with a raised eyebrow.

"No, Mom, I have not changed my mind."

"I've been giving it some thought since you mentioned it last night," Zach chimed in. "I think it's a good idea."

"You what?" their mother asked.

"I think Kate needs a fresh start." He smiled at his sister, and she appreciated that he called her 'Kate.' "She's ready for something more settled, more adult. I see it, don't you?" He looked back and forth from one parent to another. "She's not a kid any more. She's finally left home and struck out on her own. Isn't that what you've been waiting for?"

Some part of Kate knew that she should be insulted, maybe embarrassed, by Zach's words, but she wasn't. Her love for him, and his for her was the bond that allowed them to say exactly what they were thinking even if it hurt. In this case, it strengthened her resolve.

"Well, her friends seem nice and knowledgeable," her father said.

Thank you, Anne. Kate smiled as she thought of her father's liking for his new fan.

"Don't you think it's awfully, well, *remote*?" Mitzi asked.

"I had no problem getting to the hospital in time," Kate assured her. "And we're not that far in any direction from a city. Granted, I'm no longer a metro ride from anything and everything, but I'm okay with that. In fact, I like it. I even survived my first major hurricane without a hitch."

"Except that you ended up in the hospital. What about when you need to see Dr. Sprance? How will you manage that once you're further along?"

"I can still drive, Mom, and I have friends. They'll help me out. That's how it is here."

"I think it's settled," Zach said. "Katherine, I mean Kate, is staying here, you're going back to Florida, and I'm, well, I'm not sure where I'll be heading."

"What do you mean?" Kate asked in surprise. "You won't be going back to wherever you've been deployed?"

"Well, yeah, I will be going back for a few more months, but after that, honestly, I just don't know."

"Will they be sending you somewhere else? Somewhere even more dangerous?" His mother asked, fear showing on her face.

"That's not what you're saying, is it?" Kate asked. Their connection was strong, and she sensed a change in her brother. She felt it on the beach that morning, and she saw it in his eyes as they made their way through the small downtown.

"I've been in for almost thirteen years, not counting the Point. I haven't put in enough time for retirement, but I'm ready to get out. If they'll let me." He paused and then shook his head. "The things I've seen. The things I've done. I don't think I can do it anymore."

Kate laid her hand on her brother's well-muscled arm. "I told you this morning that you deserve to be happy. If this is a step in that direction, then I'm all for it. But there's something that you need to think long and hard about."

Zach's brows lifted in question.

"If you're not covert, then you should be prepared that I'm going to call you whenever I want, day and night, and I'm going to bug you to death just like when we were kids."

"Now that's a threat I can live with," Zach said, curling his arm around his little sister and pulling her close.

The door to the diner opened, and Aaron walked in, exuding confidence in his uniform, removing his hat, which Kate learned was referred to as a cover, and tucking it under his arm. He stopped when he saw Kate, slowly moved his eyes to Zach, his arm around Kate, and looked back to her with steel in his gaze.

Smiling broadly, Kate waved to Aaron and motioned him over. "Aaron, come join us." She moved over in the booth to give him room.

"Thank you, Kate, but I've got to get back to work. I just came by for a sandwich." He seemed distant, and Kate was surprised by the ice in his tone. He acknowledged her father with a handshake and said hello to her mother before nodding at Zach. "I'll see you around," he said coolly as he turned to pick up his order.

Kate didn't know what to say or think. In the time she had known him, Aaron had never spoken to her so formally or so coldly. Not even when she told him about the baby.

Nor had he brushed her off like that. She watched him pay for his lunch and walk out without looking back.

"Wow," Zach said. "That guy has it bad."

"Has what?" Kate asked.

Zach rolled his eyes. "Can't you see it? Go," he pushed her away. "Catch him. Tell him who I am before it's too late."

"What? I don't understand." Wildly confused, Kate looked to her brother for an explanation.

"Come on, *Kate*, don't be an idiot. Go after him, and let him know that I'm not Mark." Shock and then understanding flooded Kate, and she jumped up from the booth, almost knocking over her glass of water. Zach, with the instincts and reflexes of a cougar, steadied the glass.

"I can see why you're concerned," he said to her father. "But my gut tells me that you've got nothing to be worried about."

Their parents turned and watched Kate run from the deli.

***

Aaron's blood boiled as he walked down the sidewalk, an unseasonably, chilly wind biting at his face and toying with his cover.

"Aaron," he heard her call. "Aaron, wait, please."

He turned and looked at her, the way the wind blew her hair and instantly brought a bright red color to her cheeks, and his heart melted. He stood and waited for her to catch up. Realizing she was out of breath, he became concerned. He wrapped his arm around her to protect her from the cool air.

"You shouldn't be chasing after me," he admonished her. "And where's your jacket?"

"I left it. I didn't think. I just needed to talk to you. I wouldn't have to chase you if you hadn't been so curt and walked out like that." She tried to catch her breath and shivered, suddenly realizing how cold she was.

"Kayla told me you had more company. She saw you taking a walk on the beach this morning."

"She did, did she? Did she also tell you that the very rugged and handsome man who escorted me was wearing a US Army sweatshirt and had a haircut that matches your own? Did she tell you that when I gazed into his eyes, there was the same admiration and love and trust that she has when she looks at you?" Her words hit him, and he understood what she was saying.

"Zach?" he asked with hope in his voice. Kate laughed and nodded.

"I guess in all the excitement, I forgot to tell you every time we texted this morning. I seem to be so forgetful these days. Anne says it's the hormones." Kate realized she was rambling and looked at Aaron. He smiled, his dimples deepening in his cheeks.

"I thought, maybe—"

"I know just what you thought. Honestly, Aaron, don't you know that the only man on my mind these days is you?" Even Kate was surprised by her admission.

Without thinking twice, Aaron tore the hat off of his head, tightened his hold on her, and pulled her mouth to his. He claimed her right then and there on the main street of Chincoteague for all the world to see. He forgot about the cold, about his job, about her parents and brother waiting for her in the deli. His kiss went deeper and harder, and she responded by putting her arms around him and drawing him closer to her. It sent shock waves through his body, heightening his senses, making him aware that he needed to pull back. Painfully, he broke off their kiss and gazed into her eyes. Slowly, a smile spread across his face.

"The temperatures have really dropped. You're going to freeze," he said quietly.

"Not likely after that," she smiled back.

"I really do have to get back. I've got meetings this afternoon. They're going to be hard to sit through since the only person I want to meet with is you."

Kate hugged him tighter. "I better get back inside. Will you come to the house later? Dinner at six?"

"I'll be there," he said as he reluctantly let her go. Then he reached for her again, pulling her back into an embrace and planting a soft, promising kiss on her lips. "Now go before you get cold. I'll see you tonight, Princess."

She nodded and turned to go. She looked back one last time, a glowing smile on her face, before she went inside the deli.

Aaron stood on the street watching after her. Then he replaced his cover and walked back to his truck with a smile on his face and a spring in his step. It no longer felt the least bit chilly.

***

While Kate slept, her mother went to the grocery store and bought everything she needed to make her specialty—homemade lasagna and garlic bread. Kate awoke to the savory aroma of her favorite childhood dish. She rinsed her face and brushed her teeth before heading downstairs.

Nobody mentioned what had taken place at lunch, though Kate could tell by their expressions that they had witnessed her kiss with Aaron. No doubt, they noticed her glow and the way she floated back into the deli.

"It smells wonderful in here," Kate said as she came down the stairs and headed toward the kitchen.

"It's almost six," her mother said. "I was afraid you would sleep through dinner."

"Not a chance," Kate said as she blushed and gave her mother a knowing smile.

"You don't want to leave him alone and throw him to the wolves?"

"Mom, I know it's not like that." Kate went to her mother and gave her a hug. "You all love me, and I don't have the best track record. I can't fault any of you for being the least bit wary."

"We do love you, Katherine. We only want the best for you. And for you to be happy."

"I know, Mom, and for the first time in my life, I think I know what happy really feels like. For now, I'm content just knowing that. I promise not to rush things."

"Okay, then I promise to let you make your own decisions."

They laughed as a knock sounded at the door.

Kate went to the door as her mother took the lasagna out of the oven. Walter and Zach stood from their seats on the couch.

"Hi Aaron, thanks for coming." Kate stood on her tiptoes and placed a small kiss on his cheek. Aaron's dimples deepened as he smiled at her.

"Hey, Princess. Thanks for asking." He produced two bouquets of flowers from behind his back. "One for you," he said as he handed her a dozen pink roses. "And one for you." He went to Mitzi and handed her a mixture of flowers in beautiful, deep fall colors. Mitzi blushed.

"Thank you, Aaron. These are beautiful. Katherine, hand me yours, and I'll find something to put them in."

Aaron removed his cover and turned to Kate's father and brother. He offered his hand to Kate's father first. "It's good to see you, sir."

"Nice to see you, Aaron."

"And Zach," he reached for Zach's hand. "It's an honor to meet you. I apologize for my behavior earlier. I have no excuse for the way I acted."

"You have an excuse," Zach offered. "Just don't screw it up."

Aaron smiled. "I don't intend to," he said as he turned to look at Kate.

"Dinner's hot," Mitzi called from the kitchen.

Aaron took off his jacket, and hung it on the coat rack near the door along with his hat. Then he took Kate's hand and walked with her into the kitchen.

Zach surprised Kate once again when he announced that he would like the family to pray before their meal. By the looks on her parents' faces, they were even more surprised than Kate was. They clasped hands, bowed their heads, and let Zach lead them in prayer, the same one that Kate recalled from her youth that Kayla, Aaron, and the boys prayed when she joined them for dinners.

"Bless us oh Lord, and these Thy gifts, which we are about to receive, from Thy bounty, through Christ our Lord. Amen."

Kate squeezed Zach's hand when they finished and smiled at him, hoping to convey the message that she, too, had found her way to God.

Dinner was much like the ones that Kate remembered growing up. There was laughter and tears, the kind caused by laughing until you cried. Tales were told about Kate and Zach's childhood and about some of the mischief they got into when traveling with their parents and living among the Australian aboriginals. Zach and Aaron talked in general terms about their assignments, neither one going into much detail.

When dinner was over and the conversation spent, Aaron said his goodbyes to Kate's parents and took Kate by the hand, leading her onto the front step. He wrapped his arms around her as she shivered in the cold, late October air.

"I have to be at the station tomorrow for a training exercise. But will I see you on Sunday?"

"Yes, but I'm not sure about the rest of my family. I don't think my parents have been to church since I was a little girl, and I have no idea about Zach."

"It was your brother's idea to say grace," Aaron reminded her.

"It was, and I saw him pray last night before he ate. It does have me wondering." She wanted to ask her brother what led to his sudden conversion, if that's what it was called, but she wasn't sure how to approach him. Perhaps asking him to go to Mass was a good start.

"Then ask him to go with us," Aaron suggested.

Kate smiled, "You read my thoughts."

Aaron pulled her tighter to him, and leaned toward her.

"We must be in sync, Princess," he said as his mouth covered hers. It was not the same kiss as earlier, the heat and urgency were missing, but the emotions were not. Kate felt the kiss all the way to her toes. When Aaron pulled back, she felt as if a part of her was pulling away.

"Until Sunday, Princess." Aaron let her go. "Go back inside where it's warm."

"It's plenty warm out here," Kate purred, causing Aaron to grab her by the waist and pull her in for one more kiss. This time, the passion was there full force. Just as Kate felt like she would never be able to come up for air, Aaron stopped kissing and hugged her fiercely. Letting go, he smiled at Kate and winked.

"See you Sunday," he said, and he turned to go.

Kate opened the door but stood on the steps watching him until his truck was out of sight. When she was back inside, Zach was sitting on the couch by the window, a wicked grin drawn from ear to ear. Kate blushed.

"No worries, little Sis. Mom and Dad are still in the kitchen, so your hot little goodbye wasn't on full display."

"You're nothing but a peeping Tom." Kate swatted at her brother's head, but he ducked.

"Ha," he shouted. "You never could get a lick in on me." They both laughed, and Kate dropped beside him on the couch, a dreamy look on her face.

"Do you like him?" she asked.

"I do, but," Zach hesitated, and Kate looked at her brother, her eyebrows raised in question.

"What?"

"Nothing. It's none of my business."

Kat sat and stared at her brother. "What? You can't say 'but' and not continue. That's not fair."

"Unfortunately, Sis, nothing is fair in love and war."

"Zach, seriously. What's going on?"

"Has he ever talked to you about his career? Where he was stationed before getting the chance to come home? That's not normal, to get a prime station like this at our age. What did he do that got him that assignment?"

"Gosh," Kate twisted the bracelet that adorned her wrist. "I don't know. I know he graduated from the Coast Guard Academy and served some time away from here, but I don't know where or what he did. He's kind of vague on the rest…" Her words trailed off as she thought about the times Aaron and his family avoided telling her anything about his job.

A look of concern crossed Zach's face. "You should talk to him," he prompted. "The military, it's not easy. It's hard to be normal after you've seen and done the things that…"

"Zach," Kate touched his arm. "Are we talking about Aaron or about you?"

Zach shrugged. "Never mind. Like I said, it's not my business."

He started to stand, but Kate didn't let go of his arm.

"What happened over there?" she asked. "Was it awful?"

Zach wiped his brow, and Kate realized that even though the night was cool, and the room was comfortable, her brother was sweating. He shook his head and leaned forward, his arms on his thighs, and his gaze on the floor between his feet.

"It's not something I could ever talk about, partly because I'm not authorized to, and partly because, shit, because I just can't bring that home to you."

Placing her hand on his back, Kate leaned over and kissed his cheek. "It's okay, Zach. I'm here for you. Always. Even if it's just to sit beside you in silence."

He looked over at his sister and gave her a weak smile. "Thanks, Sis. Sometimes, that's just what I need."

"What's going on in here?" Walter asked as he and Mitzi entered the room. "It looks serious."

"It is," Zach said as he leaned back and put his arm around Kate, pulling her back with him. "My little sister is falling in love."

"What?" Kate said as she wiggled out of his arms. "I never said that."

"You didn't have to," Zach said. "It's obvious."

"But I, I," Kate was flustered and not sure how to respond. Was that true? She was certainly attracted to Aaron, physically, mentally, and emotionally, but was that the same thing? She thought it was love with Mark, but she had been so wrong.

"Katherine, don't worry. You don't need to rush into it," her mother reminded her.

"Well, that's good because I have no intentions of rushing into anything." Kate grabbed her stomach. "Oh," she said in surprise.

"Kate," her mother rushed to her side. "What's wrong?"

Kate looked up, a beaming smile radiated across her face. "I think, oh, yes, there it is again."

"What?" Zach asked, sitting up and moving toward his sister.

Mitzi's eyes met Kate's. Both grinned at each other. "May I?" Mitzi asked and Kate nodded.

Placing her hand on Kate's stomach, Mitzi held her breath until she felt the small kick. "I felt it," she cried.

"The baby?" Zach asked, and Kate hurriedly grabbed his hand and placed it in just the right spot.

"Wow, that's a field goal kicker in there," he said when he felt the movement.

"First time?" Mitzi asked.

"Yes," Kate said. "Wow. That was awesome. Dad?"

"I don't know. It seems weird, putting my hand on your stomach."

"Get over here, Walter. How many times in life do you get to feel your first grandchild kick for the first time?"

"Mom's right, Dad. This is pretty cool," Zach grinned.

Walter walked over to the couch and gently laid his hand on his daughter's stomach. His slow but genuine smile said it all, and the whole family took turns feeling the baby kick for several minutes.

"I think it's time for me to hit the sack," Walter finally said. "Mitzi?"

Mitzi looked at her watch. "It's awfully early for bed, but I do have a book to read, and it has been a long week."

"Wait, before you go," Kate said. "I'm going to Mass on Sunday morning, and I know it's still a day away, but I wanted to give you time to think about it. Would any of you like to go?"

"Mass?" Mitzi asked. "As in church?"

"Yes, Mom, as in church."

"I'm in," Zach said. "What time? I'd like to keep up my routine and run in the mornings."

"It's at ten, and it's just a few minutes away."

"I'm not sure what to say." Mitzi looked bewildered. "Walter?"

"Well, I guess if the kids want to go, we could go, too."

"Perfect," Kate said. "Zach can go for a run, and I'll make breakfast. Then we can all go together." She beamed as she looked around at her family. Life just kept getting better and better.

***

"Guess I can't join you." Kate was still wearing her pajamas when she walked out onto the deck.

"Mom would kill me, and so would your doctor." Zach continued to stretch without looking up at his sister.

"I know," Kate pouted, "but I miss it so much."

"All in due time, Sis," he said, standing and giving her a kiss on the top of her head. Kate watched as he headed down the beach. She felt both envy and pride. She loved her brother fiercely and wished she could help him discern what he wanted to do next. If only they lived closer and could share friends, experiences, holidays, everything. She loved that he was here now, but she knew that the month would go by quickly, and then he would return to the desert halfway around the world with little or no contact with his loved ones back home. She knew that she couldn't convince him to stay. That had to be his call. She just wished she knew a way to make his decision easier, and more to her liking.

Walking back inside, she found her mother searching through her basket of coffee k-cups

"Since when did you start going to church?" Mitzi asked as she chose a nice Colombian blend.

"Since coming here. Since finding out I was pregnant. Since I've been trying to get my life on track."

"What about Zach?" her mother asked, switching on the coffee maker and turning to face Kate.

"I've been wondering that myself. What do you think is going on with him?"

"I wish I knew. You're the only one he ever talks to. If you don't know, then nobody does."

"He barely sleeps, almost like he's forgotten how, and he's hyper-alert. Not jittery, just always aware of everyone and everything. It's like he doesn't know how to relax anymore."

"You've picked up on quite a lot in a short time. I hadn't noticed all of that."

"Zach and I have a strong connection. You know that. We always have. Plus, his room is right next to mine. I can hear him up at night,"

"Well, there were times, when we were traveling in some faraway village, when you only had each other. It's not surprising that you can probably read each other's thoughts."

"I wish that was true," Kate said as she peeked out of the window to watch her brother's long strides along the sand further down the beach. He was not alone. Another man ran with him, and Kate recognized his stride as well. She went to the back door and stood, watching the men disappear around the bend where the beach curved to the left. Her mother walked over to share her view.

"Was that Aaron?"

"It was. He must be doing a short run today before going into work. He runs here, too, sometimes if Kayla needs him or he doesn't have time for a longer run. His sister lives right there." She pointed to Kayla's house.

"Yes, I remember you telling us that on Friday. Is that how you met?"

"Actually, we met at Anne's at a cookout." Kate smiled as she thought of their first conversation. "He teased me about my name. It's why he calls me 'Princess.'"

"What made you change your name?"

"I didn't really change it. I just shortened it." Kate shrugged and continued to stare out the door, waiting for the men to come back. "A girl at work back in DC used to call me Kate. She said it was a stronger name and would bring me good luck if I used it. She was into some kind of weird name-ology or something like that, always telling people what their real names should be. When I came here, I wanted a clean break, and it made sense to reinvent myself. I guess she was right. I do feel stronger, more confident."

Kate turned toward her mother and smiled.

"I can see it. You've grown up a lot in the last few months, maybe in the last few years, and we never noticed."

"I wish I could agree with you, but I never tried to grow up. I was okay with just working the job that Dad got for me without trying for more. I watched my friends get married, have babies, and get real jobs, but I only cared about the next party. Then I fell in love with Mark without ever getting to know him and blindly trusted him without questioning things that now make me look back and wonder what I was thinking. I had no desire to grow up, and I didn't open my eyes until it was too late."

"It's never too late, Kate," her mother said. She reached over and brushed a lock of blonde hair from Kate's face. "I like it, the sound of it. My daughter, Kate. You're right. It's strong, like you."

It had been so long since Kate had felt her mother's approval. Tears formed in her eyes as she hugged her mom.

"What's going on in here?" Walter asked.

"Just some mother-daughter bonding," Kate said with a smile.

"How about some father-daughter bonding? I make a mean French toast, and if I remember correctly, you're pretty good with an omelet pan."

"That sounds like a plan, Dad." Kate started pulling out the ingredients for French toast and spinach and mushroom omelets while her mother chose a coffee blend for Walter and a decaf cup for Kate.

By the time they were finished with their culinary specialties, Zach was opening the door from the deck.

"It smells like Heaven in here," he said as he pulled off his sweatshirt. "Do I have time for a quick shower?"

"You better have. I'm not eating next to you." Kate wrinkled her nose and shooed Zach away from the stove.

Once they were all seated, Kate asked Zach how his run was that morning.

"What you really mean is what did Aaron talk about on the run."

"Well, I'm open to whatever details you want to give me."

"Sorry to disappoint you, Sis, but we didn't talk at all. He kept up with me stride for stride, which was impressive, but it left no breath to talk."

"Oh," Kate said, suppressing her disappointment. She was hoping that they had bonded over their shared military experiences, their love for running, or perhaps their feelings for her.

Zach laughed. "Don't look so dejected. I'm sure we'll have plenty of opportunities to get to know each other. In fact, we're going to run together later this week. This area isn't long enough for a good, solid run, but he gave me directions to some running path. I'll be back in time for church."

They ate breakfast and chatted, enjoying each other's company. By the time they finished, clouds began rolling in. Since the impending rain prevented them from doing anything outside, Kate directed them to the Assateague Museum. They spent the afternoon learning about the area and even caught a glimpse of the ponies. The more time Kate spent showing off the island and neighboring park, the more she felt at home.

***

Following the directions that Aaron gave him, Zach easily located the paved trail. He ran early so that he had plenty of time to shower, dress, and eat before church. It would be the first time in years that he would attend Mass in a real church and not in a foxhole or tent. He looked forward to it. There was something comforting about being in church, knowing that he could be forgiven for all the things he had done, the things he did as part of his job. Sometimes he felt like he lived a double life. In one life, he was Zach Middleton, son of Walter and Mitzi, brother of Kate, a good, All-American boy who attended Mass and liked to read, fish, and have fun. In the other life, he had a heart of stone, the mind of a robot, and a trigger finger that was worth more than the Army could ever pay him.

It had been a long thirteen years, and he was yearning to be free of the sights and sounds of war. He was already at the Point when 9/11 occurred, and he knew that day that his life would be forever changed. What he didn't know was that he would have the skill and precision to qualify him for a job at which few others could ever excel. It was both a gift and a curse.

His long legs carried him swiftly through the wooded area. He sensed the eyes on him from several paces back, but he didn't slow down or turn around. When he was in the parking lot earlier, Zach noticed Aaron pull up to the trailhead but finished his stretching and took off for a solitary run. They were about the same height and could match each other's stride, but Zach needed to run alone that morning so that he could think about his future without distraction. Being back in the States with his family had cemented his desire to return home. He was losing his grip on who he was, what he believed, and what his life's purpose was. He needed a sign, something that would give him some direction as to where to go from here and how to get there. Perhaps, like his sister had discovered, the answers could be found here on this island. One thing he knew for certain. They couldn't be found through the scope of a rifle.

***

Father Darryl greeted them the next morning when they arrived at St. Andrews Church.

"Kate, it's so good to see you. I heard what happened. The church's prayer chain was working overtime for you."

"Thank you, Father, I appreciate it. I'd like you to meet my family. My father, Walter," the men shook hands and exchanged pleasantries. "My mother, Mitzi, and my brother, Zach."

"Welcome, all of you. I'm glad you are able to join us this morning."

Kate and her family made their way up the aisle and sat in the pew behind Aaron, Kayla, and the boys. Aaron turned around and shook hands with Walter and Zach before giving Kate a smile and a wink.

After Mass, Kate introduced her family to Kayla, Todd, and EJ.

"Your chicken pot pie was wonderful," Mitzi told Kayla. "The best I've ever had."

Kayla blushed and thanked Mitzi for her compliment. "I'd love to make dinner for y'all at my house some time. It would give you a break and would allow Kate to rest for an evening."

"We would love that, Kayla. Just let us know when," Mitzi said, her hands still clasping the young woman's.

"How about tonight? It's hard during the week with the boys in school, but I'd love to have you over. We have no plans. Kate?"

"Oh Kayla, I don't want to put you to any trouble. You certainly didn't plan on us coming over tonight."

"But it would really mean a lot to me."

"Then how can I say no?" Kate said. "What time?"

They made plans for dinner, and Walter offered to bring a couple bottles of wine to complement the meal. In the meantime, Zach was anxious to get home in time for the 1:00 football game.

When it came time to get ready to go to Kayla's, Kate put on a pretty pink sweater that she and Kayla had found on Amazon, a nice pair of maternity jeans, and her favorite pearl earrings. She applied light makeup and fixed her hair, which was long enough now to pull back into a nice ponytail. It had grown to just below her shoulders, and she thought she might let it grow up a little more in keeping with her new identity. She assessed herself in the mirror and decided she liked the look. The pink sweater and ponytail made her look younger and feel prettier. She was hoping Aaron would notice.

No mention had been made of him joining them for dinner, but Kate was sure he would be there. He had been at Mass but popped in, wearing his uniform, just as it was starting and left as soon as it ended. In a text to Kate earlier that morning, he told her that he would be at the station again for most of the day but would see her that evening.

She was not disappointed when he opened the door as they were walking up the steps to the front porch. Aaron held the door for Mitzi, Walter, and Zach, but blocked

Kate's path as he met her on the porch and closed the door behind him. Without a word, he wrapped his arms around her and pulled her in for a kiss.

"I've been waiting to do that since I left your house Friday night."

"Honestly, me, too." Kate smiled.

"You look nice," Aaron said as he took her hand and walked her inside. Kate smiled, happy that she had taken the extra time with her hair and makeup.

EJ and Todd were already pulling out one toy after another to show Zach, enamored by his presence. Mitzi was in the kitchen with Kayla, and Walter was settled on the couch watching a hockey game on TV.

"Just sit, Kate," Kayla called from the kitchen. "We've got everything under control in here."

Kate and Aaron sat on the couch with Walter and watched Zach with the boys. Kate had never seen her adult brother with children, and she was amused by his attempts to keep up with everything that Todd and EJ were telling him. At one point, he gave her a confused look, and Kate laughed.

"He's talking about a television character," she told him. "I heard about him constantly during the hurricane."

Zach went back to listening as EJ talked at an incredible speed, and Todd tried several times to get his attention by pulling on Zach's arm to get the man to look his way.

When Kayla called them to dinner, Kate laughed as Todd took one of Zach's hands and EJ took the other to lead him to the kitchen.

"I think I've been replaced," Aaron whispered in her ear.

"Don't feel too bad. They'll get tired of him and come running back to Uncle Aaron. He has no idea how to relate to kids."

"He could've fooled me," Aaron said, and Kate suddenly saw the situation in a new light.

For the rest of the meal, she paid close attention to the way Zach interacted with the boys, the way he stole glances of Kayla when she wasn't looking, the way that Kayla blushed when Zach complimented her cooking.

Zach was talkative throughout the meal, something that both shocked and pleased Kate. He had been so quiet since arriving on the island, but he had the entire table laughing at stories of his Army buddies and the practical jokes they often played on one another. It was a side of Zach that Kate hadn't seen in many years.

When dinner was over, and the last piece of pumpkin spice cake had been eaten, Zach offered to help wash dishes. Kate couldn't remember a single time in their lives when Zach had volunteered to do anything in the kitchen other than eat. She and Aaron glanced at each other with raised brows.

Trying not to draw attention to the situation, Kate told the boys that she would love to play with their Legos. They rushed into the living room to break open their Lego boxes and show her the latest architectural feats they were building with the tiny blocks. She took a quick peak into the kitchen as they all cleared out of the room and saw Zach laughing at something that Kayla said and noticed how Kayla's cheeks burned bright with a rosy glow.

***

The following day was Halloween. Aaron was working late, and Kate was disappointed that she wouldn't be seeing him. She hoped that a good number of island kids would find their way to the beach houses. She laughed when she opened the door and saw Spiderman and a werewolf on her front porch. She guessed some costumes never went out of style.

"Trick or Treat," EJ and Todd chorused.

"You two look great." Kate gushed over their costumes and handed them each their favorite kinds of candy.

"How do you know what we like?" Todd asked, his eyes full of wonder.

"She lived with us for like a week, you stupid head."

"Hey, now, do you want to trick or treat or go home and go to bed?"

"Sorry, Mom," EJ said.

"Did you make their costumes?" Kate asked Kayla.

"Not Todd's. He's been obsessed with Spiderman forever. Mom and I made EJ's."

"Well you both look super cool."

"Hey, guys," Zach said from behind Kate. "Having fun?"

"We just started," EJ said. "We've got lots of houses to hit tonight."

"Then we'd better let you get on with it," Kate told them. "Have fun."

They thanked her and said goodbye. Zach peered out the window and watched them climb into Kayla's SUV.

"You can join them, you know. I bet Kayla would enjoy the adult company."

"Nah, I'm good," he said, but he continued to watch as her car drove away.

That evening, Mitzi and Walter turned in early while Kate and Zach sat up together.

"So, the kids were all cute in their costumes, especially Todd and EJ. Kayla is a real sweetheart; don't you think?" Kate tried to remain nonchalant.

"Yeah, she's nice," was all Zach said.

Deciding not to push it, Kayla changed the subject. "And Aaron? I didn't ask you last night if you approve."

"I approve," he assured her. "But I still think you need to talk to him. There's something not quite right about his being stationed here."

"He's in the Coast Guard. How bad could that be?"

"We all have our devils, Kate. You should ask about his."

Zach refused to say more, and Kate wondered if he knew something or was just trying to get Kate to be more discerning. His concern was touching, but it made Kate nervous to think that Aaron was hiding something so significant that her brother thought it might be a problem.

Kate tried to concentrate on *The Boys in the Boat* by Daniel James Brown, a book that Aaron recommended, but she found her thoughts drifting to Aaron. She thought back to the night on the dock when she poured her heart out to him, but he refused to do the same, and earlier that same day when he seemed to stop his mother from saying too much. Then there were all the clues when she was at Ronnie's house. Each of those times, Kate knew that there was something that they were all hiding. She supposed that it was time to get Aaron to open up about his past and about whatever it was that brought that shadow over his features whenever she asked about his service. She was afraid that Zach might be right. There was something in his past that haunted Aaron, and Kate needed to find out what it was.

Although many countries banned the enlistment of Indigenous Peoples, many such people from around the world proudly fought for their countries in both World Wars as well as Korea and Vietnam. Each of these men and women fought for their own reasons, obeying commands, and often partaking in fights that left them scarred physically and mentally. As with all people, reassembling into normal lives after returning to their homelands was sometimes a greater hardship than the war itself.

From the *Studies of Indigenous Peoples* by Walter Middleton

CHAPTER ELEVEN

Kate had a hard time sleeping after her conversation with Zach. The next morning, the first of November, she told her parents that she needed to run out for a little while. Against their protests, she held firm and insisted that she go alone. Pulling up in front of the Coast Guard station, she was suddenly nervous. Was she doing the right thing? Aaron was at work, and she shouldn't just go busting in there demanding that he make time to talk to her. She sat in her car and tried to decide what to do. Rain poured down around her as she sat, lost in thought, with the windshield wipers slapping back and forth to a hypnotic tempo.

After a few minutes, a rapping on the window startled her, and she jumped at the noise, her heart leaping into her throat. She exhaled in relief as she rolled down the window partway. Raindrops landed softly on her arm, nose, and cheek.

"Needed some time away from the doting fam?" Aaron smiled.

"Something like that." Kate offered a weak smile, and Aaron frowned.

"What's wrong, Princess. Is everything okay?"

"I'm not sure." Kate looked away and stared out the front window.

"Are you okay? Is it your heart?" Alarm sounded in Aaron's voice, and panic filled his eyes.

"Yes, I mean no. I mean, I'm fine. I just—"

"Hold on." Aaron walked around the car, and Kate hit the button that unlocked the doors. He opened the passenger door and climbed in. "That's better," he said as he removed his hat and shook the water onto the floor. "Now, what's bothering you? Is it Zach?"

Kate was taken aback and looked at Aaron with surprise. "Zach? What about Zach?"

"Nothing," Aaron said. "I shouldn't have said anything."

Was this a dream? Or a nightmare? First Zach implies that Aaron was hiding something, and now Aaron was implying the same about Zach. What was going on?

"Tell me," Kate insisted. "What's going on here?"

"It's probably nothing. I shouldn't jump to conclusions, but when I saw the way he was looking at my sister, well, she's been through so much, you know? I just started to worry."

"Worry? About Zach? Why? He would never do anything to hurt Kayla, to hurt anyone."

Aaron just looked at Kate. His expression was unreadable, but Kate felt the weight of what he refused to say. "Aaron, talk to me. What are you worried about? That she will fall for him, and then he'll leave? If that's it, then you should know that he's considering getting out. He says he doesn't want to live that life anymore."

"That's not it, but it's good to know."

Kate's ire was on the rise. "Then what is it? I have a right to know what you're thinking."

"Kate, you've told me that your brother is covert, that he has some kind of high-level clearance or something. Do you know what he actually does? Has he ever given you any clue?"

"What do you mean? He's covert. He can't share anything with us. It's classified."

Aaron nodded. "I get that, but haven't you ever wondered? Have you ever noticed how serious he is, how focused? How he's always looking around him, but not in a jumpy way, more observant, like he's on the prowl. He misses nothing. He's in better shape than most military men are these days, and he takes that very seriously. He's introspective and calm. And then there's the callous."

"Callous? My brother isn't callous. He's one of the most caring men I know."

"Not *he's* callous, *the* callous. On the pad between his thumb and forefinger." He took her hand, opened it, and pulled on her skin between her thumb and finger. "Here. He's calloused right here. Very much so."

"I don't get it," Kate said. "What does that mean?"

"Nothing by itself, necessarily. But put it all together, and I can't help but wonder."

"Wonder what?" No longer annoyed, Kate was becoming worried. What was Aaron trying to say? He let out a long puff of air and looked through the windshield.

"What did he say about getting out? About his reasons?"

"Not much really. Just that he's tired of the things he's seen. The things he's done… What do you think he meant by that?"

"Anything else?"

"Well, he did make a strange comment the other night when he mentioned getting out. He said 'if they let me,' or something like that. I wondered what he meant."

"Kate," he held her hand. "This is going to sound strange, but do you go to the movies much? Action movies?"

"Kind of. It was the one place that Mark didn't mind taking me. Go figure." She frowned. "Why?"

"Did you ever see *American Sniper*?"

"I did. It was intense." She stopped and looked at Aaron. "Wait, you don't think? No, that's not possible. Zach doesn't have it in him. He's kind and caring. He could never—"

"Never rise above the crowd? Never be the very best at something? Never take an order and do something he didn't want to do? Never take on the responsibility of saving lives by taking out a life?"

"Oh, God. He would do all those things. He's super smart, good at everything he ever put his mind to. He firmly believes in sacrificing all for his country, and he would do anything if it meant he was saving lives."

"I could be wrong. It's not like I know anyone in that line of work. It's not something we specialize in. But I read, I talk to other military, and I've served in the Middle East. I could just sense it. From just one evening with him, I could see that he was different. Not bad," he assured Kate when her expression hardened. "Just different, like he saw life differently than the rest of us, like he saw things through eyes that see everything in a very focused way. I don't know how to explain it."

Aaron looked at the digital clock on the dashboard. "Look, I've got to get back inside. Was there something else you wanted to talk about?"

Kate realized that until that moment, she had completely forgotten why she was there to begin with. She shook her head. "No, not now. It's okay." She looked down at their hands that were still entwined, and squeezed his fingers. "Thanks for letting me know what you were thinking. I need honesty in the people I trust. I need complete honesty." She let her words sink in, and Aaron held her gaze for several seconds before slowly nodding. He let go of her hand and lifted his to her chin. Pulling her gently to him, he kissed her. It was soft and slow, but as his hand trailed from her chin to the back of her neck, he pulled her closer, and the kiss deepened. Kate let herself go, melting into his embrace, his lips. Without realizing it, she moaned, and Aaron pulled back.

"Sorry, Princess. That's all I can give right now." He let go of her and smiled a lazy, provocative smile.

"That's okay. It's going to be all I can give for a while."

"So it is, Princess. So it is." He turned and opened the car door. Looking back, he said, "I'm coming over for dinner tonight. I just thought I'd warn you." Then he winked, and she watched as he closed the door, walked around the car, and went back inside.

"Well, crap. That's not what I bargained for," she said out loud to herself. "What is it about me and men with secrets?" Kate shook her head and put the car into drive. A trip to the grocery store was in order. Kate groaned. She hated hauling in groceries in the rain.

***

For the rest of the day, Kate watched her brother and did indeed see the things that Aaron had seen, including the callous on his palm. No wonder Zach was suspicious of Aaron. He didn't want his sister involved with a man who might have seen and done the things that Zach may have. But those things didn't make Zach a bad person. Was that why he was suddenly so religious? Was he looking for a way to right his soul, to make amends, to convince himself that he wasn't a bad person?

By the time Aaron appeared at the door, Kate had worked herself up into quite a state of nerves. She knew it wasn't good for her or for the baby, and she felt the need to set things straight between them all, but how? She couldn't just come out and ask her brother if he was a cold-blooded killer, and she didn't want to put the blame for the suspicion on Aaron. Nor did she want to alarm her parents. These thoughts consumed her as she opened the door and pushed Aaron from the doorway, stepped onto the porch, and closed the door behind her. She wrapped her arms around Aaron and collapsed into his embrace.

"Princess, what's wrong?" Aaron held her tightly to him and felt her shivering in the cool, evening air.

"I don't know what to say to him," she said into Aaron's chest. "Do I pretend that we don't suspect anything? Do I confront him? How do you ask such a question? How do I act around him? He's my brother, my best friend. I've never felt uncomfortable around him."

Aaron took her elbows and pushed Kate gently away so that he could see her face. He moved his hands up her arms, across her shoulders, and to her cheeks. Gently holding her, he looked into her eyes. "You love him. Just the same as always. Let him know that you're here for him if he wants to talk. Be his sister, and let him do the rest."

Kate slowly nodded and closed her eyes. It was then that she realized how safe she felt with Aaron, how dependable he was, how strong and capable yet at the same time, gentle and kind. She opened her eyes and smiled up at him. "How do you always know the right thing to say?"

"I let my heart be my guide," he said as he leaned down and kissed her slowly and sweetly, turning her insides to a churning wave of physical and emotional tingling more powerful than any she had ever felt with anyone. She knew that her hormones couldn't be trusted these days, but, as Aaron suggested, she was listening to her heart.

"We should go inside," Aaron said quietly against her lips.

"We should," she agreed but made no attempt to move as his breath warmed her face, and his arms sheltered her from the cold and from everything else that threatened to ruin her happiness.

Reluctantly, Aaron loosened his hold and reached for the door. When they entered the house, the living room was empty, and they could hear voices in the kitchen.

Mitzi looked up and smiled when they walked in. "I've put out some cheese and crackers, a secret family recipe."

"It's not that big a secret, Mom. You've been telling people how to make this cheese spread for years."

"Only those who can be trusted," Mitzi answered with a smile.

Licking a bit of cheese off his upper lip, Aaron winked at Mitzi. "No need to share the recipe with me as long as you keep it coming. This is one helluva good cheese. Just don't let my sister taste it. She'll be selling it before you know it."

"Hmm," Mitzi mused. "Perhaps I should draw up a contract giving me a percentage."

They all indulged themselves with the appetizer while Mitzi and Kate finished preparing the meal, a pork roast with baked sweet potatoes, fried apples, and pumpkin muffins. It was Kate's favorite fall meal, and it reminded her of autumn days spent with her family in Georgetown.

They kept the dinner conversation light until a challenge went up, and the dishes were hastily cleared as cards and scoresheets were brought out. They played rummy until Aaron decided he had better hit the sack.

"You're just quitting because I'm so far ahead," Zach chided him.

"Hey, somebody in this house has to go to work tomorrow. The rest of you can enjoy your R&R, but I've got to report at 0700 hours."

"I've got three weeks left of R&R, and I'm going to enjoy every minute of it." Zach tilted back his bottle of beer and finished it off like a champ.

"You do that, Sergeant. Enjoy your time off," Aaron said.

Kate noticed a look that passed between the two men and wondered if, somehow, Zach knew. Her brother slowly nodded at Aaron.

"That's Staff Sergeant to you, Commander," Zach said with a smirk. "And I will, Aaron, I certainly will."

Kate felt her brother's eyes on them as they walked from the room. Or was it her imagination?

"He knows that you know, or that you suspect," she whispered at the door.

"Probably not, but maybe he'll talk to you, or even to me. I think he has a lot on his mind."

"I hope so. I guess we'll see." She leaned up and draped her arms around his neck. "Until we meet again." She smiled coyly and enjoyed the sweet taste of the kiss he planted on her lips.

"I'll be in touch, Princess." He kissed her one more time and then let go. Kate watched through the screen door as Aaron walked to his truck. He waved one last time before getting in and driving away.

"Aaron gone?" Kate jumped as her brother's voice broke the silence.

"You scared me," she said as she closed the door.

"Can we talk? Alone."

That was fast, she thought. Or was it? She had a feeling that Zach had been trying to come clean since he arrived.

"Sure. Where?"

"I don't know. Where do you suggest?"

"It's getting cold outside. How about my room?" Zach nodded and followed his sister upstairs.

They each sat on her bed, Kate by the pillows and Zach on the end. He played with a crocheted seashell on the afghan that was draped across the foot of the bed.

"He's a good guy. Aaron. I'm sorry if I led you to believe that he might not be. I haven't see any signs that his job or his past might be an issue."

"Thank you. I haven't either, but you'd know more about that than I would." Kate let the words hang in the air, but Zach didn't seem to take them as an invitation.

"I just worry about you, you know. I don't want to see you get hurt again."

"I know that, Zach. No hard feelings. My track record speaks for itself. I appreciate you looking out for me."

Zach nodded and continued to concentrate on the seashell.

"Zach," Kate began "Is there something bothering you? Something you'd like to talk about?"

He remained silent, as if the answers to all her questions could be found in the delicate, blue shell that seemed so dainty and out of place in his fingers.

"You know, you can tell me anything, anything, and it would never change my opinion of you. No matter what happens with Aaron, you will always be the one man who means more to me than anyone in the world."

Zach nodded. "I know. Thanks. I guess I just needed to hear that." He started to stand, but Kate reached over and laid her arm gently on his.

"Anything, Zach," she stared at him until he lifted his gaze and met hers.

"Do you think—" He started but then looked away. "Never mind, it's a stupid question."

"What?" she prodded. "Ask me anything."

He thought about it for a minute as he looked around the room. "Do you think I'd make a decent dad?"

Kate was taken aback by his question. It was the last thing she thought was on his mind. "Well, of course. You'd make a wonderful dad." Then a thought occurred to her. "Zach, is there something I should know? I mean—it's obvious that something is bothering you, and you've said more than once that you want to get out of the service. Are you? Is there?"

"Hell no," he said emphatically as he stood and began pacing. "Absolutely not. No offense, but one unexpected baby is enough right now, and you've got that covered."

Kate frowned, "Then why the question?"

Zach shook his head and ran his hand through the several-days of growth on his chin. "I don't know. It's those boys. I keep thinking about how they don't have a dad, and their mom has to do everything on her own. I know that her husband didn't intend to be killed, but what kind of father puts himself in that situation? What kind of man risks his life every day; sees, knows, and does horrendous things; and is able to go back home and hold his kids and kiss his wife and act like everything is normal?"

"I'm sure that Kayla's husband didn't have any idea that those men would kill him."

"Yeah, but he knew he was risking his career, his family, and possibly his life. More than that, he knew that he was in dangerous territory, that what he was doing could change him as a human being, that it could leave a mark on him that he might never be able to erase."

"Zach," Kate said quietly. "You can erase it. It doesn't have to become *you*, to define who you are."

Zach stopped abruptly and stared at his sister. A look of desperation and defeat overshadowed his face. "What if it already has?" He turned and left the room, and Kate felt a tear escape from her eye. Her brother was in so much pain, and she had no idea how to help him. It broke her heart.

***

"Father Darryl, do you have a few minutes?" Kate bit her lip as she stood in the door of the priest's office a few days after her talk with Zach.

"For you, Kate, of course I do. I have all the time you need. Come sit, and talk to me." The young priest gestured toward the chair where Kate had once before poured out her heart to him.

"Have you spoken to the baby's father?"

Kate shook her head. "No, I'm sorry. So much has happened since we talked about it. Honestly, I haven't had time to even think about it. But I still have time." She tried to smile. "Actually, I'm not here about me this time. It's about my brother. I'm not sure how to help him."

"Is he sick? Or is this more of a spiritual matter?"

Kate offered a weak smile. "I'm honestly not sure. I think he needs someone to talk to, and normally, I'm that person, but this time, well.... He seems to want to open up to me, but he's having a hard time doing it. It's like he's dropping these little bread crumbs for me to follow, but just as I get to the end of trail, he swoops in and gathers them up again, and I'm more lost than before."

"Perhaps he's not quite ready yet. You know how that is." He gave her a knowing look, and Kate blushed. "How long before he goes back?"

"The Sunday after Thanksgiving. But he doesn't want to go back. I can tell. He keeps talking about getting out, about not re-upping in March. But I think he doesn't even want to go back for the time he has left. I think," she tried to figure out what to say without divulging Aaron's suspicion. "I think his job entails doing things that he doesn't want to do any more."

Father Darryl nodded. "It is war. It happens. Young men go over to do what they think is best and then find that what is best for the country or the world is not what is best for the soul."

"Exactly," Kate said emphatically. "He seems to be concerned with how his actions will affect his soul, not just his heavenly soul, but the very essence of his personhood."

"Yes, that can be a concern. Your brother was at Mass on Sunday. Do you know if he goes regularly?"

"I don't know, but I suspect he does. Or as regularly as circumstances allow. We never went as kids, and I don't ever remember him being religious at all when he's come home before, but now, he's different. He says grace, and I noticed that he knows all the prayers at Mass, even the ones that changed since I graduated from high school and stopped going. I'm still struggling with those, but he knows them all. So I'm assuming he must go pretty often."

"Then he's seeking answers in the right place."

"I guess, but I wish there was someone more tangible who he could talk to." She looked at the priest and raised her brow.

"Kate, I'm happy to talk to him, but he needs to come to me."

Sighing, Kate nodded. "I know. I guess I was hoping, well, I don't know what I was hoping."

Father Darryl smiled, "You were hoping for a miracle of some sort?"

"Aren't we all?" she asked honestly.

"Life is a miracle, Kate. The fact that we are all here, living and breathing with knowledge and forethought. You have a miracle growing within you, and I believe you've experienced many miracles since coming to the island. Am I right?"

Kate thought about it and then slowly nodded. "You're right. It's an island of miracles. Maybe Zach's miracle can be found here, too. You never know, right?"

"You never know. It all depends upon how you look at the world. There are miracles that take place every day.

We just have to be open to the possibility to recognize them."

"Father, there is something you could do for me, if you don't mind."

"What is it, Kate?"

"Would you come for dinner? Tonight? Tomorrow night? Whenever you're free? Perhaps just having you there will help Zach see that I'm not the only one he can talk to."

"Dinner that doesn't come from the freezer? There's no way I would pass up that opportunity. Tonight's not a good night. We have a parish council meeting. But tomorrow sounds great. What time?"

They came up with a time that would work for both of them, and Kate thanked him for his help and advice. Now she just had to hope that after they got to know each other, her brother would feel comfortable seeking out the priest for advice. She wasn't sure where else she could turn, but she did know that her brother needed help.

At least one good thing was coming out of whatever was going on with Zach. Kate was spending less time worrying about her life and problems and more time thinking about someone else. It was a welcome change in her life, and she had a feeling that she had the island to thank for that, too. Her friends and neighbors made her realize that life isn't about what you have or need, but about meeting the needs of others. It was a lesson that took Kate a long time to learn, but one that would leave a lasting imprint on her life.

***

Dinner was a loud and crowded event. With six people huddled around the little kitchen table, and Kate taking up more room than anyone else, she felt claustrophobic. Excusing herself between the main course of ham, green beans, mashed potatoes, and homemade rolls and the decadent crème brülée that Kayla taught her to make, Kate went to the bathroom. She stared at herself in the mirror and marveled at the roundness of her belly, the way it curved in the most beautiful way to show off the life growing inside of her. If anyone had told her a year ago that this would be happening, all of this, she would have laughed at them. Now it seemed like the most natural thing in the world for her to be caressing her stomach and thinking about the life within it.

A light knock at the door broke into her thoughts. "Katherine, honey, are you okay?"

"I'm okay, Mom." She opened the door. "I just needed a minute. It was a little stuffy in the kitchen."

"Yes, we're going to move into the living room for dessert. Your priest friend is quite the charmer. How did he ever escape the loving embrace of a good woman and end up as a lonely priest?"

"Mom," Kate gasped. "I'm sure he doesn't look at it like that at all. He's a wonderful priest."

"Yes, but it's so sad, to see a young man alone in the world."

"Are you sure you're talking about Father Darryl?" Kate leaned against the doorjamb and eyed her mother.

"Well, maybe I'm thinking a little of your brother. Don't you think he would be happier if he had a woman in his life?"

"I do, Mom, but I think he has other things to work out first."

"Like what?" Her mother's eyes widened. "What has he told you?"

"Very little, unfortunately. But I'm working on that." Kate switched off the light and started from the doorway, but her mother grabbed her arm.

"Katherine, is everything okay? Should I be worried about Zach?"

Kate hesitated. "I don't think so Mom. Zach is a big boy, and he's quite capable of taking care of himself."

Mitzi looked into Kate's eyes for several seconds. Seemingly satisfied that her daughter was right, she nodded and let it go.

Once they entered the living room, Kate's eyes immediately caught Aaron's. He raised his brow in question, and she smiled, letting him know that everything was fine. She saw the relief on his face and went to the seat that he offered her on the sofa next to him.

"Here's your dessert, Sis," Zach said as he handed her a crème brülée. "Father Darryl was just telling us about his recent trip to the Holy Lands. It sounds like quite a different view of the Middle East than I've ever seen."

"I spent some time in Bahrain, but that's pretty friendly territory." Aaron looked at Zach for his input.

"Yeah, Israel and Bahrain are quite different from what I'm used to. Iraq and Afghanistan are hostile places. Were you on a ship or at the base?"

"I was on the base," Aaron confirmed. "I oversaw RAID operations and conducted demonstrations for visitors."

"You mean visiting VIPs. Wow." Zach was genuinely impressed. "You were one of the top dogs. How'd you manage that assignment at such a young age? The Army and Coast Guard ceased RAID a couple years ago, so you had to have been there a while back."

Aaron shrugged. "I got lucky. It wasn't a big deal." But as he said it, Kate sensed that it was a big deal. Zach had hit on something, and by the look on his face, he knew it. Their eyes met for just a split second, and she knew that Zach was telling her that there was more to Aaron's story than a lucky break.

"What's RAID?" she asked.

"Redeployment Assistance and Inspection Detachment," Aaron answered. "It was a joint op between the Coast Guard and the Army. To sum it up in quick and easy terms, we used our expertise in inspecting cargo containers to determine whether the ones being used in the Middle East were seaworthy. There was more to it than that, but that's the gist."

"Did you convoy or stay at the base?" Zach asked.

"Just the base. I commanded the inspections there. It was a pretty nice gig." He turned to the others in the room. "Most of the guys in RAID were stationed on the island but traveled throughout the Middle East to do their inspections. It made more sense than bringing all the containers to Bahrain. Sometimes, they ran into problems, but we were pretty sheltered on the base. I didn't have to see or do anything compared to what Zach has probably been through."

"So, Father," Zach changed the subject. "Tell us more about your trip."

Kate sensed her brother's desire to move on and chimed in. "Yes, I'd love to hear what it's really like in Bethlehem. Why are Mary and Joseph often depicted in the snow if the Holy Land is in the desert?"

"Ah, that's a good question," the priest said, his eyes twinkling. "It actually does snow in Bethlehem."

"No way, seriously?" she asked.

"Seriously," he nodded. "I've never actually seen it, but a friend was there when it was snowing a few years ago."

They spent the rest of the evening hearing stories about Father's trip. They listened in rapt silence as he told them about saying Mass inside the tomb in the Holy Sepulcher and laughed at his story about baptizing fellow pilgrims in the River Jordan as dozens of babies cried all around them. Zach was very attentive and seemed to connect with the young priest. The three men made plans to go deep water fishing the following week if Aaron could work some magic and find a ship with an open reservation. Kate had no doubt that he would make it work. She knew that she was witnessing one more island miracle.

***

"Katherine Middleton." Kate rose when the nurse called her name. "This way please."

Kate followed the nurse down the white hallway into a white room with a white paper sheet pulled across the green exam table. On the walls were posters of gestational periods and healthy reproductive systems. A small corner of the countertop held pamphlets about an array of problems that could plague one's pregnancy. Kate was glad that hers was mild in comparison to other issues some women faced.

The nurse introduced herself as Mary Sifka and proceeded to take Kate's vitals.

"You can leave on your underpants, but everything else needs to come off. Here's a gown," the nurse said with a smile as she picked up the paper gown from the exam table and handed it to Kate.

"Thank you." Kate smiled back as she took the gown and watched the nurse close the door. She changed and then sat on the edge of the table. She had barely settled herself when there was a knock at the door, and Dr. Sprance poked his head inside the room.

"Are you ready for me?" he asked with a broad smile, those bright blue eyes twinkling as he greeted her.

"Yes, come in," Kate said. He entered and was followed by Mary who wheeled in a portable sonogram machine.

"How are you feeling? Any shortness of breath or dizziness?" He put his stethoscope in his ears as she shook her head, and he leaned down to listen to her back and chest.

"How's the monitor? Not too much of a bother?"

"What can I say? It's not the most up to date fashion accessory, but as far as life-saving wear, it's not too gauche."

"What more could we ask for, right?" He smiled as he put the stethoscope back around his neck and took his reading glasses from his pocket. He read her chart and made some notations on his iPad. "I'm trying to get myself and my office into the 21st Century, but I sure do miss my good, old-fashioned pen and clipboard of papers." He said as he put the device down on the counter. Mary rolled her eyes, and Kate laughed. "I have to keep my staff happy, though, and they say this makes things much easier for them."

"I tried using a Kindle once. I think it's back in DC sitting on my nightstand. I'm not sure it even has any books on it other than the ones that came pre-loaded. It just didn't feel right in my hands when I settled down to read at night."

"I understand just what you mean," he said as he examined her reflexes and asked her to lie back. He lifted her gown and examined her stomach. Kate flinched as he squeezed some cold gel onto her belly.

"Now, let's see what's going on inside here today."

"We're going to see the baby today?" Kate asked, her excitement showing on her face.

"We sure are," Dr. Sprance answered as he began to roll the sonogram wand around on her belly.

"Oh my gosh," she said as she watched the monitor. "Everything in the hospital was so surreal, and the heartbeat was so quiet. It was all like a dream. But this, this is amazing."

"It is pretty amazing. Is there anyone with you who you would like Mary to go find and bring in?"

"Oh my, yes! Please get my mother. She was so disappointed that she wasn't there the first time. I almost feel like I wasn't there the first time."

Dr. Sprance pointed out some of the baby's features while Mary went to get Mitzi.

A gasp sounded from the doorway. "Come here, Mom." Kate held her hand out, and Mitzi took it as she went closer to the table, her eyes fixated on the monitor.

"Oh, my," she said. "I never had one of these with you or Zach. This is, he's, she's, it's beautiful. I never knew that there was so much detail to be seen. The pictures never look like this."

"This is a 3D sonogram," Dr. Sprance told them. "State of the art. It's the most realistic view of your baby you will see until birth."

"It's almost as good," Kate marveled.

"You just wait," her mother told her. "This pales by comparison."

"That it does," the doctor agreed. "That it does."

"Can you tell, no, wait. I don't know if I want to know. Do I want to know?" She looked to her mother for advice, biting her bottom lip.

"I don't know," Mitzi hesitated. "I always believed in being surprised, but…"

Kate wasn't sure what to do, and she knew why. What if it was a boy? A boy who looked just like Mark? How would she handle that? What if she ran into him someday, and he took one look at their son and just knew? She thought about Father Darryl's warning that she should tell Mark about the baby. Maybe he was right. But was he? She felt a sense of panic coming on and began breathing heavily.

"Kate," Dr. Sprance stopped moving the wand and looked at his patient. "Are you all right?"

Swallowing and blinking back tears, Kate nodded. "I think so. I'm just, it's all so much. I don't know what to do."

"It's okay. You don't have to decide today. Even though we're usually able to tell with this advanced machine, it's better to wait another week or two to be sure."

Kate felt a sense of relief. She had a little more time before she had to make a decision. The problem was that there was more than one decision she was having a hard time making.

***

The elementary school was decorated with red, white, and blue everything. Banners, flags, flowers, tablecloths. There wasn't a surface on the cafeteria that wasn't decorated with something patriotic. The Coast Guardsmen of Yesteryear Breakfast was a big deal on the island, and Kate was honored to be included. Aaron had asked her to attend as his guest, though she was covering it for the paper and would have to split her time between Aaron and the other Servicemen and women.

She spoke to as many of the retirees as she could, asking about their time in the Service: highlights, scares, important things they had witnessed. As the band played the Coast Guard anthem, she watched the grown men weep. She had witnessed many tribal ceremonies and more than her fair share of college graduations when her father was a professor, but she had never had the privilege of seeing anything like this.

"Did you notice that my date is the most beautiful woman in the room?" Aaron whispered to her as they sat down following the Pledge of Allegiance and the blessing.

"I didn't," she said, blushing. "But I did notice that I'm with the most handsome seaman, next to Rear Admiral Gehrig, of course."

"Old Ty? I could take him."

"You wouldn't dare. He's not only handsome, but he outranks you."

"Wow, you sure know how to hit a man when he's down."

Kate was so happy that she felt like a giddy teenager. She beamed as she looked at Aaron. Several of the wives had told her that she was glowing, and while she knew what they meant, she attributed it to much more than her healthy, normal second trimester. She had never been so happy in her life. The truth was that her life hadn't really started until the day she arrived on the island. She was blessed to be there, to be with Aaron, to have her mom around for a couple more weeks. Her father had returned to Florida and would be back for Thanksgiving.

After the breakfast and the ceremony, Kate proudly watched Aaron attend to his duties. Seeing the other men salute Aaron made her swell with pride. She was sure that there was whispering and tongue clucking going on behind their backs when Aaron escorted her in and to their seats, her newest maternity dress showing off her now prominently displayed belly. But she didn't care. If Aaron wasn't ashamed to be seen with her in public, then why should she let it bother her? It was nobody else's business but theirs.

Going to Mass the next day was harder, though. She could feel the stares of the some of the older women, the ones who didn't know her personally, and she wondered how many of them mentioned her sinful condition to Father Darryl. It didn't seem to matter, though, as he always wore a smile when he greeted her and asked how she was doing. She didn't mention Mark, and neither did he, but she knew that the time was coming. At some point, she needed to decide what to do, and she was afraid that it was going to have to be sooner rather than later. She and Aaron were now seen as a 'couple,' and it wasn't fair to him to have this hanging over them. She knew that there was a chance that it could all come out someday, that Mark would know and might try to do something to find her or see the baby. But as much as she hated telling him, carrying around the secret, and the guilt, was beginning to affect her.

***

"Father Darryl thinks I should tell Mark about the baby."

Mitzi's fork stopped mid-air. Zach stopped chewing the large piece of roast beef he had just popped into mouth. Aaron slowly swallowed his mouth full of water and put down his glass.

"What did you just say?" Zach asked, his expression showing his disbelief.

The kitchen that, only moments ago, had been filled with the happy sounds of laughter, multiple conversations, the clinking of silverware, and ice settling back into the tea pitcher, was now silent as Kate's words washed over everyone at the table.

"Father Darryl thinks that it would be best for everyone involved if I tell Mark about the baby."

"How the hell is that what's best?" Zach exploded. Mitzi, always even-tempered, laid her hand on her son's arm.

"Zach, why don't we let Kate explain."

"I don't really know how to. He just thinks that not telling him is a lie of omission and one that would weigh on my heart and soul."

"And how do you feel about that?" Mitzi asked. All eyes were on Kate as she swallowed and looked around the table from one person to another, stopping on Aaron who had remained quiet thus far, letting her handle the situation in her own way.

"I thought it was a really bad idea." She looked away and bit her lip. "But now, I'm not so sure." She moved her gaze back to Aaron and hoped to communicate her feelings, pleading with him for understanding through her expression alone. He nodded for her to go on.

Taking a deep breath, Kate continued. "I thought that the best thing to do was to never contact him again, to keep the baby a secret and raise him or her on my own. But," she hesitated, not wanting to give voice to her fear. "What if I run into him someday, or he tracks me down for some reason, or someone in DC sees him and tells him that I had a baby? What if the baby looks just like him? How could I deny it?"

"Kate, dear," Mitzi said as she placed her hand over her daughter's. "The decision is yours, and yours alone. I know that you like and respect that priest, but he isn't the one who has to live with this."

"That's exactly the point, Mom. I have to live with this. I have to live with the fact that I kept a man from his child or that I'll have to share my baby with a man I want nothing to do with. The bottom line is that, whatever I decide, I'm the one who has to live with the consequences, and which consequences are going to be worse in the long run?"

"I get it," Zach said quietly, having given it some thought. "It's not the truth that is the problem. It's the secrecy and the pain that you'd have to keep bottled up inside of you forever."

"He's right," Aaron agreed. "Sometimes keeping something in the past is harder than facing it in the present and future."

Silence filled the room as each person looked around and wondered what the answer was. When is it time for a secret to no longer be a secret, and how do you tell those with whom you least want to share it?

Contrary to popular belief, it was not the Pilgrims who introduced the concept of Thanksgiving to the Native Americans. In fact, the Wampanoag Tribe held harvest celebrations long before the Europeans survived their first winter in the New World. Giving thanks came naturally to the Wampanoag peoples, and they celebrated small thanksgiving rituals daily. Larger celebrations took place at the beginning of each harvest season in gratitude to the Creator for giving sustenance to the people. These celebrations included singing, dancing, and feasting.

From the *Studies of Indigenous Peoples*
by Walter Middleton

CHAPTER TWELVE

As Thanksgiving approached, Kayla worried about what to do about Mark, but she was more worried about Zach's imminent departure. They had planned on having dinner at home with just their family, and Kate assumed that Aaron would spend the holiday with his family. Her father had returned from Florida, and Kate was feeling strong, healthy, and happy, surrounded by those she loved. She was surprised on that Tuesday by a call from Father Darryl.

"I'm so sorry to bother you, especially in your condition, but I need a few extra hands and was hoping that your family could help."

"Of course, Father, what can we do for you?"

Kate put her groceries down on the counter and let her mother begin unpacking them while she moved into the living room and sat in her favorite chair.

"We're holding a Thanksgiving dinner on Thursday for those on the island who have nowhere to go. Some might be homeless, some perhaps just can't afford a big, fancy dinner, and others are elderly islanders with no family in the area. It's early in the day, one o'clock, and everyone comes and eats at once, so it won't take up the entire afternoon. Would you all be willing to help?"

Kate peered around the corner and watched her mother put the large bird into the refrigerator. The counter overflowed with the traditional ingredients: potatoes, salad fixings, cans of cranberry sauce, stuffing mix. She hated to disappoint her mother who was used to having their Thanksgiving meal early in the day, followed by football and naps and maybe a board game later. But something inside of her told her that this was the right thing to do. She stood up and walked to the doorway where her mother would hear her.

"We would love to help with the Thanksgiving dinner, Father. What time should we be there?"

Her mother gave her a quizzical look, hands on her hips and an eyebrow arched over her blue-shadowed lid.

"Ask Kayla. She's in charge of the cooking."

"Will do."

When Kate disconnected the call, she looked at her mother apologetically. "I couldn't say no."

Two days later, her entire family, along with Aaron, Kayla, Todd and EJ, Ronnie and Trevor, Anne's family, and Shannon's family, worked side-by-side cooking and serving a traditional Chincoteague Thanksgiving dinner. Walter had made it back from Florida the evening before and thought that helping at the church was a splendid idea.

Kate had never had turnip greens or corn pudding, but she proclaimed herself the test taster and enjoyed every bite of the new-to-her foods. Trying the green sweet potatoes had taken a bit more courage, but she found them to be absolutely delicious. Having had her share of fried oysters back in the seafood restaurants in DC, she was pleasantly surprised to find that the ones that were freshly caught and shucked that very morning were the best she had ever tasted. Zach concurred, and Kayla had her hands full keeping him from eating them as quickly as she could put them on the serving trays after Trevor fried them.

Kate watched her brother interact with Kayla and was mesmerized by the scene.

"It makes you wonder, doesn't it?" Aaron whispered, coming up behind Kate and laying a soft, gentle kiss on her neck below her ear.

"They seem so, what? In sync? It's like watching bees dance."

"What?" Aaron asked with a laugh. "What does that mean?"

"A few years ago, the Smithsonian ran an article about bees. It was around the time that the book was such a big hit, *The Secret Lives of Bees*, you know?"

Aaron murmured that he didn't know, but he wrapped his arms around her and held her close while they watched their siblings. He nuzzled his cheek against her ear.

"Anyway, the writers who interviewed the beekeepers videotaped them taking care of the bees. When the bees mate, they do this kind of dance. It's beautiful and indescribable, and that's what I think of when I watch them together."

Aaron rocked Kate back and forth, his hands around her belly. "Like this," he whispered as he rhythmically swayed her to the beat of his heart.

"Just like that," she purred, closing her eyes and inhaling the scents around her – the frying oysters, the baking corn and potatoes, the stewing turnip greens, and him, his freshly washed and shaven body so close to hers that she could feel his heartbeat.

And at that moment, she forgot about the bees, her brother and her dearest friend, her parents, thanksgiving, and everything else. Only one word came to her mind. Love.

***

Back at the house that evening, they ate turkey sandwiches and watched the Cowboys get whipped by the Redskins. After they ate, Kate laid on the couch, her head on Aaron's lap, and her feet propped up on a pillow at the other end. Zach sat in the chair that Kate usually claimed for herself while Kayla sat in the chair next to his. The boys colored while half-heartedly watching the game, and her mother sat on the loveseat, reading a book, while her father dozed next to her. Kate looked around the room and marveled at her family, all of them. She thought about all her father's research, the many things he explained to her about the different peoples they encountered in villages all over the world. This was the true meaning of family, of a community that looked out for one another, cared for one another, and saw each member as an extension of himself. It was the most beautiful revelation she had ever had.

***

Sunday came much too soon. Kate started crying the moment she awoke. Their family breakfast was quiet as each person at the table kept their thoughts to themselves. Kate knew that Zach had enjoyed his fishing trip with Father Darryl and Aaron, but he never made any attempt to speak with the priest, and he hadn't opened up to Aaron. Kate looked at her brother as he put his dishes in the sink. He stopped at the kitchen window and gazed at the house across the marsh.

"I think I'll take a short walk," he told them, and Kate knew just where he was headed.

"Zach, we don't have much time."

"I know, Dad. I won't be long."

Kate cleared her dishes and watched her brother close the distance between the two houses. She wished she could go, too, and hear what was being said, but she had to trust that there was a bigger plan in this.

By the time the kitchen was clean, Walter was pacing back and forth in the living room.

"Kate, go get your brother."

"Dad, he'll be back soon. Give him a minute."

"He's had ten. He's going to miss his flights. Norfolk isn't just around the corner, you know."

The back door opened, and Zach walked in. "Ready?"

"Yes, let's get going," Walter said, his patience already more than worn thin.

"As soon as I say goodbye to everyone."

Zach held open his arms, and Kate fell into them. The tears flowed as she clung to her brother.

"I don't want you to go."

"I know, Sis, but it's okay. I'll be back before you know it."

Nodding and wiping the tears from her face, Kate pulled back and looked up at him.

"There's so much more to be said and done."

"Shhh, it's okay. I will be back, I promise."

"Did you promise Kayla?"

Zach looked surprised. "Kate, there's nothing—"

"Don't lie to me, Zach. Not now. I've had enough of secrets and hiding things and holding back."

A small smile appeared on his lips. "Okay, then. Yes, I promised her that I would be back. I promised the boys, too. Are you happy now?"

"No, but it's a start."

"Come on, Zach." Walter was at the end of his patience, and they all knew it. He was nothing if not punctual even if that meant hours earlier than necessary.

"One more thing," Kate grabbed his hand and pulled him outside.

"What now?" her father groaned.

"I'm only going to ask you this once, and I expect an honest answer," she said as she closed the door behind them and wrapped her arms around herself. "Are you, or are you not, a sniper?"

Zach tried to act surprised, tried to laugh it off. "What? Are you crazy? Why on earth—"

"No more lies, Zach. I need to know."

Suddenly, he became serious. "I can't talk about it, Sis. I won't let you into that world."

"Then Aaron was right."

"Aaron? Is he the one who put this crazy idea in your head?"

"I knew from the minute you got home that something was going on. Aaron just helped me put together the clues. Now you listen to me. I don't care what you do, and neither does Aaron, and neither will Kayla, but you finish it up, and come home. We can get you whatever you need to get that stuff out of your head and live a normal life, but that job isn't you. It's what you do. And when you get out, it will be in the past. Do you hear me, Zachary Michael Middleton? It is not what defines you. This," she jabbed her fist into his chest. "This is what defines you, and it's good and solid, and unlike mine, it works in all of the ways that count. You got that?"

With tears in his eyes, Zach pulled his sister into a tight embrace. "I love you Katherine Rebecca Middleton. Don't you ever forget that."

"I love you, too, Zach. Now, go do what you have to do to get back home to us. All of us."

When they went back inside, Aaron was waiting for them. He reached out his hand to Zach.

"Good luck soldier. I look forward to having you back here soon."

The two men embraced in a man hug, slapping each other's backs and wishing each other well.

"You take care of my sister, man. I only expect to hear good things from her."

"No worries, Zach."

Walter went to Mitzi and hugged her. "I'll be back in a few hours." He looked at Mitzi. "You know, I hate that I'll be making this trip twice in one week."

"I know, Walter, and I'm so glad you're okay with us staying for just a few more days. I want to make sure Kate has everything under control before I leave and that her doctor's appointment goes well."

Kate resisted rolling her eyes. She knew that her mother just wanted to stay for the Island's Christmas house tour but that Walter was anxious to get back home. The two weeks he had spent in Florida while Mitzi remained in Virginia had given him ample time to get his golf swing back, and he didn't want to lose any more time on the course.

After another round of tearful goodbyes, Walter and Zach left for the airport.

The rest of the day was somber. Aaron left Kate and her mother to be alone, and the two women folded laundry and talked about unimportant things. The house felt empty without Zach's huge presence, and Kate missed him terribly already.

The Achuuar tribe of Ecuador subscribes to a type of vision quest involving the spirit of the forest, Arutam, who lives in the great Kapok tree. At the age of thirteen, a young man is sent into the forest alone where he prepares and ingests the forest medicines, Datura and Natem, which produce hallucinations. Arutam will visit the boy in the form of an animal of strength, perhaps a jaguar or other predator of the forest. If the boy is afraid, the Arutam will disappear; but if the boy shows courage, his true calling in life will be revealed to him.

From the *Studies of Indigenous Peoples*
by Walter Middleton

CHAPTER THIRTEEN

There were so many events to cover the first week of December that Kate barely had time to stay sad. There was the Homes for the Holiday Tour, the annual Waterfowl Show and Auction, the Christmas tree lighting, the Kiwanis Christmas breakfast, the Christmas parade, and the gingerbread house contest. Kate was exhausted when the week was over, but it felt good to be out in the community, constantly meeting new people, and saying hello to those who were now old friends.

Aaron tagged along to as many events as he could, but he bowed out of the homes tour, much to her mother's delight. She was looking forward to taking the tour with her daughter and having just a little more time together before she headed home. It was Sunday, and she and Walter were to leave on Tuesday. For the first time in Kate's adult life, she wished her mother didn't live so far away.

Aaron couldn't accompany the women to the Christmas parade because he was in it along with many of the other servicemen from the island. Todd and EJ rode in the church's float which depicted the Christmas story. Kate couldn't help but notice the way that Todd, as Joseph, blushed each time that Mary, played by Anne's daughter, Lizzie, looked up at him as she held baby Jesus.

The island, which had been so quiet for the past few months, seemed to come alive with all the hoopla of the holidays. There were people everywhere, and stores that were usually closed up tight during the colder months were now open on the weekends as visitors filled the town for a festive getaway, some of them lured there by Anne's newly updated website.

When Kate arrived at her doctor's appointment on Monday, she knew what she had to do. Much to her mother's disliking, she had insisted that she go to the appointment by herself. Since her parents were set to leave the following day, Mitzi wanted the doctor to assure her that Kate would be okay once they were gone.

Dr. Sprance grinned as he told her that he could indeed see the gender of the baby she carried.

A tear rolled down her cheek as Kate looked at this kind and gentle man.

"Please," she said, barely above a whisper. "Please tell me. I need to know."

Noticing the catch in her voice, Dr. Sprance stopped and looked over at Kate. With the wand suspended above her belly, he raised his brow. "Are you sure?"

"Yes," she nodded emphatically. "Yes, I'm sure."

Placing the wand back on her belly, he rolled it around until they had the view they wanted. Smiling, he looked at Kate. "You have a beautiful, baby—"

***

"Hi," was all she managed to say.

"Hello? Who is this?" He sounded irritated, perhaps thinking she had the wrong number or was a telemarketer.

"It's me."

"Katherine? Is that you? Where the hell are you?"

She flinched at his tone and held the phone away from her ear as she caught her breath.

Had he always sounded that curt, that mean? Looking back, she realized that he had. Whenever she called him at what he considered an 'inopportune time.' Now, of course, she knew that those times were probably when he was at home, his real home, with his wife within hearing distance.

As if sensing her distress, he changed his tone. "I've been waiting for you to call, baby. Where are you? Tell me, and I'll come get you. I miss you."

"I have something to tell you." She tried to keep her voice even, but her entire body was shaking as she sat in her car outside of the doctor's office. Even with the heat on, she trembled like she was standing on the bridge to the island in a cold, battering wind.

"Sure, baby. I'm listening."

"It's a girl. And she's mine. I just thought you should know."

There was silence on the other end, and as the moments ticked by, Kate was sure that they had been disconnected, but a look at her screen told her that he was still there.

"A girl?" he finally said in a hushed voice.

"Yes, but I don't need anything from you. I don't want anything from you. I just thought that you should know." She closed her eyes. No, she didn't think he should know. She regretted telling him instantly, but now it was done.

"When? You weren't…" He sounded angry before his voice softened. "A girl? And she's mine?"

Kate's blood boiled. She clenched her jaw and spoke in a low, even tone. "No, on second thought, I'm not sure that she is. In fact, I know she's not yours. Forget I ever even told you."

"Katherine, wait-" But there was no waiting. She had done what Father told her to do. Whether Mark believed her was his problem. As far as she was concerned, that was the last contact she ever had to have with Mark Leahy.

***

By the time Kate got back to the beach house, her heart was racing, and her breathing was shallow. It was difficult for her to climb from the car. Pulling herself from the driver's seat, she clung to the door, trying to catch her breath. Before she even realized what was happening, she was falling.

"Mitzi, help me. She needs to go to the hospital." Kate heard her father's voice somewhere in the distance. She was being carried, a little girl again, in the forests of Brazil, fighting for her life.

***

Once again, Kate awoke to a bright light above her, machines beeping and hissing on each side of the bed. As she blinked her eyes, she felt the squeeze of her hand.

"Thank God you're awake. I've been going crazy here."

Kate turned to see Aaron by her bedside. The look on his face sent a panic through her.

"The baby—"

"is fine," he completed the sentence. "It's you that we're all worried about. Your mom and dad went to get coffee, and Zach has called a million times. He's still stateside. Everyone is worried about you."

"What happened?"

"You tell me. You got home from seeing Dr. Sprance, who by the way said that you were fine and healthy when you left the office, and you almost collapsed getting out of the car. Your father was watching from inside the house and made it to you just in time to catch you as you fell to the driveway. Lucky for you, your mother was a nervous wreck about you going alone and had him standing guard at the front window. What were you thinking? Your mother would have gone. I would have gone."

Memories came flooding back to her: the sonogram, seeing the baby, the nurse, Mary, handing her a picture of her baby girl, the call to Mark. Kate closed her eyes and lifted her arm to her face, laying it across her forehead.

"Oh God, I called him."

"Who?"

"Mark. I called him when I left the office." She moaned and tried to take a deep breath, but her chest still hurt. She winced in pain.

"I'm going to get a nurse," Aaron said, letting go of her other hand and racing from the room.

What have I done? The thought came over and over again. Kate berated herself for not waiting until she was home, for not giving herself time to prepare. For ever listening to Father Darryl to begin with.

"Well, good evening, Kate. Remember me?"

"Nurse Lloyd, I do remember you." She gave the nurse a weak smile.

"Just call me Michelle. How are you feeling?" Michelle checked Kate's vitals and increased the flow of the IV tube that was connected to her arm.

"Weak, tired, out of breath."

"That's normal. Dr. Sprance will be in soon. Do you need anything? You missed dinner. Are you hungry?"

Was she? She should be, but her thoughts were all jumbled, and she couldn't concentrate on anything, not even the signals her own body was sending her.

"I think so. I haven't eaten in a while. She's probably hungry." Kate laid her hand on her stomach and rubbed it gently as she thought about the news that she had a daughter. "I'm having a girl," Kate lazily smiled.

"I heard. I'll get you something to help with the pain and something to eat. Hang tight."

Mitzi and Walter rushed into the room as Michelle was leaving. Mitzi wrapped Kate in a hug.

"Oh darling, why didn't you let me go with you? Why didn't you at least call for someone to come get you and bring you home?"

"I'm so sorry. I thought I would be okay. I won't do it again."

"No you won't. This just proves that you can't be left alone. Why not come to Florida with us for the next few months?"

"No, I can't do that." Kate looked at her mother with distress.

"Why not?"

"I just can't. Dr. Sprance knows my case, knows what I need. I can't leave and just start over with someone else. I'll have Aaron and Kayla and Anne. They'll help me."

"Kate, dear, Aaron has a job, an important one. And Kayla and Anne have children, families to take care of. They can't worry about you, too."

Was her mother right? Was she placing too much responsibility on her friends?

"I can be there."

They turned to see Zach in the doorway.

"Zach, what are you doing here? How? What's going on?" Kate was confused. Was she dreaming? She looked back and forth from one parent to the other, but they both seemed as shocked as she was to see Zach.

"There's a helicopter pad on the roof. I had someone bring me as soon as I got word. I'm not leaving. I'll have to make a few calls, maybe compromise some on my discharge date, but I'll work it out."

"Are you sure?" Kate asked. She hated putting her brother in this situation. As much as she wanted him out of the military, and as much as he talked about getting out, she knew that this would not look good for him or his record. "Are you AWOL, or whatever they call it?"

"Not quite," Zach told her. "I was being briefed. I can't tell you where, but I was still in the States." He crossed the room and stood by her bed. "Look, I can't tell you much, but I'm kind of important to the Army. They've depended upon me for a long time, and as far as I see it, and my Sergeant First Class agrees, they owe me. Hell, a lot of people owe me." He took a deep breath and exhaled through his cheeks. "I've been in for a long time, and I've done my job well. Very well." He looked at Kate and held her gaze. He emphasized his next set of words. "But I'm not my job. I've done it a lot longer than other men in my position, and it's time to get out. Period."

"Zach, how are you going to get permission to just leave?" Walter placed his arm on his son's bicep and turned the younger man to face him.

"I'll apply for a Chapter Six," he said as he sat in the chair by the bed. "I might need Dr. Sprance's help to get the proper paperwork, but if we can prove that you need around the clock medical help, and that I'm the only person who can provide it, then I should be okay. It should help that I'm due to be discharged soon. They won't like that it comes on the heels of a month of emergency leave, but I'll deal with that."

"Son," Walter asked, "is this what you really want to do? I know how much being a soldier means to you."

They all knew that it pained Walter to even ask the question. It took a long time for him to accept that Zach wanted to go enlist after college and an even longer time for him to accept that Zach re-upped after his first term. Their father was a pacifist, and though he was very proud of his son, he had seen the devastation of war throughout the world and wished that his son had no part in that kind of destruction.

"It is, Dad. Kate needs me, and I need a change. It's a temporary fix. Eventually, I'll need to find my own place and get a job, but in the meantime, I can be there to help. I have a feeling that I won't be the only man coming to her rescue, but she's my sister, and I should be the one on the front line."

A knock on the door was followed by Dr. Sprance's entrance into the room. "Well, how's the patient?"

"Okay, I guess. But you tell me." Kate looked at the doctor and hoped for good news.

"Everything is fine." Everyone breathed a sigh of relief. "However, I'm going to prescribe bed rest for you, Kate. No more reporting on events, driving yourself to appointments, or cooking meals for dozens of people."

"They told?" She looked from one family member to another.

"You weren't totally honest with me this morning. You haven't exactly been resting and taking care of yourself."

"I haven't been running every day or working out or even working a full-time job. It's not like I've been exerting myself."

"No, but you haven't been taking it easy either. Kate, let me explain something." He propped himself on the edge of her bed. "If your heart condition worsens, if you are no longer able to breathe and live a normal life while pregnant, then we will need to perform surgery."

Her eyes opened wide in alarm. "While I'm pregnant?"

"Yes, Kate, while you're pregnant. And while the mortality rate for babies of mothers in your condition has gone down significantly in recent years, surgery does complicate that. We can't guarantee that your baby would survive or that she would be born without problems."

"What if Kate doesn't have any more issues and the heart remains stable?" Mitzi asked.

"Then we hope and pray that she carries the baby to term and that her symptoms retreat post-partum."

"That can happen?" Kate asked. "I can go back to being normal?"

"For the most part, yes. You'll still need to be monitored and might not be able to run quite as long or as hard, but you should be able to live a full, normal life."

"Then bed rest it is. Whatever you say, Doc, I'm on board."

"Okay then. I'd like to examine you one more time before I leave for the night, and we're going to keep you overnight for observation, but you should be able to go home tomorrow."

Kate's family cleared the room so that Dr. Sprance could examine her. When he was finished, Kate brought up her brother's idea.

"A Chapter Six, huh? We might be able to make that work."

"Really? To be honest, I don't even know what that means, but if you can make it work, I would be ever so grateful."

"I was an Army doctor in my early years, before I decided to re-train and specialize in at-risk pregnancies. I might have the connections we need to get this rolling."

Kate breathed a sigh of relief, thanked the doctor, and tried to get herself comfortable as she watched him leave. She remembered what Father Darryl said about miracles and hoped that she wasn't pushing it with the man upstairs. Was there a limit on how many miracles one person could obtain? So far, Kate was receiving more than her fair share, and she was still praying for more.

***

"You look terrible," Kate said when Zach arrived the next morning.

"I was up most of the night making and accepting calls. Nothing moves easily or quickly with the military unless someone important thinks it's worth it. Lucky for you, my CO's wife almost lost their first child. He bent over backyard to rubber stamp my request."

"Wait, you mean that's it? You're out?" She sat in bed and looked at her brother.

"Not quite. There's the administrative overview bull, and the red tape, and the discharge papers, but I'm good to stay while it's happening."

"Are you serious? Nothing in this world moves that fast."

"Okay, confession time." Zach leaned closer and whispered. "I actually started the process the first week I was home."

"What? Why didn't you tell us? What was with the big goodbye and all of the tears?"

"I hadn't heard anything yet. I had to report for duty, go to my briefings, attend a bunch of bull crap meetings and hearings. I wasn't sure how long it would take or even if it would go through. Honestly, I don't think it would have gone through at all if you hadn't pulled that little stunt and landed yourself back in here. That gave them the impetus to push it forward expediently." He grinned at his sister who could do nothing but sit up and stare incredulously at her brother.

"Oh my gosh. I can't believe it. So, you're moving in?"

"I guess so."

"It's done?" Mitzi asked from the doorway.

"It's done," Zach affirmed as he rose from his seat by Kate's bed.

"Oh, Zach, I'm so happy for you. For both of you. This is a gift from Heaven."

In her mind, Kate saw the miracle ticker go up another number and said a silent prayer that her quota hadn't reached its limit.

"So I hear we have a caregiver?" Dr. Sprance said as he walked into the room.

"Yes, Sir. We do indeed." Zach shook the doctor's hand. "Thank you for faxing all of that paperwork last night. It sealed the deal."

"I must say, I've never seen anything with the U.S. Government or Military move so fast."

"It appears that Zach has been working on this for much longer than he indicated," Kate told them.

"Then I give Zach a lot of credit for his foresight. Now, let's see how you're doing this morning so we can get you home. Zach, you may need to start your new deployment right away."

"Nothing would make me happier, Sir."

"We'll be right outside, Dr. Sprance." Mitzi shooed them out of the room so that Kate could be examined.

After several minutes, Dr. Sprance opened the door. He smiled at Kate's family as he placed his glasses in his coat pocket. "She's all yours, Zach. Take good care of her, and have her call the office tomorrow to set up a follow up for two weeks. I know it's a busy time, but I'd like to start seeing her more frequently to keep an eye on things."

"Yes, Sir. We'll see you in two weeks." The men shook hands again.

Mitzi and Walter thanked the doctor for all that he had done and then went to get Kate ready to leave. Zach saw a familiar face coming toward him in the hallway and reached out his hand.

"All set, Commander."

"That's great, Zach. I'm relieved to say the least. I want you to know that I would have done it. I would have taken care of her."

"Hey, no need to say anything. I know that. You've got a job you love, and I was ready for a change. It's all good."

"I hope you don't mind if I'm around a lot."

"I wouldn't have it any other way."

"Thanks, man. She means a lot to me."

"She means a lot to me, too. Don't you forget it."

"You've got nothing to worry about."

"Except," Zach offered.

Aaron looked at Kate's brother and frowned.

"The baby. Look, I know you love my sister. That's obvious, even if you haven't said the words. And that's great. But the baby is someone else's. How are you going to deal with that?"

Aaron nodded and pursed his lips. "Zach, I'm not going to lie to you. I think I've been in love with your sister since the first day I laid eyes on her. I teased her and flirted with her and did everything in my power to get her to notice me. When she finally did, I figured everything would just fall into place." He took a deep breath and blew out the air to the side before turning back to Zach. "When she told me about the baby, I was pissed. I was ready to take her home, dump her on the sidewalk, and walk away. But I couldn't do it. Then after she told me the story, I knew that there was a reason all of this happened. A reason she ended up here."

Aaron walked away and went to the window that looked out across the parking lot. Zach joined him and gazed out beyond the lot to the busy streets and hustle and bustle of the morning.

"Do you believe in God? I mean, really truly believe?" Aaron asked Zach as they looked outside.

"I do. It's hard to understand why things happen the way they do. Why men do the things they do, but I had this chaplain back in Afghanistan. The two of us would sometimes sit up all night talking about God and His plan for us. I've seen a lot of horrible things, and I've had to do some pretty ugly things myself, but somehow, I know that He still has a plan for me. I just have to figure out what it is."

"I think you're right, Zach." Aaron turned back toward the other man. "And I think that His plan for me is to take care of Kate and that baby. She was lost when she first came to the island. But now she has a whole group of people who love her, she has found peace, and she has found God."

"And she found you."

"Yeah," Aaron shook his head. "She sure did. And I didn't even know that I was lost."

***

The second set of goodbyes was easier than the first. Kate knew that her parents were a phone call away, but she was going to miss her mother terribly. They talked about coming back at Christmas, but Kate told them it might be hard on her, feeling like she had to entertain them. Her mother protested, but her father agreed.

"Let's let Kate and Zach get settled and get into a routine. Having us back so soon would complicate that. We'll Skype each other, and we'll be back when the baby comes."

"But that's so far away," Mitzi cried.

"Mom, if I need you to come back, I won't hesitate to call. It's okay. I'm going to be fine. It's not like we've never been apart for Christmas."

"That's true, but things have changed. We've changed." Mitzi looked around at her family. "We've all changed."

"We have, Mom, and next Christmas there will be even more change," Zach said. "And a little one to celebrate with."

The group finally said goodbye, and Zach took his parents to the airport while Aaron drove Kate home. He reached across the seat of the truck and took her hand in his.

"How are you doing?"

"I'm okay. It's going to be quiet with them gone, but I think I need quiet." She put her head back and closed her eyes.

"You've given me a couple of heart attacks myself, you know that?"

Opening her eyes, she turned toward him and grinned. "Sorry about that. I promise to do better."

They came to a stoplight, and Aaron turned toward Kate. "I don't want to lose you. Got that, Princess?"

"I've got it, Aaron. I feel the same way."

"Good. As long as we've got that settled." He smiled and turned back to the road.

Kate kept her gaze on Aaron as he drove. *How did I get so lucky? After all my screw-ups, how did I end up here, with him?*

She squeezed his hand, closed her eyes, and drifted off to sleep, secure in the knowledge that she was safe and loved.

***

"The new Alexa Jacobs novel," Kate squealed. "How did you know I wanted this?"

"I remembered you telling me that she's one of your favorite local authors. I looked her up and saw that she had a new book come out. Open it," Kayla prodded.

"To Kate, Best wishes and sweet dreams, Alexa Jacobs."

Kate looked at her friend. "How did you do this?"

Kayla shrugged. "I just emailed her. She's so nice, and she was happy to sign a copy and send it to me."

"Oh, Kayla," Kate reached over and hugged her. "I can't wait to start reading. I've read everything in sight. And I've watched every show on television, and every show on Netflix, and every movie. Oh my gosh, I'm so bored!"

"I figured. That's why I decided not to wait until Christmas to give it to you."

"You are, without a doubt, the best friend I've ever had. And now look, I'm crying again."

Kayla laughed. "No surprise there."

"Jeez, is she crying again?" Zach put the car keys down on the table as he came in the door carrying a load of groceries.

"I'm sorry. I can't help it."

"Everything makes her cry. Especially my cooking."

"Your cooking doesn't make me cry. It makes me gag."

"Then let us bring dinner to you tonight," Kayla suggested.

"What? I just got back from the store. Don't tell me I went grocery shopping for nothing."

"It will keep. I'm testing out a new recipe, and I'd love for you to try it out."

"Are you sure you have enough for everyone?" Kate asked hesitantly.

"If you mean, me, the boys, you two, and Aaron, yes. I always have enough. I have to see how many people the meals truly feed before I can sell them as family meals. I'm opening right after the New Year, you know."

"Then I guess we have to have you cook dinner for us. It's for the business, after all." Zach said as he headed to the kitchen.

"Need help?" Kayla asked.

Kate watched them from the sofa. They chatted as they unpacked the groceries, and Kate saw, once again, how easily they worked together. She asked Zach what he said to Kayla on the day that they thought it was goodbye, and he said that Kayla knew about his plan all along. He was giving her an update and letting her know that he hoped to be back soon. In the meantime, he wanted her to keep an eye on Kate. It wasn't the romantic goodbye that she had pictured, but he was here now, so there was still a chance for something to spark between them. How could they not see how perfectly they fit together?

Once the groceries were put away, Kayla headed home to begin cooking dinner. Kate didn't say anything to Zach. She knew he was just beginning to find himself again, so she was willing to give him the time and space to do it. She just wanted him to be happy, and she was sure that Kayla was the key to making that happen.

"Hey, Sis, did Mom call you?" Zach asked once Kayla left.

"No, why? Is everything all right?"

"Yeah, but your security alarm went off last night."

"In DC? Did they send someone to check it out?"

"Yeah. Mrs. Iverson next door heard it and called the police. She didn't know how to find you, so she called Dad. There wasn't any sign of breaking and entering, so they just did a cursory check before having the company re-set the alarm."

"Huh. Maybe a squirrel in the attic? It wouldn't be the first time."

"Maybe. I desperately need clothes, so I thought I'd go up there tomorrow and get some of my stuff from the attic. I'll check it out. Is there anything you want?"

Kate's eyes lit up. "There is. Actually, there are few things I'd like you to bring, but one thing in particular. I'll make a list, but first, I have to call Dad."

"Just let me know. I'm going to shower before Kayla and the boys get here."

"Will do," she said as she reached for her phone. "Hi Dad, I have a huge favor to ask. You know your special collection of first editions? I'd like to know if I can have one."

***

Zach didn't see anything out of the ordinary when he arrived at the house in Georgetown. The alarm had been re-set, and the house was locked up tight. Zach looked around at the mess that his sister had left behind. She told him that she hadn't been up to cleaning those last few weeks before she left, but she assured him that she had tidied the house before heading to Chincoteague. If this was her idea of tidying up, Aaron was in for a rude awakening if they ever got married.

The dishes were all clean and put away, and all the sheets and towels had been washed and stored in the linen closets. Thankfully, she hadn't left any trash behind and had been cognizant enough to clean out the fridge. What amazed Zach was the state of the living room, the library, and his sister's room, once their parents' master bedroom.

Zach stood in the doorway and looked at the room. The bedspread was a mess, revealing the absence of sheets, and the pillows were strewn around the room. The closet doors stood open, and clothes were haphazardly lying in piles on the floor. Kate's dresser was a mess, the drawers pulled open, undergarments and t-shirts hanging out without care. Kate's makeup and jewelry that she hadn't taken with her covered the top of the dresser as if someone had…

The hair stood on the back of Zach's neck. His senses heightened, and the instincts that he had perfected over the past thirteen years took over. Zach inspected the room with a different perspective. The pillows and bedspread looked more like they'd been ransacked than causally left undone. Zach turned to the clothes by the closet. On closer inspection, they weren't just random clothes. They were dresses, very nice ones, that would have been worn on dates and special occasions. He turned toward the dresser and looked at the undergarments. Instead of underwear and bras, these were sexy pieces like those exhibited by Victoria's Secret models. He cringed when he thought of his little sister wearing them. The drawer on the nightstand stood open, its contents dumped on the floor beneath it.

Zach took his phone from his pocket as he made his way down the hall to the library. He dialed 911 and relayed his circumstances and address to the dispatcher while he searched for the book his sister requested. Thankfully, it was still on the shelf. It hadn't been thrown on the floor in what looked like an attempt to find something, or someone.

Kate answered the phone on the third ring, and Zach hoped that the officers wouldn't be blasting their sirens when they arrived. His sister had enough to worry about.

"Hey, Zach. What's up?"

"Hey, I'm at the house. I found the book you wanted."

"Is everything okay there?"

Zach looked around at the books lying on the floor and then turned toward the living room where pillows and afghans were tossed about, and books and magazines littered the coffee table and area rug.

"Everything's fine. Hey listen, I got a call from an old army buddy who now lives in Salisbury. He wants to get together. I might not be home until late. Will you be okay?"

"No problem," she answered. Zach heard the lift of her voice. "I'm really glad you're meeting up with a friend. Have fun."

He knew that Kate had been worried about him, and her cheerful tone made him feel less guilty about lying to her.

"Thanks, Sis. Have a good evening."

"You, too, Zach. Be careful driving home."

"Roger," he said as he pushed the end button. He watched through the windows as red and blue lights reflected off the glass.

***

"What are you and Zach doing for Christmas?" Aaron and Kate were alone for the evening. Kate was tremendously happy that her brother was spending the evening with an old friend. He needed to have his own life apart from taking care of her. She and Aaron had just finished watching a movie and were snuggling on the couch. As much as they could with Kate's five-month-along belly taking up more room than either of them. Aaron had his legs stretched sideways over a pillow on the coffee table, and Kate used the back of the couch to support her back and laid her head on Aaron's chest.

"We haven't really talked about it. We're planning to go to Mass on Christmas Eve and then have dinner. Zach's becoming quite the cook." She smiled a she pictured her macho brother leaning over the stove.

"Mom thought you could join us if it's not too much for you."

Her lips curled up, and she snuggled closer to him. "I'd love that. I'm sure Zach would, too. It means he won't have to worry about grocery shopping."

"I'll let her know."

They were silent for a few minutes, and then Kate felt a familiar movement. She took his hand and, lifting her shirt, laid it on her belly. She placed her own hand on top of his and pressed down until she heard and felt him suck in his breath.

"That's her," he said quietly. "She's moving."

"Yeah, she moves a lot these days."

Aaron kept his hand on her stomach for several minutes. When the baby moved, he moved with her. The gentle caress she felt as his hand moved over her belly stirred a multitude of emotions within Kate. She couldn't ever remember a time when she felt so content. She tilted up her head and looked at Aaron. Awe. That was the best way to describe what she saw on his face. He looked down at Kate, and she saw another emotion. Her eyes began to fill with tears.

Sliding his hand from her belly to her back, Aaron turned Kate and eased her up a little higher.

"You are the most amazing woman I have ever known," he whispered to her.

"You're pretty amazing yourself," she whispered back and grinned up at him.

"I don't think I've ever really told you how special you are. I've known it since the first night I saw you, at the—"

"Boy Scout ceremony," they said in unison and chuckled.

Aaron placed a light kiss on her forehead and then looked at her. He kissed her beside her eye and looked in her eyes again before moving down to her cheek, and finally to her mouth. The kiss was soft and chaste, but the longer it lasted, the more heat it created. They moved their hands along each other's backs and curled toward each other. He kissed her chin, across her neck, and worked his way back up to her mouth. When he moved back to her neck, she groaned, and he pulled back.

"You are so sexy, Princess," he whispered to her.

A sly smile spread across her face. "All one hundred and fifty pounds of me?"

In a flash, he pulled her under him and raised himself above her in a push up, his arms extended, holding him above her belly.

"All one hundred and fifty beautiful pounds of you. Kate," he hesitated and then pushed himself up and away from her, easing the coffee table away and kneeling on the floor beside her. She pushed herself up onto her elbows. "Kate, I've been alone for a long time. I mean, I have Kay and our parents, and all my friends, well, now our friends, but I've been on my own since I was eighteen. I haven't even dated in years. I wasn't in a good place, and I needed space, time on my own. In fact, I wasn't sure I'd ever want anyone else in my life, and then I found you. Or you found me. Either way, you're all I've wanted for months now. Okay, that's not true." He put his hand back under her shirt and lifted the hem away so that her belly was exposed. Leaning over, he kissed her soft, smooth skin. Butterflies danced in her stomach along with the little girl who squirmed inside of her. "For a while now, all I've wanted is the two of you." He looked up into her eyes. "I love you, Kate. With all my heart, my soul, my being. I love you."

Kate had known for a while that she was indeed falling in love with Aaron. She had fought the feelings at first, and then she wasn't sure she trusted them. But once she gave into it, began following her heart, she knew that she would never again feel for anyone what she felt for Aaron.

"I love you, too, Aaron. I have for a while."

He leaned over her, placed his hands behind her head, and pressed his mouth to hers. He took her for his own, pouring all his feelings into his kiss, and she did the same. When he pulled away from her, they were both breathing heavily, and Kate yearned for more.

"I'm supposed to be taking care of you while your brother is out."

"You're doing a good job of it."

"Not like this. We're going to do this right. You were cheated out of the real deal, and I'm not going to do that to you. Besides, my heart is doing flip flops right now, so I don't even want to think about yours is doing."

"Ugh," she cried as she collapsed back onto the couch. "Darn heart. It's always getting in the way."

"But it led you to me," Aaron said. "So it's perfect as far as I can see. Now, let's get you to bed."

"Whoa, boy, those are some mixed signals there."

"Very funny. Your brother will be back soon, and I know what he did in the Army. I'm getting you to bed so that you can sleep."

"You're just a tease," she said as she sat up.

"But you've known that since the beginning, Princess." And he winked at her as he helped her up off the couch.

***

Instead of the vigil Mass, the entire Kelly family, along with Kate and Zach, attended Midnight Mass. Kate took a nap earlier in the day so she could stay up, and she was so grateful that she had. The Mass was said by candlelight, and the church glowed with a flickering luminescence that gave off a magical aura. Kate sat between Zach and Aaron holding each of their hands at different points of the Mass. She felt as if her entire being was overflowing with joy.

After Mass, Father Darryl told Kate that she looked fabulous and asked how she was feeling.

"Better than ever, Father. Thanks to you and your advice. I'm a free woman, no longer bound by guilt or lies of omission."

"I'm very proud of you, Kate, and very happy for you. It looks like you've finally figured out who you are and where you belong."

"I have, Father. Thank you."

"And Zach, how are you doing on this beautiful Christmas morning?"

"I have to say, I agree with Kate. Better than ever."

"Monday afternoon?" Father asked him.

"Yes, Sir," Zach responded. Kate eyed her brother, but he looked away as if he didn't notice. She elbowed him as they walked away, but he shrugged and kept walking.

The next morning, Kate and Zach returned to the Kelly home for a mid-morning brunch. After a hasty cleanup of the dishes, they took their dessert to the family room where they began handing out presents. As they sat and ate their pumpkin pie, they watched Aaron and Zach make piles of each person's gifts.

When it was time to start opening, Kate and Zach were told that there was a tradition to be followed, the youngest to the oldest opened one gift at a time. Kate had a feeling they might be up all night, but she looked forward to the fun.

"I'm first," yelled Todd as he dove into his pile searching for the perfect gift to open first.

"How does he have so much energy after being up so late?" Kate whispered to Aaron.

"It's a gift. I'm ready for a nap."

"By the looks of this place, that's not going to happen any time soon."

"Bet? We'll be done by 2:00 tops?"

Kate raised a brow but didn't argue. She was anxious to get a look at whatever Todd was whooping and hollering about.

"It's the new Spiderman Lego set. I wanted this more than anything."

"Ten bucks says he says that about every gift he opens," Aaron leaned over and whispered.

"Kate, honey, why don't you sit on the couch instead of the floor?" Ronnie called across the room.

"Thanks, but I'm fine. I just might not be able to get back up again."

They watched as EJ opened a new baseball glove.

"Wow, this is a real nice glove, Zach."

Kate looked at Zach with wide eyes. Her brother had dutifully bought every present on the list she gave him, and she spent a lot of her time in bed perfectly wrapping each gift. Zach never once mentioned that he had done his own shopping for everyone.

"Yeah, I'll teach you some fancy plays once the weather warms up. You'll be the envy of every kid in town."

"Who's next?" Todd asked as he looked around the room.

"I think that would be Kate," Aaron said, reaching into her pile to hand her a gift.

"Really? I haven't felt this young in a long time." She took the box and opened it. Inside was a beautiful gold and sterling silver crucifix on a chain. "Oh, Ronnie, I love it. Thank you."

"You're welcome, honey."

Aaron helped her put it on, and she held it out in front of her to see it.

"I have no idea who's next," Aaron said, looking at Zach.

"It's not me, buddy. I wish I could say you've got a foot in the grave ahead of me, but no such luck."

"Then I guess it's Aaron," said Kayla. "By six whole minutes."

Aaron chose the smallest box in his stack and read the note from his father. Tears came to his eyes before he even touched the wrapping.

"What?" Kate prodded.

"It says, 'Dear Aaron, I've waited a long time to see this day. These are yours. Wear them well. Love, Dad.'" He looked up at his father. "Are these?"

"Open them," said Ronnie.

Inside the box was a pair of gold cufflinks with the Coast Guard insignia on them.

"They were my grandfather's," Aaron told Kate.

"Regulation, too. I expect to see them on your uniform on the next special occasion."

"You can bet on it, Dad. Thanks."

Next was Kayla, who received a cashmere scarf from Kate. "I thought the green would go well with your eyes." Zach rolled his eyes as he was the one who picked them out, remarking to Kate that the color would bring out the tiny flecks of green in Kayla's hazel eyes.

"I love it, Kate. Thank you," she said as she wrapped the scarf around her shoulders.

"Zach, your turn," Kayla said as she handed him a box.

Zach's eyes widened as he opened the handcrafted chess set. "I hear you were once quite the player. I thought maybe we could teach the boys to play."

"Kayla, this is magnificent. It's too nice to play on."

"Nonsense, life is too short to not play chess with a handmade chess set."

Zach smiled at Kayla and nodded. It was the first time Kate had ever seen him at a total loss for words.

Ronnie was next, and she oohed and ahhed over the embroidered jacket from Trevor. Then Trevor opened his present, a handmade birdhouse from EJ.

"Zach helped me finish it. It's so you can watch those birds you always like looking for. Now they can come live in your own backyard."

"Thanks, EJ. I'll put it up as soon as I get some birdseed."

"Then you should open my present next, Granddad," Todd told him. Everyone laughed, and the fun continued for several more rounds.

On Kate's final turn, she looked at the pile but saw nothing more to open. "I guess I'm out," she said.

"Not quite," Aaron told her as he shifted to one knee. A hush came over the room as he pulled a box from his pocket. "Katherine Rebecca Middleton, Princess," he grinned. "We've only known each other for three months, but I have never been as happy, or as scared, as I have been since meeting you. You are my world, and though it's soon, I know that it's right. And honestly, you don't have a lot of time left to give this little girl a daddy." He chuckled, and Kate's heart skipped a beat. "So, I've spoken to both your father and your brother, and it would make me the happiest man in the world if you would do me the honor of allowing me to be your husband and the father of your child."

"Aaron Noah Kelly, I would be honored," Kate said through a river of tears.

Shouts went up around the room as Aaron placed the ring on her finger and hugged her.

Next to her engagement ring, Kate's favorite present was another gift from Ronnie. It was the painting of sunset in the cove that she had admired at the art festival. The two teary-eyed women hugged as Kate thanked Ronnie profusely for the painting and for welcoming her and the baby into their family with open arms.

The last two presents given, before EJ and Todd finished opening their mounds of gifts, were Kate's to Aaron and Zach's to Kayla.

"Kate, this is beautiful," Aaron said as he gently held the first edition, *Moby Dick*, in his hands. "Where did you find it?"

"I got it from a collector," she told him, casting a glance toward her brother who nodded in agreement. "Every seaman should have a special copy of Melville's classic, if for nothing else, to read his descriptions of the sea."

A gold bracelet with a heart dangling from it was Zach's gift to Kayla. "You didn't have to get me anything," she said, blushing as he placed it on her wrist.

"I know I didn't, but I wanted to. You deserve some happiness, too."

By the time the boys finished opening their gifts, eyelids were drooping all around the room. Despite it being just after 1:00, the late night combined with the excitement of Christmas morning were taking their toll.

"I think it's time for a nap," Kayla said, and the boys protested for the first time in Kate's presence. But their protests were sleepy ones, and it didn't take much for Kayla to scoot them down the hall.

"We'd better head out," Aaron told his parents. "I'm sure Kate is exhausted."

"I can't argue with that," Kate agreed though she would have been perfectly happy staying and enjoying the family time. However, she could hear Dr. Sprance's disapproving voice in the back of her head and knew that she needed to go home and rest.

Kisses and hugs were quickly exchanged as each person headed to bed, the couch, or their vehicles. After helping her into the Mustang, Aaron gently caressed Kate's cheek.

"I'll see you later, Princess," he said before kissing her, a soft, loving kiss full of hope and promise.

“Do I get a goodbye kiss, too,” Zach cooed from the driver’s seat.

“If you insist,” Aaron said with a wink. Kate laughed and pushed him out of the doorway.

“See you tomorrow,” she said as she closed the door.

Aaron watched the car drive away before heading to his truck. He couldn’t ever remember a better Christmas.

In many Indigenous cultures, a man was prohibited from taking a woman for his wife until he proved that he could protect her. At times, this meant that two men, both vying for her love, would be forced to face each other in a series of physical competitions. In some societies, the betrothed male underwent tests of endurance to prove that he would be capable of providing for and protecting his future wife.

From the *Studies of Indigenous Peoples*
by Walter Middleton

CHAPTER FOURTEEN

New Year's Day brought the promise of snow to the island. Though accumulation was normally low in this part of the Mid-Atlantic, Kate was ready to see a blanket of white.

"I keep telling you not to get your hopes up," Aaron told her as they left Mass that morning.

"But it's freezing, and the weather map shows snow."

"And we're on the ocean. It's a whole different climate than you're used to in DC."

As if Mother Nature was listening to their conversation, a light snow began to fall.

"See? I knew it would snow," Kate triumphantly turned to Aaron with a smirk on her face.

"It's snowing, but don't expect it to amount to much."

Several hours later, when the precipitation subsided, there were two inches of white powder on the ground. It wasn't a major snowfall, but Kate was satisfied.

"All I wanted was to see the yard covered with snow. I got my wish."

"I'm glad you're happy Princess. Now put on your coat and boots. I've got a surprise for you."

"You're not taking her out in this frigid weather are you," Zach asked in concern.

"I sure am. We won't be long, and she'll be safe. I can assure you. I won't let anything happen to her."

Zach backed off, but Kate could tell that he was uneasy about her going. She had already been to Mass that morning, and she knew that she didn't need to be going out again, but Aaron would be there, and he wouldn't let her do anything she shouldn't.

Aaron refused to tell Kate where they were going, but she immediately recognized the route.

"Why are we going to your Mom's?"

"We're not. Just be patient."

She watched as he bypassed the road to his parents' house and continued down toward the cove.

"Aaron, there is no way I'm getting into a kayak or even walking on the dock. Are you out of your mind?"

"Give me some credit, Princess. Just wait."

As they pulled up to the dock, Kate saw the most beautiful site, perhaps even more beautiful than the sunset she witnessed the first night they came to the cove.

Twilight had arrived, and the sky and water were once again bathed in color. The sky glowed bright orange, and a paler shade covered the water where the light had melted the snow. Along the edges of the sound, snow lay in soft drifts, and in a long line across the center of the frozen water, before it headed out into the Bay, a gaggle of geese stood on the ice. It was like a painting, and she could envision Ronnie, standing in this spot, creating a masterpiece.

"It's breathtaking," Kate whispered, unwilling to mar the tranquility of the scene.

"It sure is," Aaron whispered. Kate turned to him and realized he wasn't looking out the window but at her. Simultaneously, they reached for each other. Their kisses were long and slow, not rushed, not heated. They were the kisses of two people who knew that they had all the time in the world to be together.

"There's more," Aaron said when they broke apart.

"What could be better than this?"

"You'll see," he said as he put the car in reverse and made a three-point turn to head back down the road.

They once again passed by his parent's lane and continued back out to the main road until they turned onto another familiar road.

"Your house?"

"Yep. I've got something to show you."

Kate watched as they drove up to the modest house, wrapped with a white deck, that Aaron called home. Since the afternoon of the crab feast, she had been there on a couple of occasions, but not for any length of time. Once, when she had forgotten a sweatshirt and they ran by to grab one of his, and another time when he had her over for Chinese take-out. They spent most of their time at Kate's house since her family was there for so long, and Kayla was right next door, where Aaron was accustomed to hanging out. Kate looked forward to spending time in his secluded little house once they were married.

Opening the door for her, Aaron helped Kate out of the truck and up the path to the front porch. He pushed open the unlocked door and led her inside. Without a word, he held her hand as they ascended the stairs to the second floor where Aaron slept in one room, and his home office occupied the other.

When Aaron gently pushed open the door to the office, Kate gasped.

"I knew that you wanted it to be a girl's room but not too girly."

"Aaron, it's beautiful."

Kate slowly walked across the hardwood floor taking in the décor. The walls were a light shade of turquoise, and a bright pink rug lay on the polished floor in front of the white crib. A pink and turquoise chair sat in the corner. A small, crystal chandelier hung from the ceiling, and above the crib, was painted the verse from the book of Jeremiah, "Before I formed you in the womb I knew you."

"I didn't buy the linens or put up pictures or anything because I wanted to save those things for you. I hope you don't mind that I did this much without you."

"Aaron, how could I mind?" She ran her fingers along the railing of the crib before turning toward him. "It's perfect and certainly not something I could have done in my condition. But when did you find the time?"

"I've been working on it here and there. And I had some help." He put his hand on the crib. "Zach helped me bring it up one of the nights that Kay was keeping you company. It was mine." He nodded at the verse. "And Mom helped, of course. Do you like it?"

"Like it? I love it." She wiped a tear from her cheek and wrapped her arms around him. "And I love you, Aaron Kelly. More than you will ever know."

"I love you, Princess," he said before kissing her.

Before leaving, Kate took pictures of the room on her phone so that she could show her parents. She was looking forward to going online and finding the perfect finishing touches for the room. As she stood on the porch waiting for Aaron to make sure the lights were all off, Kate peered at the woods surrounding the house and shuddered. Aaron came up behind her, wrapped his arms around her, and nuzzled her neck.

"What's wrong," he asked, always able to sense her mood.

"Nothing, I guess." She tried to dismiss the eerie feeling that crept up her spine as she looked around. "I'm just not used to being in the woods. It's kind of spooky, like someone's watching us."

Aaron looked up and surveyed the area. "It's just your imagination. We're not close enough to another house for anyone to see us, and the trees block the view from the road."

"I'm sure you're right." She shook her head as another chill ran across the back the back of her neck.

"You're freezing," Aaron said, running his hands up and down her arms. "Let's get home and settled in by the fire. That will make you feel better."

Kate hoped he was right. She examined the woods as they drove away, unable to shake the sensation of being watched.

***

January was cold, and Kate spent little time away from the couch near the fireplace. Though Aaron had set up the nursery and was in the process of making room for Kate and her things at his house, Kate remained in the beach house with Zach. She was going to do things right this time and that included not moving in with Aaron until they were married. In the meantime, she was enjoying every minute she had with Zach.

The lease on the house was up at the end of February, and Zach was considering purchasing the house. It was more house than he needed, but he told Kate that he hoped to have a family someday, and the four bedrooms would come in handy. Kate suspected that its proximity to Kayla's house also played into his decision. Making minor repairs around the house and thinking about things he might want to change, kept Zach from getting bored.

There was no boredom for Kate either. She spent hours online, looking for baby clothes, toys, and accessories to fill the beautiful nursery waiting for their baby girl. She ordered frilly dresses, dainty shoes, play clothes, and even a dress that resembled a sailor's outfit, much to Aaron's delight. She was on a first name basis with the UPS guy, Tom, who couldn't help but get caught up in her enthusiasm each time a new package was delivered.

Once everything arrived that Kate ordered for the nursery, she was anxious to finish the room that Aaron had so lovingly created. Zach agreed to drive her over and do the work if she promised to do nothing but sit in the chair and give orders. Kate was fine with that. She was looking forward to sitting in her rocking chair and daydreaming about holding their little girl while her brother did all the work, hanging pictures, filling drawers, and putting together and stocking the changing table.

They arrived at the house to find the door ajar.

"The wind must have pushed it open," Kate said. "Aaron never locks it. I guess he didn't make sure it was latched."

That wasn't like Aaron, and Zach knew it. The man was detail oriented and would never have left the house without making sure the door was completely closed. The hairs on the back of Zach's neck stood. He became hyper-alert as he looked around. The house was completely surrounded by trees, one of the few like it on the Island. And it stood empty most of the time since Aaron worked all day, many weekends, too, and spent almost all his spare time with Kate.

Zach eased the door open all the way.

"Stay here," he commanded his sister.

"But it's cold out here," she protested.

"Then get back in the car." It wasn't a suggestion, and she knew it. Kate went back to the car, keeping her eyes on the house as her brother went inside.

Zach went through the downstairs making sure it was clear. Nothing seemed to be out of place, but he'd only been there once, when he helped Aaron put the antique crib in the nursery. They had gone online to check the crib standards and had to adjust the spindles in the gate, but otherwise, the crib was in perfect condition; and it didn't take long to carry it upstairs and put it in place.

Zach checked the downstairs first. For the second time in just over two months, the first being the day he went to the house in Georgetown, Zach wished he had his rifle. Kate had no idea that he kept one in his closet, but it was a hard habit to break. He needed the security. It didn't stop the nightmares, but he kept it anyway.

Easing up the staircase, Zach held onto the knife he took from the kitchen. Something in the air wasn't right. An odd scent, paint perhaps, mixed with human sweat, the smell of something else. Fear? Rage? The human body gave off many scents that went along with different emotions. Most people never noticed the difference, but he did. He noticed everything, like the crooked picture on the wall outside of the nursery. That was something that Aaron would have seen and fixed before leaving the house.

When Zach arrived at the threshold of the nursery, he stopped in his tracks. His blood ran cold as his instincts proved correct. Over the crib, where the Bible verse was so lovingly scripted by Ronnie's hand, a giant red X obliterated the text. Wet, red lines dribbled down the wall like blood from a wound.

A gasp from behind him had Zach spinning on his heels, the knife in his hand ready to take out the intruder.

Kate stood with tears in her eyes, her hand at her heart. "Oh God, who would do such a thing."

***

The police took the report, snapped some photos, and talked to Aaron, Zach, and Kate in turn about what they knew. Aaron had left at six thirty that morning for work at the Coast Guard station. Zach and Kate had gotten to the house just past ten. Somehow, whoever vandalized the house knew that nobody would be at home. The paint was still wet, so the perpetrator hadn't been long gone with Kate and Zach arrived.

Ronnie, who Aaron had called on his way to the house, held Kate in her arms while she wept. "It's okay, sweetie. I can fix it. It won't take long for Aaron and Zach to have the wall all ready for me. Don't cry."

"But who would do this? Why?"

Zach and Aaron exchanged looks. They had each filled in the responding officers on Kate's background. While neither of them ever had the sense that Mark was dangerous, based on what they knew from Kate, he couldn't be ruled out as a suspect, nor could his wife. Out of range of Kate's hearing, Zach filled the officers in on the break-in back in DC and told them that he suspected that Mark was trying to learn Kate's whereabouts. Upon hearing about Kate's precarious condition, the officers agreed not to question her about her former husband but told the men that they would not rule out needing to speak with her about him in the future. For now, they would check him out and go from there.

Once they had Kate back home and in bed, Zach and Aaron sat at the kitchen table and devised their own plan.

"Doors locked at all times. Got it. I don't operate any other way."

"And you've got ammo?" Aaron asked. Zach nodded.

"She's not going to like knowing that it's here, but it's for her own good," Zach said as he eyed his rifle, now sitting in the corner of the room.

"Do you think it was him?"

"Hell if I know, but I imagine he's pretty pissed. I'm sure it was Mark who broke into the house last month. I'm betting his happy marriage fell apart, and if the wife told his superiors, he may have lost his job, too. Then Kate calls him to give him the good news. It was bound to set off something," Zach surmised.

"I think so, too. We could be barking up the wrong tree entirely, but I'm with you. We'll see what his alibi is, and his wife's. For all we know, she could be the one who snapped and is out for revenge."

"I'd say they're both good possibilities," Zach agreed.

"Do you think Kate suspects him, too?"

"Maybe. She didn't say anything to me. You?"

"No," Aaron said, shaking his head. "And I don't want to ask. She's got enough to worry about right now."

"Agreed. Let's just let this play out for now. She's not going to be alone, that's for sure."

"I've got somebody installing cameras in and around my house," Aaron said. "If it was anybody else but you staying here, I'd board this place up and move her in with me, but I have a feeling you've got things here well covered. And I don't want her to know how bad we think this might be. Let her believe it was vandals and that we're operating as normal."

"Except for old Betsy in the corner."

"Yeah, except for that. Tell her whatever you want about that. Just don't tell her the truth."

"Speaking of the truth," Zach ventured. "How'd you know? About me, I mean? It certainly wasn't Kate who figured it out."

"About you? I didn't, not for sure. But after all the time I spent with your brothers in Bahrain, and then watching you, I had a pretty good inclination."

Zach nodded. "Does it bother you? That I did that kind of work? That I'm living here, with Kate, and next door to your sister?"

"About my sister," Aaron said. "What's the deal with you two?"

"At the present time, there isn't anything between us, but would it bother you if there was?"

"Zach, I've gotten to know you pretty well over the past couple of months, and I've been listening to your sister talk about you since I met her. If I had a problem with you and my sister, I'd have let you know it by now."

Again, Zach nodded. "Thanks, man. I've got a long way to go to recovery, as they say, but it's good to know. Now, about you."

"What about me?" Aaron asked, obviously surprised by this shift in the conversation.

"How'd you end up in Bahrain? And when are you going to tell my sister? She knows, you know, that you're hiding something. She's known for a while and is letting you tell her when you're ready, but I'm ready now. After what happened this morning, I think it's time to lay all of the cards on the table."

Aaron sat back in the chair and looked at Zach. "Mind if I get a cup of coffee?"

"Only if you're going to add a shot of something to it."

"Whiskey work for you?"

"Damn straight it does."

The men let a comfortable silence fall between them while Aaron made them each a cup of strong Colombian coffee and added a shot of Jack. When he sat back down, he was ready to talk.

"I was in command of a cutter. Our main mission was drug interdiction in the Gulf of Mexico. It was routine stuff. We stopped the merchant ships, checked for illegal substances, confiscated what we needed to, *et cetera*." He took a sip of his coffee. "One night, things got a little out of control." He looked Zach square in the eye. "Look, man, this is classified stuff. I lose everything if this comes out. The only reason my parents know is that my father was already a Vice Admiral when it took place. He was informed, and he told my Mom. He wasn't supposed to, but they have no secrets from each other of any kind. I intend to have that with Kate, but I must ask that you understand where I'm coming from. Even Kay only knows the smallest details."

"I got it, Aaron. You have to know that my head is full of classified info that will never be divulged."

Satisfied, Aaron went on. "So back to this night. It was routine except for the fact that the cargo ship was on a route well known to be one used by El Chapo. We had a feeling that the load was going to be big and that they would use any and all means to protect it. I didn't normally board the vessels, but this time was different. It was all hands on deck. We left just a skeleton crew on the cutter and boarded the ship at night, hoping that we were surprising most of the crew. Boy, were we wrong." He took another drink and sighed heavily.

"As soon as they got below decks, my men were surrounded. It was like a scene from a movie. They were under heavy fire, and then before they knew what was happening, two of my men were being held at gunpoint. Everyone was told to lay down their weapons and surrender, or they were going to be killed. You know as well as I do that none of us were going to walk out of there alive. They were going to kill everyone as soon as the weapons were down, and then they were going to kill the ones they were holding captive. It was a no-win situation. Except that they didn't know I was there. All my men were surrounded and had been identified except for me. Call it skill or call it luck. Hell, call it the hand of God. I don't know. I just knew as I looked down from my hiding place above the engine room, I had a clear shot of both men. Aaron, I'm no sniper. Hell, I couldn't ever have imagined that I could do what you did, that I could be that skilled, that calm under pressure, but at that moment, I knew what I had to do. I hadn't made sure the ship was secured before they went down into the hold; therefore, it was my fault that my men had been ambushed. Maybe not in the eyes of anyone else, but in my own. I watched one of my best friends die that night in the firefight because I was too cavalier in thinking that we knew where all their crew was. I knew that I had to take both men out who were holding my guys, and that meant that I had no more than a split second to do it. I lined up the shot, pulled the trigger and never saw the first man fall back before I took aim at the second one. Again, all hell broke loose, but this time, it was our guys who had the upper hand. When we left the ship that night, not one of their men was standing." He stopped and took a long swig of his coffee.

"I take it that the Coast Guard has never confirmed knowledge of this, shall we say, alleged situation."

"What situation? None of it ever took place. There were no witnesses left on their end, and our men did what they needed to do. Rather than create an international ordeal, the ship was burned and sunk into the Gulf. Maybe El Chapo suspected. Hell, maybe the Mexican Government suspected, but the Coast Guard wasn't talking."

"And you ended up with a nice, new appointment in Bahrain, the envy of every Serviceman who ever served in the Middle East."

Aaron shrugged. "I couldn't be promoted or welcomed home as a hero, as the incident never happened, so they did the next best thing. I was given a move via deep selection, an internal decision that resulted in a higher rank and better job without a recorded explanation. After a few years, they let me pick where I wanted to go. From that night on, all I wanted was to be home."

"Did you ever consider getting out?"

"Every day, but this is my life. It's what I do. What my dad did and my grandfather before him. It's in my blood, and I just couldn't walk away."

"What if you were faced with that kind of situation again? The need to kill someone to save a life?"

"Kate's life? I wouldn't hesitate."

Kate sat on the stairs, her heart beating faster than she should have allowed it to. Having heard voices, she had headed down the stairs to see what was going on, but she couldn't bring herself to interrupt the conversation. She held her breath as she listened to Aaron tell his tale. She knew that he would one day share the story with her, but she vowed never to bother him about it again. She trusted him with every fiber of her being, and she would protect him fiercely, just as he had vowed to protect her.

***

Another snowstorm hit the island before the month ended, and the temperatures dropped below twenty degrees. After Aaron repainted the wall, he, Zach, and Ronnie finished the nursery while Kate watched and gave directions. But the cold temperatures, the short drive back and forth, and the stress of the growing baby became too much for her.

"No more," Dr. Sprance told her at what was now her weekly visit to see him. "From now on, bed rest means just that. You're in bed. Period."

"But I haven't actually been doing anything."

"And still, your heart is working overtime. I'm getting concerned, and you're still too early for me to deliver the baby."

"I can't even go to church?"

"Not even to church. I don't want you out of bed except to use the bathroom. And no showers. I want you in bed with your feet elevated. You can sponge off and maybe take a bath once or twice a week."

"Once or twice a week?" Kate groaned in despair.

"She'll do whatever you say," Aaron assured him. "Between Zach and myself, we've got it covered."

"Good. I'm going to hold you to that. Now," Dr. Sprance smiled, his blue eyes dancing in the light. "Do we have a name?"

Kate looked up at Aaron and smiled. "We're close," she said, "but it's such a hard decision. We want something that has to do with the water. I like Lorelei, which means 'luring rock' and comes from a myth about woman who lures men to the sea."

"Yes, but then she kills them," Aaron said. "I'm not sure that's the right name for a baby."

"But it's a strong name, and perhaps she didn't kill the man with whom she finally found love and happiness."

Dr. Sprance laughed. "Keep working on it. I'm sure you'll find the right name."

"Maybe by next week," Kate said as she sat up from the table. She took one last look at the image that was frozen on the screen. "Isn't she beautiful?"

"The second most beautiful female I've ever seen," Aaron said as he leaned over and kissed Kate on the forehead.

After the appointment, Kate waited in a wheelchair by the door while Aaron went to get the car. While she was waiting, her phone vibrated. Megan's number lit up the screen, and Kate wondered why Megan was calling her after all this time.

"Hello?"

"Kate, thank God you answered." Megan sounded upset, and Kate worried that she was in trouble. It was a little early in the day to be drinking, but one never knew with Megan.

"Megan, what's wrong?"

"It's Mark. Has he called you?"

Panic hit Kate like an ocean wave, and she grabbed a nearby directional sign to steady herself.

"Mark? No, he hasn't called. At least I don't think he has. I blocked his number from my phone. Why?"

"He called here, at work, looking for you. I told him that I had no idea where you'd gone. Hell, you didn't tell me you were leaving."

"What did you tell him, Megan?" Kate's legs felt like they were going to buckle under her as Aaron pulled up in his truck. Seeing the look on her face, he jumped from the truck and rushed to her side. Kate held her hand up to silence him.

"I didn't tell him anything. I have no idea where you are. But Kate," Megan hesitated, "he seemed…desperate. He sounded like he'd been drinking, and he used language that I've never even heard my old man use, and that's saying something."

"Megan, when did he call you?"

"I don't know. A few days ago. I would have called you sooner, but I didn't think it was a big deal. Only, the more I thought about how he sounded, the more worried I got, and I figured you should know."

"Thanks for calling me. I appreciate it."

"You're welcome. And Kate, I hope you're okay."

"I am, Megan." Kate started to say goodbye but added, "Hey, Megan,"

"Yeah?"

"Watch out for yourself. Don't walk home alone, and don't talk to Mark again. I'm not sure what he's capable of."

"Same to you, girlfriend."

Kate heard the cell drop and looked up at Aaron.

"What's wrong?" he asked as she put his arm around her and helped her to the truck.

"That was a girl I used to work with, a friend actually." Kate thought about the way she treated Megan that night in the bar when Megan had the best of intentions for Kate. "She called to warn me that Mark is trying to find me."

Aaron stood in the door on the truck and looked at Kate. He took her hands in his and rubbed them, trying to comfort her.

"He's not going to find you," Aaron assured her, "but if he does, I'll be waiting. I won't let him hurt you again."

Kate nodded, and Aaron gave her hands a squeeze before letting go, shutting the door, and walking to the driver's side.

Once they were out of the lot and headed back toward Chincoteague, Kate spoke.

"Do you think Mark was the one who…. Never mind." She shook her head. It wasn't possible. He couldn't know where she was.

"Who vandalized the nursery?" Aaron supplied.

"Yes," Kate admitted. "Do you think he did that?"

Aaron tightened his lips and stared through the windshield. After a moment, he nodded. "I do, and so does Zach. So do the police."

"And you didn't tell me?" Kate's tone revealed pain, not anger.

"We didn't want to worry you."

"Did the police question him? Check out an alibi?"

"They can't find him. He's disappeared. Did Megan say where he was when he called."

Kate shook her head. "She didn't, and I didn't get the impression that she knew, or she would have told me." She thought about it for a moment. "His wife must know where he is. Did they ask her? What about the airline?"

Aaron shook his head. "They checked her alibi, too. She was at work. She kicked him out some time after she learned about you, and he started drinking, lost his job, probably took a downward spiral to nowhere good. Your brother suspected as much. Mark's gone completely AWOL."

Silence engulfed the cab of the truck. Finally, Kate spoke.

"How long have you known? Or when did you first suspect?"

Aaron glanced at Kate and then returned his eyes to the road. "From the beginning. Zach, too. Who else would do that to your house, and then my house, our future home, our baby's nursery?"

"My house? Do you mean in DC?" Kate's mind raced as she put together the events of the past few weeks.

"Yeah. When Zach went there, he realized that someone had been there, had gone through your things." His jaw twitched as he clenched his teeth in anger.

"Is the house okay?"

"It's fine. Zach cleaned up the mess and alerted the neighbors that someone had broken in so that they'd be more aware if lights were on or there was movement."

"That's why Zach has had a rifle at his side for the past couple of weeks."

"Yeah. He's on high alert, as is my team. And the whole police force on the Island. Plus, the Guard."

"But he's here. He knows where I am. I don't know how, but he's found me." She looked out the window and tried not to cry.

Aaron swallowed but didn't say anything.

“What are we going to do?” she asked, fighting back the tears.

Aaron reached for her hand. She was trembling and breathing in small gasps. He glanced over to make sure she was okay.

“Nothing. We’re going to live and love each other and have a baby. He’s going to slip up, and we’re going to be ready.”

Kate turned away from Aaron and stared through the windshield. What more would she have to endure? Her life had become a nightmare from which she was unable to wake.

The Yoruba peoples of Nigeria believe all human beings possess a fate, or a destiny, that will one day bring their spirit into communion with Olodumare, the divine creator. They believe that the thoughts and actions of every living person interacts and intersects with all living creatures to influence everything on earth. They believe that their spiritual lives are constantly growing and transcending life on earth until they are bound with the creator. Life and death are but cycles on this transcendence toward perfection in communion with the creator.

From the *Studies of Indigenous Peoples*
by Walter Middleton

CHAPTER FIFTEEN

By the time February rolled around, Kate was going stir crazy being cooped up in the house and was worried that Mark had to be located. She knew that stress and anxiety were bad for the baby and for her heart. She struggled every day to maintain her composure and remain calm. At Ronnie's urging, she ordered a book from Amazon on yoga and meditation for pregnant woman and even found one on yoga for the bedridden. She was determined to keep her mind and heart at peace even as chaos reigned around her.

Zach and Aaron were keeping vigil night and day. Even Trevor began staying at the house during the day when Aaron felt that he needed to sleep to stay vigilant at night. Paul had men stationed at Zach's twenty-four hours a day and had someone always positioned between Kate's house and Kayla's. Sometimes, lookouts were in a police car out front; and sometimes, they were in a Coast Guard vessel offshore. In either case, there were eyes on the houses at all times.

Lying in bed all day was taking its toll on Kate, and she became restless and irritable. Her back ached, and her body almost felt bruised from lying in the same position all the time. She was sore and fatigued even though she rarely moved from her bed. She looked forward to her checkups with Dr. Sprance, the only man in her life these days who didn't seem to be living like a soldier in enemy territory. She missed going to Mass but enjoyed her one-on-one visits with Father Darryl.

"So tell me how you're feeling," he asked one Sunday after their private Communion service in her bedroom.

"Like the man on the mat who had to be lowered through the roof of the house so that Jesus could heal him. I just want him to tell me that I can pick up my mat and go home."

"Ah, yes, there are many times in life when we wish that all troubles could be so easily lifted. But Jesus also said 'Take up your cross and follow me.'"

"But for how much longer do I need to carry it? Jesus was the Son of God. I'm only human."

"When Jesus carried his cross, he was human as well. He felt the pain, the scorn, the humility. He was probably bitter and angry and upset that he was going through all of that. Remember, even Jesus asked that this cup pass from him, but then what did he say?"

"Something about God's will being done?"

"'Yet not as I will but as You will.' He understood that God had a plan, and he has a plan for all of us. One that will lead to eternal salvation. I once heard someone describe God's plan as being like an Impressionist painting. You've traveled. Have you been to the Louvre or the Orsay?"

"I have. I was very young, but I remember seeing the paintings of the great masters."

"Well, if you look at, say, a Renoir, up close, what do you see?"

"Just dots of many colors."

"That's correct. But let's say you stand back and look at the painting from across the room. Then what would you see?"

"Well, the painting, of course. As it was meant to be seen."

"Yes, and that's what God sees. Right now, you're seeing your past with Mark, your mistakes, your flight to the island, your pregnancy, meeting Aaron, coming back to the church, all these things, as just separate events, happenings in your life that you have to muddle through until the next event occurs. They're dots on the canvas. What God sees is the painting as a whole, the finished work that will only be visible to your eyes when you're seated at His table looking down on the course of events that made up your life."

"Wow. That's a beautiful analogy."

"It is, and I believe that you will see that work of art someday, Kate; but for today, and tomorrow, and the rest of your life, just keep connecting the dots."

When Father Darryl left, Kate thought about their talk. For the first time since New Year's, she felt truly calm. This, too, would pass, and she and Aaron would be able to get married and live the rest of their lives together. The baby was due in April, and they were planning on being married in the fall. It wasn't perfect, and she would have preferred they not wait, but she knew that planning a wedding would add unneeded stress in her life. And Father Darryl insisted on a longer engagement. What they would tell the baby as she got older, they still didn't know, but they had time.

"Knock, knock." Anne poked her head through the open bedroom door. "Are you up for company?"

"I'm always up for company," Kate replied with a smile.

"Then how about a party?"

"A party?"

Before Kate could figure out the meaning of Anne's words, the door swung open, and half a dozen women filed in yelling, "Surprise" and carrying presents wrapped in pink bows.

"We know it's a little early, but we thought you could use some cheering up."

"I sure can. Please, come in, everyone."

Luckily, the bedroom was large and airy, and everyone fit, followed by Aaron and Zach carrying folding chairs for all the party guests.

"The chairs are courtesy of the Chamber," Shannon said as she went to the bed and gave Kate a hug.

Once everyone had greeted Kate and taken a seat, the shower began. There were games, and gifts, and even a bowl of punch and platter of cookies that the men carried up the stairs and set up in the room. Kate opened one present after another, remarking on the tiny shoes, the pink, frilly dresses, and the adorable baby accessories.

Anne, who could count knitting as one of her many talents, made Kate a beautiful layette complete with sweater, booties, and a baby blanket. Tammi crocheted an afghan in the colors of the nursery that was large enough for Kate to drape over herself as she sat in the chair nursing the baby or reading while the baby slept. Woven into the afghan was the image of a heron standing on the shoreline. It was exquisite. Ronnie painted a lampshade with a magnificent beach scene that also encompassed the nursery's color scheme. Kayla provided a cookbook with homemade baby food recipes as well as easy-to-cook meals for two. Each entry was hand-written and accompanied by whimsical sketches that showed that the proverbial artistic apple doesn't fall far from the tree.

By the time everyone left, Kate was exhausted but overwhelmed by the feelings of love and gratitude.

"A good day?" Aaron asked as he slid into the bed beside her.

"A wonderful day. A perfect day." She snuggled close to him, and they both lay with their hands on her belly as the baby moved and kicked. Zach found them that way an hour later, sound asleep. He left them there and went to take his watch over their happy home.

***

In the early hours before dawn, on Valentine's Day, a cold draft pulled Kate from her sleep. Shivering, she pulled the covers up tightly around herself and tried to get warm. The sound of the outdoors was louder than it should have been, and she turned toward the French doors to find them open, allowing the cold air to drift across the wood floor. She felt as if she was walking on ice as she stepped from the area rug by her bed to the cold floor and shut the doors. She didn't remember having them open recently and wondered if a shift in the wind had caused them to sway open during the night.

Once she was up and standing on the icy floor, she couldn't fight the urge to use the bathroom, a sensation that was all too familiar these days as she inched toward her seventh month of pregnancy. She was twenty-five weeks and didn't know how she would survive another fifteen weeks in bed. Then she remembered Father's words about bearing her cross and knew that she would carry a hundred crosses if it meant delivering a strong, healthy baby.

She went to the bathroom and emptied her bladder, washed her hands, and filled a bathroom cup with cold water to soothe her nighttime-dry throat. When she walked back into the bedroom, her blood ran as cold as the floor. The doors were open again. Frantically, she searched the room with her eyes. The full moon bathed the room in light, and as far as she could tell, nothing was off or out of place. Still, her heart raced as she tried to decide whether to close the doors or flee from the room.

As she took a tentative step toward the hallway, her closet door silently opened behind her, and a hand snaked its way around her head, covering her mouth.

"Hello, Katherine," the familiar voice whispered in her ear. "Daddy's home."

Fear seized her, and she was unable to move. This was a man she didn't know, never knew despite the nights they spent together, the baby they created.

No, her mind protested its own thoughts. *This is the baby that Aaron and I created together, maybe not biologically, but out of love and trust. You have no claim to her, to either of us.*

She struggled to break free, but his other hand went around her belly showing her a long blade that glinted in the moonlight. Her eyes widened with fear, and her body went rigid with the understanding that he had, indeed, gone mad.

"We're going to leave here, together, the three of us. Do you understand me?"

Kate nodded, too afraid to not obey.

"That boyfriend of yours is downstairs, and your brother is in the next room," he whispered. "If you make a sound, I'll slit open your belly and let you watch as I rip that baby out of you. Got it?"

Tears spilled down her face as she nodded. She was having a hard time breathing with his hand over her face, and she struggled to take breaths through her nose. Her chest was tight, and she had never felt so afraid.

"We're going to go out onto the balcony and down the steps to the side of the house. And you're going to be nice and quiet and do exactly as I say every step of the way. Is that understood?"

Again, she nodded. She tried to think of a plan, of a way to break free, to call for help, but the sight of the blade near her stomach prevented her from fighting or trying to get away. She had no idea what Mark was capable of and wasn't willing to risk her baby's life to find out. She knew that, somehow, Aaron and Zach would find her. They wouldn't stop looking until they did. She only hoped it wouldn't be too late.

They shuffled toward the open doors, and Kate prayed harder than she had ever prayed in her life. She said every prayer that she had ever learned, even ones that didn't make sense in the present situation. She called on every angel and saint in Heaven. When the cold blast of wind hit her as she edged near the balcony, she sucked in the salty air and closed her eyes. The pain in her chest radiated through her body, and she knew that this was it. One way or the other, she was going to die that night.

"Stop and turn around." The command came from an unknown voice, one that contained steel and was as cold as the ocean air. Mark froze, his body tensed, and he slowly turned, taking Kate with him, the blade touching her belly.

Kate saw the man in the doorway, recognized his face but not his eyes. They were the eyes of a stranger, the eyes of someone stalking his prey. He was as still as a statue and as calm as a late spring day.

"Now put down the knife, and let her go."

Almost ten years earlier, Aaron watched his best friend and brother in arms die on the floor of a cargo ship in the Gulf of Mexico because, in his mind, Aaron had not successfully planned for every scenario. For all those years, Aaron carried the guilt of not being able to save Mack. He swore that if he was ever again in a similar situation, he would be prepared for anything and everything. Once he returned to Chincoteague, Aaron assumed that he would never again be faced with a gunfight of any kind. Apparently, he was wrong.

"I said, put the knife down, and let her go."

Mark just laughed. "That pistol in your hand doesn't scare me. You can shoot, but you might hit Katherine, and

I don't think you'll take that chance. Now drop the gun, and kick it over here, or I'll slash her throat faster than you can take aim."

Aaron nodded and carefully put the gun on the floor, but instead of kicking it toward Mark, he kicked it toward the bathroom, well out of Mark's reach.

"I've seen you," Mark said, not seeming to care where the gun landed. "I've seen the way you look at Katherine. You seem to think that you have some kind of claim to her, but you're wrong."

"Do you have a claim to her, Mark?" Aaron asked, his voice calm and steady.

"She's my wife." Mark spat out the words. Despite the cold, sweat dripped from his forehead, and a piece of hair fell onto his face above his left eye.

"Really?" Aaron asked. *Keep it cool. Don't antagonize him.* "I'm confused by that. What happened to your first wife?"

"She left me. And she took our kids."

Mark moved his hand away from Kate's mouth to wipe away the sweat. Kate gasped for air. Aaron slid his gaze from Mark to Kate. She didn't look good. She was too pale, her breathing too shallow.

"Where did they go?" Aaron asked as he shifted his eyes back to Mark's. He tried to sound concerned, even compassionate.

"Hell if I know," Mark answered. He put his free hand around Kate's stomach, his other hand still holding the knife to her throat. "She had divorce papers sent to me at the airport. Then she up and left. I called her parents, but they wouldn't take my calls. They changed all of the numbers and blocked them from all directories."

"So why come after Kate?" Aaron said, taking a small, hopefully unnoticeable step closer to Mark and Kate.

"Because I know she still loves me. We can make it work, us and the baby. *My* baby."

Aaron shuffled a bit closer. He was calm, but desperation began to set in as he subtly moved his gaze between Mark and Kate. Pain radiated from her. She was barely holding herself up.

"Mark, Kate's sick. Did you know that? She has a heart condition. She's not looking too good right now, Mark. I think she needs a doctor. How about you let me call a doctor?"

Using his training, Aaron made sure to use Mark's name, to reason with him, to make it seem like Mark was holding all the cards. To most people, it would appear that he was.

"You're lying. You're trying to make me take my eyes off you, but I'm not stupid. I know what you're trying to do." Mark's eyes were wild with a mix of emotions—anger, desperation, fear, and madness. There was a look in his eyes that reminded Aaron of Vincent Price's character in Poe's *Telltale Heart* that they watched way back in high school.

Aaron took another step toward Mark hoping that their plan didn't backfire. This was it. This was the make it or break it moment.

"Stay back. Do you hear me? Stay back, or I will hurt her." Mark's shrill order filled the room.

"Don't take her, Mark. Please let me call the doctor." Kate's eyes were closed, her breathing almost non-existent as far as Aaron could tell. It took a level of determination that he didn't know he had to stay calm.

"I said, stay back," Mark yelled as he took a step backwards onto the balcony.

The crack of the rifle fire was barely audible. Aaron watched Mark's expression go blank. His body stiffened for a second and then fell backwards. Aaron leaped forward and grabbed Kate as she crumpled into his arms. She was so cold, and he felt no movement in her chest as he pulled her into the bedroom and stretched her out on the floor. Without hesitation, he began CPR.

"How is she?" Zach said, stepping over Mark's body and coming in from the balcony as calm and sure as an eagle in flight. He laid the rifle down on the floor.

"I don't think she's breathing," Aaron said as he pumped air into her chest. "Her pulse is barely perceptible."

"The ambulance and police are on the way. Let me take a turn."

Aaron let Zach take over long enough for him to catch his breath. He bent down close to Kate's ear.

"Don't you leave us, Princess. You're safe. Zach and I are here. Don't you leave us. I love you."

***

After what seemed like an eternity, Aaron watched helplessly, for the second time, as Kate's body was lifted into an emergency vehicle, but this time it was a helicopter. He and Zach continued to take turns giving her CPR until the EMT arrived. They stabilized her in the ambulance and took her to the closest place for the chopper to land—the Coast Guard Station. This time, the EMT moved aside to let Aaron climb into the chopper beside him.

"En route to Norfolk General with a female, thirty-two years of age, twenty-five weeks pregnant, suffering from a possible cardiac arrest. Patient has been diagnosed with Mitral Stenosis and is in the care of,"

"Dr. Sprance, Dr. George Sprance," Aaron shouted over the noise of the chopper. He could hear the EMT through the headphones he had been handed before takeoff.

"Dr. George Sprance at NGH."

"Copy that. We will have Dr. Sprance on standby. What is the patient's current condition?" the voice radioed back.

Aaron listened as the EMT conveyed Kate's status and watched as he opened an IV line and administered medication to her.

"Yes, patient is breathing on her own, but breathing is labored. CPR was given at the scene."

During those critical moments on the balcony, when Aaron could feel no pulse nor detect breathing, life as he knew it came to a halt. Pulling himself together, he let his training and his instincts take over just as Zach had when he took out Mark and fired a bullet that hit just two inches from his sister's head.

Within minutes, they were landing on the roof of the hospital, and Dr. Sprance was racing out to the chopper. They wheeled Kate inside before Aaron had even exited, and he hurried to keep up. A nurse stopped him at a set of double doors.

"I'm sorry, but you can't go in there."

"I have to. I'm the father." It was the first time he had said the words, but they rang true in every sense of the word.

"I'm sorry. You can wait in that room over there." She pointed down the hall. "Someone will come out to talk to you soon."

After what felt like an eternity, Nurse Lloyd appeared at the doorway. She headed straight for Aaron who stood and tried to read her expression.

"She's stable, but she needs heart surgery, stat. A cardiac surgeon has been called."

"The baby?"

"That's why I'm here. They're prepping her for a C-Section. At her last visit, she made Dr. Sprance put into writing that he would do whatever necessary to save the baby."

Her expression told Aaron what he knew in his heart. Kate would choose the life of the baby over her own if that's what it came down to. His chest ached at the thought.

"Are you ready to go?" Nurse Lloyd asked.

"I can go?"

"If you hurry. They won't waste any time. The anesthesiologist is already giving her meds."

She didn't have to say another word. Aaron was on her heels. He washed up as quickly as he could and slipped on the scrubs that she handed him.

"You're just in time," Dr. Sprance said when Aaron walked into the OR. "Stay up there by her head. Hold her hand. Talk to her. I promise you, she can hear and understand every word you say."

"Hi, Princess," Aaron managed to say through tears. "I'm here with you. Hang on, Princess. You're about to be a mom." He brushed her hair back and kissed her forehead, whispering over and over again that he loved her and was not leaving her.

When the small, baby girl was lifted for him to see, Aaron's own heart lurched. She was so tiny. Her entire body fit across Dr. Sprance's two hands. Aaron was sure that she hadn't made it, but when he looked up at the doctor, he saw a smile.

"She's small, but she's breathing, Aaron. That's as good as it gets right now."

Aaron cried as his daughter was handed off to another nurse who quickly wrapped her in a blanket and laid her in an incubation basket. The baby was whisked from the room as Dr. Sprance finished working on Kate.

"Aaron, I'm sorry you didn't get to cut the cord, but next time, okay?"

"It's a deal, doc, but there has to be a next time." He looked down at Kate, her face so pale it was almost blue.

"I'm almost done here, and then you and I will both need to leave. We've done all we can do except pray. Dr. Carter is an excellent cardiologist. He'll do the rest."

***

"How is she?" Zach asked as he rushed down the hall toward Aaron.

"Which one?" Aaron asked, his eyes full of more tears.

"You mean?"

"One pound and six ounces. So small I could hold her entirely in my two hands, but yeah. Come with me."

The men walked down the hall toward the NICU.

"Kate's in surgery. They said it's going to be a while. She missed the birth. She was out cold. But I was there." He stopped and pointed to the tiny, baby girl who was being attended to by a nurse. "I saw her when Dr. Sprance reached in and pulled her out. She was so small, and she didn't cry, but he said she was breathing, and that was good."

He couldn't stop the tears that flowed from his eyes, but that didn't matter. Neither could Zach.

"Mom and Dad are on their way. It's going to take them some time, so maybe she'll be out by the time they get here."

"Zach, Aaron." Both men turned to see Father Darryl hurrying down the hall. "Tell me what's going on."

Through more tears, Aaron told the priest what transpired. He was barely able to choke out the words when he told them that Kate had chosen the baby's life over her own.

"They need prayers, Father. The biggest, strongest ones you can muster," said Zach.

"Is there a chapel?"

"Down the hall," answered a passing nurse. "That way."

The three men followed in the direction to which she pointed and entered the quiet room. Kneeling together, they prayed, Father Darryl leading them in a heart-felt prayer that pleaded for God's hand to work through the hands of the doctors, for God's healing to be with Kate, and God's strength and mercy to be with the baby.

As soon as he was allowed, Father Darryl went into the NICU to pray over the baby. He was followed by both Zach and Aaron, all wearing scrubs from head to toe with strict instructions not to touch the sleeping infant.

"Should she be baptized?" Zach asked. Father turned to Aaron for an answer.

"No," he said firmly. "Her mother should be here for that. There's time. I know there is. She's going to thrive and flourish and grow to be a strong young woman with all of her mother's talent and beauty."

It was still hours before a young doctor emerged from the O.R. Half the eyes in the waiting room looked up when he called Aaron's name. Ronnie and Kayla held each other's hands. Trevor stopped pacing. Zach turned from the window as Anne, Shannon, and Tammi looked up from their praying. Mitzi and Walter stood and followed Aaron to the door.

"She's stable, and she's lucky. I don't know who she had in her corner rooting for her today, but as a man of science, I'm happy to say, she's a living miracle."

"You have no idea," Aaron told the doctor. "You have no idea."

Long before Christianity was introduced to the people of Brazil, there was a profound belief in God. It was believed that all living things and all things in nature have a spirit. Good spirits were believed to bring blessings to the people and were called upon to drive bad spirits away.

From the *Studies of Indigenous Peoples*
by Walter Middleton

EPILOGUE

At Aaron's insistence, Miren, an Irish name that means 'born of the sea,' was baptized while in the Neonatal unit, but not with all the pomp and ceremony that usually accompanies a Catholic Baptism. With Kate and Aaron looking on, she was brought into the faith by Father Darryl, but no Godparents or other witnesses were present. That had to be saved for another occasion. Three months, one week, and two days after her birth, Miren Lorelei Kelly was ceremonially baptized in front of the entire congregation of St. Andrew's Church.

The baptism took place in June, exactly two months and five days after Kayla and Zach stood up for Miren's parents, Kate and Aaron in the same church. Father Darryl relented and allowed the early wedding. He knew that no man could stop something that God put into motion.

Middleton weds Kelly

On April 10, 2016, the marriage of Katherine Rebecca Middleton, daughter of Mr. and Mrs. Walter Middleton of San Marco Island, Florida, and Aaron Michael Kelly, son of Vice Admiral (ret.). and Mrs. Trevor Kelly of Chincoteague, Virginia, was performed by Father Darryl Millette. The double ring ceremony was performed at St. Andrew's Church in Chincoteague.

Given in marriage by her father, the bride wore a white, floor-length satin gown adorned with pearls and sequins. Her veil was hand made by her friend, Tammi Warren. She carried a bouquet of lilies, pink roses, and seashells.

Kayla Reynolds, sister of the groom, was the Maid of Honor. Zach Middleton, brother of the bride, was the Best Man. The flower girl was Lizzie Parker, daughter of Mr. and Mrs. Paul Parker, and the ring bearer was Edward Reynolds, Jr, son of Kayla Reynolds and the deceased, Edward Reynolds, Sr.

A reception, catered by the Maid of Honor's company, Homemade Helpings, was held in the church hall. The couple will reside on the island of Chincoteague, Virginia, with their daughter, Miren.

About the Author

Amy began writing as a child and never stopped. She wrote articles for magazines and newspapers before writing children's books and adult fiction. A graduate of the University of Maryland with a Masters of Library and Information Science, Amy has resided on the Eastern Shore of Maryland for 21 years. She worked as a librarian for fifteen years and, in 2010, began writing full time.

Schisler's first children's book, *Crabbing With Granddad*, is an autobiographical work about spending a day harvesting the Maryland Blue Crab. Sarah Book Publishing released Schisler's novel, *A Place to Call Home*, in August of 2014. A revised second edition was released in March 2015. *Picture Me, A Mystery* was released in August of 2015 and won a 2016 Illumination Award as one of the top three ebooks of 2015 among Christian writers. Schisler followed up her success with the critically acclaimed, *Whispering Vines*, a 2017 Illumination Award as one of the best Christian romance novels of 2016.

Amy is the author of a weekly blog which has over a thousand followers around the world. Her topics range from current events to her daily life with her husband, three daughters, and two dogs.

Follow Amy at:

http://amyschislerauthor.com

https://amyschisler.wordpress.com

http://facebook.com/amyschislerauthor

https://twitter.com/AmySchislerAuth

https://www.goodreads.com/amyschisler

References

Bothamley, Judy and Boyle, Maureen. *Medical Conditions Affecting Pregnancy and Childbirth*. London: Radcliffe Publishing, 2009.

Bourke, Eleanor Bourke and Colin. *Families and cultural diversity in Australia*. December 1 1995. 1 October 2016.

Foley, Andrew Rumbach and Dolores. "Indigenous institutions and their role in disaster risk reduction and resilience: evidence from the 2009 tsunami in American Samoa." *Ecology and Society* (2009): 19(1): 19.

Healthline Editorial Team. *Mitral Valve Stenosis*. Ed. Steven M.D. Kim. 12 November 2015. 1 October 2016.

Kannan, M. and Vijayanand, G. "Mitral stenosis and pregnancy: Current concepts in anaesthetic practice." *Indian Journal of Anaesthesia* (2015): 439–444.

LaFleur, Sandra. "Spurning Syrian Refugees Is Inhumane." December 13 2015. *Indian Country Media Network*. 1 November 2016.

Littlejohn, Nate PA2. *Chincoteague Island, a Coast Guard Community*. 20 August 2005. 1 November 2016.

Mendelson, M, Glob. "Pregnancy in the Woman With Preexisting Cardiovascular Disease." 1 September 2008. *Global Library of Women's Medicine*. 1 October 2016.

Nunkai, Anank Nunink. "Meeting Arutam." *Cultural Survival Quarterly Magazine* (2008): 32-34.

Robinson, B.A. *Ifa: The Religion of the Yoruba peoples*. 17 May 2012. Ontario Consultants on Religious Tolerance. 1 November 2016.

Sheffield, R. Scott. *Indigenous Peoples and the World Wars*. 4 April 2016. 1 November 2016.

Smith, Derek G. *Indigenous People: Religion and Spirituality.* 23 July 2015. 1 October 2016.

Sullivan, Lawrence. *Religions of the World: An Introduction to Culture and Meaning.* Minneapolis: Fortress Press, 2012.

Svensson, Bjorn. *Indigenous People of the Amazon Native Amazonian Tribe.* 1 January 2007. 1 October 2016.

Toensing, Gale Courey. *What Really Happened at the First Thanksgiving? The Wampanoag Side of the Tale.* 23 November 2012. 1 November 2016.

Univeristy of Colorado. "Study highlights indigenous response to natural disaster." 13 February 2014. *EurekAlert.* 1 November 2016.

Wise, Sarah. *Improving the early life outcomes of Indigenous children: implementing early childhood development at the local level.* Issue Paper. Closing the Gap Clearinghouse. Sydney: Australian Government, 2013.

Book Club Discussion Questions

1. At the outset of the novel, Katherine Middleton seemed to live a charmed life, but her relationship with her parents was strained, her career was at a dead-end, and her marriage was not what it seemed. Are there people you know, who seem to have it all, whose life may not be perfect? Why do you think we are all so quick to judge others based on outward appearances?

2. Kate spent her youth traveling the world; but, as an adult, all she longed for was a place to belong. Do you think that her nomadic youth contributed to her decision to marry Mark and her inability to leave a job in which she was unhappy?

3. Do you think that Katherine's decision to escape to Chincoteague was brave or cowardly? Was she too quick to give up her life and run away, or do you think that events in her life led to her move? Would you consider that fate? Do you believe in fate, destiny, or divine providence; or do you believe that we chart our own paths? Is there such a thing as coincidence, or does everything happen for a reason?

4. Zach and Aaron both kept secrets from the ones they loved. Knowing what those secrets were, would you have done the same? Why or why not? How would you have handled Kate's questions?

5. Kate harbored a secret of her own and spent a great deal of time debating whether to tell Mark

the truth. If you had been in Kate's shoes, what would you have done?

6. In Kate's eyes, everyone sees her a failure who can't get her life together. Have you ever felt that way about yourself? About another person? What advice would you give to someone who seems to always make poor decisions?

7. The residents of Chincoteague, for the most part, welcome Kate with open arms. Have you ever lived in or visited a place where the people make you feel like you belong there? Did it make it hard for you to leave?

8. Aaron's love for Kate was simple, pure, and true. He was willing to do anything for her and for her baby and to accept her for all that she was. It seems like that kind of love is hard to find these days. Do you think that people, too often, have lofty expectations of people and aren't able to fully accept people for whom they are? Why do you think that is?

9. Which character spoke to you the most and why?

10. What, if anything, would you change about *Island of Miracles*? What would you tell the author if you could talk to her about her book?

CPSIA information can be obtained
at www.ICGtesting.com
Printed in the USA
LVOW12s1447090517
533873LV00001B/28/P